PRAISE FOR THE
STEEL BROTHERS SAGA

"Hold onto the reins:
this red-hot Steel story is one wild ride."
~ A Love So True

"A spellbinding read from a
New York Times *bestselling author!"*
~ BookBub

"I'm in complete awe of this author. She has gone and
delivered an epic, all-consuming, addicting, insanely
intense story that's had me holding my breath, my
heart pounding and my mind reeling."
~ The Sassy Nerd

"Absolutely UNPUTDOWNABLE!"
~ Bookalicious Babes

LEGACY

LEGACY

STEEL BROTHERS SAGA
BOOK FOURTEEN

HELEN HARDT

WATERHOUSE PRESS

ISBN: 978-1-64263-222-4

To all survivors of mental illness.
I'm humbled by your strength.

PROLOGUE

Brad

Present day . . .

Other than Talon, my children don't visit me in prison.

Not that I blame them. I've betrayed them. I've betrayed their mother. I've betrayed the legacy I wanted more than anything for them.

Ryan and Ruby had their child—a little girl they named Ava Lee Steel. One of the guards got wind of it and told me.

My sixth grandchild, including Marjorie's stepson, and I'm certain more will come.

If only I could be the doting grandfather they deserve.

But even if I weren't incarcerated, their parents wouldn't let me near them.

How can I blame their thinking?

I wouldn't let me near them either.

Do they take the children to see their grandmother? Daphne won't know them, but somewhere inside her, she'll remember how much she loves her children, and by extension, her grandchildren.

How well I remember the first year of Jonah's life. Daphne chose his name because it meant "dove." She'd taken to calling him "little dove" as he grew inside her, and when he was born and we saw he was a boy—as she'd always suspected—she told me his name.

She insisted his middle name be after me. Who was I to say no? At that time, I thought I'd be his hero.

For a while, perhaps I was.

Now?

I'm no one's hero.

Not my wife's.

Not my children's.

Not my grandchildren's.

Most certainly not my own.

No one's.

No one's hero.

CHAPTER ONE

Brad

Forty years earlier . . .

I stood and followed Jonathan back into the house.

"About that nightcap," he said.

"No, thank you."

"You don't have to have one, but I do, and we're not having it here."

"You want to go somewhere?"

"A little Irish pub about a mile away from here. I want to talk to you in private."

★ ★ ★

Jonathan ordered an Irish whiskey, and I decided to join him. One drink wouldn't hurt, and I could use a little relaxation. Jonathan seemed so serious.

I took a drink of the liquor and let it burn a trail down my throat. Then I turned to him. "I really do love her, Mr. Wade."

"Jonathan, please."

"All right. Jonathan."

"I know you love her, son. She's a very special girl."

"She is."

"It's soon, but I see it in your eyes. You want to take care of her."

"I do. And I will."

"I believe you want to. I truly do. You certainly have the means, and I believe that you used protection."

"I did. A condom, like I said."

"Things happen," he said.

"Yes," I agreed, not sure where he was going.

"So you love her, but you haven't known her long, and you're both so young. Is this really what you want?"

"It is, sir. I've thought of nothing but Daphne since I first laid eyes on her. Would I have liked to go a little slower? Of course. But what's done is done. It can't be undone."

"Well, it could be."

"Neither of us wants an abortion."

"I understand. And adoption?"

"We talked about it. But I love Daphne, and I want her to be my wife. I'd hate knowing we had a child out there who wasn't in our home."

He nodded, took a long drink of his whiskey, and set the glass down on the wooden bar. He turned to me and met my gaze. His blue eyes were stern. "I think you're a good man, from what I can tell by only talking to you for a couple hours. I do think you mean well."

"I do. I love her, and I already love this baby."

"I want you to succeed. I want Daphne to be happy."

"That's what I want as well."

"Then there's something about Daphne that you need to know."

CHAPTER TWO

Daphne

My mother didn't speak as I helped her clear away the dinner dishes and load the dishwasher.

She didn't speak as she wiped down the kitchen and then removed the tablecloth from the dining room table, took it outside, and shook off the crumbs.

She didn't speak as she laid the cloth back on the table and straightened the chairs.

She didn't speak as she returned to the kitchen, opened the cupboard above the refrigerator—my mother was as tall as I was—and withdrew a bottle of liquor.

Vodka. My mother wasn't a drinker, but she'd turned to it more and more lately, it seemed. I didn't remember her ever drinking before my junior year of high school.

"Mom?" I finally said.

"What, honey?"

"I'm . . . sorry."

She poured the clear liquid into a glass, sniffed it, and then took a drink, wincing. "How could you let this happen?"

"I didn't. He used protection."

"You're sure?"

"I saw him take the condom off when we were done." I winced this time. Describing that to my mother felt all kinds of wrong.

"You wouldn't lie to me." More a statement.

"That's right, I wouldn't, especially not about something this important."

She sighed and took another drink, grimacing once more. "I'll never get used to the taste of this stuff."

"Then why drink it?"

She sighed again. "It takes the edge off, Daphne."

The edge. I didn't have to ask. *I* was the edge. Me. She'd sent me off to college with Dr. Payne's blessing, and I came home pregnant after three weeks.

Not what she had planned.

Not what I'd planned either, for that matter.

One more sip, and she turned to me, her dark eyes unreadable. "Please, honey, don't pin all your hopes on this boy."

"Boy? He's a twenty-two-year-old man, Mom."

"Twenty-two is still a boy. He may look like a man, even act like a man, but inside, he's still a boy, just like you're still a girl."

"I'm eighteen."

"God, Daphne, that's a baby, especially after . . . "

"After all I've been through. Yeah, I get it, Mom." Now *I* kind of wanted some vodka myself, but drinking wasn't the answer. It was never the answer, and my mother should know better.

"I don't mean it that way," she said. "I just mean . . . I wish you'd waited a little longer."

"Why? How old were you when you had sex for the first time?"

It was a daring question. My mother and I didn't discuss this kind of stuff. We used to, before junior year. She was always open to talking about boys and sex and my body when I had questions. Now, she seemed to clam up at the thought.

"That's not really relevant."

"Sure it is."

She took another swallow. "If you must know, I was eighteen."

I couldn't help a slight scoff. "I see."

"But I was different. I didn't plan to marry the guy, and I didn't..."

"Get pregnant?"

"No, I didn't, and if I had, I would have—"

"Gotten an abortion? It wasn't even legal then, Mom."

"No, I wouldn't have gotten an abortion, Daphne. I hate the thought of abortion for you or anyone. I would have seriously considered adoption, though."

"I *did* seriously consider it, but Brad and I want this baby."

She stayed silent for a few minutes and finished her drink. Then, "Just don't pin all your hopes on this. If it doesn't work out, Daddy and I will take care of you."

"It *will* work out," I said adamantly.

"But if it doesn't," she insisted, "we're here for you. You can live at home this year and have the child. We'll find a nice couple to adopt it, and you can start college next year. You'll still have your scholarship, and you'll only be a year behind. Everything will work out."

"Why are you doing this, Mom? Why are you assuming Brad and I won't work out?"

She didn't answer again for a few minutes—a few minutes that dragged much like the minutes while I was waiting for Kathleen at the student health center to give me my pregnancy test results.

Finally, "You've only known him three weeks. You don't know anything about him, and he doesn't know anything about you."

Ah. That was what she was getting at. "For your information, I told Brad the truth about junior year. He still loves me, and he still wants me. So there."

Yeah, the "so there" was childish and immature from a woman about to become a wife and mother, but I couldn't help myself.

Again, she was silent. Her arm trembled as she reached for the vodka bottle. I placed my hand over hers.

"Don't, Mom. We're going to be okay."

"I hope so, honey. I truly do." Her gaze seemed to go through me, as if she were seeking something she couldn't see. "Your dad and your boyfriend will be gone awhile."

"So? They're getting to know each other."

She nodded. "Yes. Getting to know each other."

Her words skated over me in an eerie way.

As if they had some deeper meaning.

CHAPTER THREE

Brad

"Okay," I said. "What is it?"

Jonathan Wade stared down at the clear glass holding his Irish whiskey. "It's about her junior year of high school."

Was that all? He probably thought Daphne had told me the London lie. She had, at first, but she'd come clean before we made love.

"She told me." I smiled. "I guess you brought me here for nothing."

"What exactly did she tell you?"

"That she spent much of the year hospitalized for anxiety and depression, and that there's a lot she doesn't remember because of the medication she was on."

"I see."

"I'm okay with all of that. My mother spent some time in a facility herself. I understand a lot about what Daphne went through."

"Oh? What happened to your mother?"

"Exhaustion, mostly. Neither she nor my father was ever the same after the accident that left her unable to have more kids. My father blamed her, and it wasn't pretty. My mother broke down when I was in high school and spent nearly a year at a mental hospital, or a sanitarium as my father called it."

My mother's hospitalization had affected me more than I knew at the time. I got involved with the Future Lawmakers during that time, made decisions I now regretted. Looking back, I saw clearly how her absence had taken its toll.

"Does Daphne know this?"

I nodded. "When she told me her story, I told her my mother's. It helped us both."

"And how did you deal with your mother's absence and your father's . . . "

"The word is abuse. I told you it wasn't pretty, though the physical abuse had stopped by then."

"Did he abuse you as well?"

"Not physically. Maybe mentally or emotionally, but he did it to make me strong. It worked."

My mind raced briefly to the two calves I'd grown to love when I was a kid. My father had forced me to go with him to have them slaughtered. I never forgave him for that, but I never got close to another one of our animals. I also could never forgive him for how he treated my mother. I'd put a stop to it once I was big enough.

Despite his flaws—and his flaws were many, some horrifying—I'd learned to have an odd respect for the man who'd taught me . . . well . . . everything. Especially since he'd helped me have Wendy Madigan put away so that Daphne and I could marry and have our baby in peace.

"You're okay, then? You're strong?"

"I feel like I am. Don't get me wrong, Jonathan. I know I'm twenty-two and have a lot to learn about life and everything else. But I can run that ranch when my time comes, and I can take care of Daphne and our baby."

He nodded.

"Daphne also told me she sometimes has strange dreams that scare her, but when she wakes up, she can't remember them."

He nodded again. "Did she tell you anything else?"

"Just that you guys made up a story about her living in London for a year." I swirled the whiskey in my glass. "Oh, and that her best friend moved away after sophomore year."

"Yes. Sage Peterson."

"Daphne said she and Sage lost touch."

He didn't reply.

"I suppose it's hard when you're young, writing letters and all." I took a sip of my drink.

Jonathan cleared his throat. "Sage didn't move away, son."

"Oh? Then why did—"

He gestured me to stop talking. "Sage didn't move away. She committed suicide."

My eyebrows nearly flew off my forehead, and my heart thudded. I didn't say anything because I couldn't form the words.

"Sage was a lovely girl, very smart. She and Daphne met in kindergarten and were inseparable through sophomore year."

"Why didn't Daphne tell me?"

Jonathan sighed. "About the suicide? Because she doesn't know."

Huh? I wrinkled my forehead. "How can she not know?"

Jonathan drained the last bit of his whiskey and set down his glass. "Listen, Brad. I want to make this very clear from the start. Lucy and I will always take care of Daphne. No matter what. You have my word."

"Of course. She's your daughter. Why are you changing the subject? You can't drop a bomb on me like that and not tell me what's going on."

He cleared his throat and signaled the bartender. "Two more, please."

I shook my head. "Not for me." No way did I want another drink, even if I wasn't driving. This shit was getting heavy, and I wanted my mind at full capacity.

Once the bartender was out of earshot, I faced Jonathan. "What the hell happened to Daphne's friend?"

"I'll get to that in a minute. First, you need to understand that Lucy and I will see to Daphne's needs—and the baby's, if necessary—if things don't work out between you two."

"What do you mean 'if necessary'? Of course the baby will have needs."

"I mean, if she decides to keep the baby."

Damn. My muscles tightened, and everything in me went on alert. My hands curled into fists, and the anger inside me coiled like a snake ready to strike. "We've already decided to keep the child. You know this."

"Just in case things don't work out with the two of you."

"Why wouldn't it work out? And don't tell me how young we are. We already know that. We took precautions, and this happened anyway. Seems kind of like it was meant to be."

He smiled then. A small smile, but a smile nonetheless. "I understand what you're feeling."

The urge to do Jonathan Wade physical harm hadn't lessened, but I forced my fists to unclench. "I'm not sure you do."

"You've fallen in love. First-time love is quick and powerful. It's almost magic. It's what I had with Larry's mother. Of course, you see that Larry's mother and I are no longer together. We divorced when Larry was just a toddler."

Rage swept through me once more, but I vowed to keep it in check. If I showed my anger, I'd only be proving to him that I *was* young. Young and hotheaded. "Daphne and I are different."

"I believe you. That is, I believe that's what you *think*. I thought the same about Lisa, and we were older than you two are."

I shook my head. "You're wrong. I felt something different for Daphne the first time I saw her, and she says the same. She says fate brought us together."

"You believe in that?"

"I never did before, but I do now."

Jonathan sighed. "My daughter is an old soul. She's always found pleasure in the small things, even more so since her hospitalization. When she was little, she insisted a nest of fairies lived outside her room, that they came to her and sang to her at night. She's one of a kind, an almost ethereal spirit. It's that spirit that has gotten her through the rough times."

His choice of words made sense to me. Ethereal meant light and delicate in a way that was almost too perfect for this world.

That was Daphne to a T.

Jonathan continued, "Somehow, she's able to pick anything apart and find the good, no matter how minute it is, even if it means tossing everything else aside. It doesn't surprise me to hear that she used the word *fate*."

Again, Daphne to a T. She found the beauty in a simple sunrise, a yellow tulip. Was it any wonder I loved her?

"I've told you before that I believe your intentions are honorable, Brad. I know you love my daughter. I see it in your eyes when you look at her."

"Still, you think it's just puppy love."

"I don't know, son. But I'll find out."

"How exactly can you do that?"

The bartender set his second drink in front of him. "I'll find out in the next few minutes. After I tell you the rest of Daphne's story."

CHAPTER FOUR

Daphne

I loved my father. He was a good man, and he took care of my mother and me. He'd never treat my mother the way Brad's dad treated his mom. He'd never treat Brad badly, either.

So why were my nerves jumping on trampolines under my skin?

Getting to know each other.

My mother's words had seemed ominous, but why shouldn't they get to know each other? Brad was going to be his son-in-law, the father of his grandchild. Of *course* they should get to know each other.

Mom had finished her second drink and had gone to her bedroom.

I now sat on my bed—a bed that was still home to Puppy, my stuffed cocker spaniel I'd slept with since I could remember. His golden fur was matted down, and his nose had fallen off years ago, but I loved him. I hadn't taken Puppy to college. Now I snuggled him, wishing he were real so he could give me doggy kisses like Ebony had at Brad's ranch house. My mom was allergic to dogs, so I'd never had one. I'd named Puppy when I was a kid. I'd thought many times about renaming him to something a little more original, but I never did. He'd always be Puppy to me.

I lay down, still snuggling him. My favorite pillow was at school, and the one Mom had replaced it with wasn't nearly as fluffy and comfy. My bed was, though. So much better than the dorm bed.

I closed my eyes.

I remembered the most comfortable bed I'd ever slept in—the one in the guesthouse on Brad's ranch.

The one where we'd made love.

I touched my abdomen.

The bed where we'd created our baby.

Was it the bed that was so comfortable? Or was it being with Brad?

Probably both.

"Hello in there," I said to my belly. "It's me. Your mama. You're a boy, aren't you? I'll love you no matter what, but I really think you're a boy. You're like a peaceful dove that flew into me to save me. I have to be okay now, because you need me."

Not that I thought I wasn't okay. I'd proved I was strong. I'd gotten through the hell that was junior year, and now I forced myself to remember every little detail of my life. I'd faltered a few times, but no more than anyone else.

At least that was what I told myself.

Now, though? No more faltering. "I promise, little dove. I'll be the best mother in the world, because that's what you deserve."

I closed my eyes.

No one else knew yet. I hadn't told Patty or Ennis or anyone at school. Brad hadn't told Sean. Or his parents. Next weekend we'd tackle that.

Tackle. That was the word, all right. But with Brad at my

side, loving me, and our baby nestled safe in my belly, I could tackle anything.

I could tackle the world.

I'd tackle the world gladly for Brad and my little dove.

Fate had brought Brad Steel into my life. Fate had put this baby inside me. And fate would guide us the rest of the way. I touched my abdomen—

Crash!

I jerked upward.

I scrambled off my bed and out of my room. "Mom? Mom, what happened?"

The house was dark, and my parents' bedroom door was closed. Mom had gone to bed after her two drinks. How long ago had that been? An hour or so, but no longer.

I knocked on the door. "Mom?"

No reply.

"Mom!"

Still no reply. I turned the knob and entered—

"Mom!"

She lay on the floor next to her bed. I raced to her, knelt down, and shook her shoulder. "Mom, you fell out of bed. Wake up."

Nothing, so I nudged her harder.

Still nothing—

"Oh my God!"

Next to her on the floor lay several pills and an open prescription bottle. I'd nearly missed them in the dark. I picked up the bottle and read the label.

Valium.

Three white pills lay on the carpeting. How many were in the bottle?

"Damn it, Mom. Wake up!" I shook her hard. "Wake up! How many pills did you take?"

God, what was I supposed to do? This was my mother. She wasn't perfect, but she was mine, and I couldn't lose her.

Keep your head, Daphne. Call an ambulance. She needs help.

I'd read about the new 9-1-1 service to call in an emergency. Did we have it in Colorado yet? I had no idea. I kept the bottle in my hand and picked up the princess phone on her nightstand. I dialed zero.

"Operator? I need an ambulance."

"I'll connect you."

Tick. Tock. Tick. Tock.

Finally someone came on the line.

"I need an ambulance. My mother's passed out. She took Valium."

"Yes, ma'am. Address please."

I hastily gave our address.

"Thank you. Dispatching now. How much did she take, ma'am?"

"I don't know."

"How many pills were in the bottle?"

"I don't know."

"The bottle will say how many were prescribed."

I couldn't read the small print in the dark. Why hadn't I turned on a light? I hit the lamp and read the bottle. "Thirty pills."

"How many milligrams per pill?"

"Can you please just get the ambulance here?"

"I've already called for the paramedics, ma'am. I'm getting information from you that I can dispatch to them while they're on their way."

"Oh." That was good. Very good. "Five milligrams."

"And when was the prescription filled?"

"What?"

"The date on the bottle, ma'am."

"Right, okay." I quickly scanned the small print. "Oh, shit. Yesterday."

"How many pills are left in the bottle, ma'am?"

Tears fell from my eyes. "Three. Only three," I sobbed.

"Thank you, ma'am. Help is on the way."

I hung up the phone.

"Brad!" I cried. "Daddy! Where are you?"

I had to find them, tell them what was going on.

Nightcap. My father had asked Brad to go for a nightcap. What was the name of the bar he went to sometimes? It was an Irish pub. An Irish name.

I shook my mother once more. "Mommy, please wake up!"

Her pulse was still visible on her neck. I placed my hand on her flesh. She was cold. So cold, but at least her heart was beating. I lay down next to her and snuggled into her. *Please, Mama. Please, don't leave me.*

Be strong.

The words cut into my mind. Dr. Payne's words. My father's words. My mother's words—words she hadn't heeded herself.

My own words.

Be strong, Daphne.

I had to find my father. What was the name of that pub? I rose. I hated leaving my mother, but I had to find the phone book. Where was it? If I could only remember the name, I could call information.

McFall's Pub. The memory hurled itself into my mind. That was it!

Lucy, I'm meeting Bud for a drink at McFall's.

How many times had my father said those words?

He drank a lot at McFall's.

My mom drank a lot at home.

I knew this, and I'd never given it much thought.

They were drinking too much.

Most likely because of me.

And now my beautiful mother had taken pills.

Because I'd come home pregnant.

I quickly dialed information and got the number for the pub.

CHAPTER FIVE

Brad

What kind of story did Jonathan have to tell me? I already knew everything, except for why Daphne didn't know the truth about her best friend.

Was that what had sent her into anxiety and depression? But how could it have if she didn't even know?

"I'm listening," I said. "But nothing you tell me will make me love Daphne any less."

"I hope that's true, son. I sincerely hope that's true." Jonathan cleared his throat. "It's not an easy story to tell. Not for anyone, and especially not for me."

"I can't imagine it's easy for anyone to talk about the death of a young girl," I agreed.

"If only that were all there was to it." He took a sip of his second Irish whiskey.

I wished, then, that I'd let the barkeep make me a second as well.

No. Better to stay focused. Whatever Jonathan had to tell me, I'd remain calm.

Nothing would sway my love for Daphne and my unborn child.

"You know Daphne was hospitalized. What you don't know is why."

"It wasn't anxiety and depression?"

"Son, most cases of anxiety and depression don't require hospitalization."

"But my mother ... "

"From what you've described, your mother most likely had a mental breakdown brought on by your father's emotional and physical abuse."

"But I stopped it. She was hospitalized after I stopped it."

"You may have stopped the physical abuse. That doesn't mean it ended for her. I'm not a doctor, Brad. I'm not going to try to diagnose your mother. But I do know this, from experience. Most anxiety and depression can be treated with therapy, medication, or both. Rarely is hospitalization necessary, and certainly not hospitalization for an entire year."

"So Daphne wasn't anxious and depressed? Is that what you're saying?"

"Oh, she was, but there was much more to it than that."

Again, I wished for that second drink. Was I ready to hear this?

Didn't matter. I loved this man's daughter. She was carrying my child. I'd made a commitment to her—a commitment I'd stand by, no matter what.

But I had to know what I was dealing with.

"She's told me she doesn't remember a lot about that year."

"She doesn't, and she's better off for it."

"All right," I said. "Let me have it."

Jonathan rubbed his chin. "It's very complex, and it's not pretty. In fact, it's horrific."

My heart sped up as my blood thundered through my veins. "God. Okay. I get it. Please. Just tell me."

"It happened in August, right before Daphne's junior year was to begin. Daphne told Lucy and me she was spending the night at Sage's. Only that's not what happened."

I nodded, unable to speak. Jonathan's voice was muffled beneath the noise of my own blood gushing through me. At least that was what it seemed like.

"Sage told her parents she was spending the night at our house."

It took me a few seconds to register his words and then reply. "That's an old trick. Most teens have tried it."

"And most teens get away with it, no harm done," Jonathan said. "That wasn't the case for Daphne and Sage."

My bowels clenched as nausea clawed its way up my throat. I knew this feeling. The fight-or-flight response.

Flight was tempting.

But this was Daphne. My love.

I chose to fight.

"Go on," I said.

"It was a Saturday evening. No one knows the details of where they were going or why, but they ended up at the high school after dark."

After dark. Already I knew where this was headed.

I swallowed back the puke that threatened.

"Someone found them behind the stadium bleachers early in the morning and called the police and an ambulance."

"Oh, God."

"They'd been beaten and raped, Brad. Both of them."

No.

No. No. No.

Not my Daphne. Not my beautiful Daphne. I clenched my fists. Fight. I'd fight. I'd fucking kill.

"No," I finally said aloud, my eyes squeezed shut.

"I know how you're feeling."

My eyes shot open. "How can you possibly know?"

"Because I'm her father, Brad. Three men—"

"Three? Oh my God." I buried my head in my hands. Three men who'd die at my hands if it was the last thing I did.

"Look at me."

I stayed buried.

"Look at me, Brad."

Be strong. Be fucking strong.

I raised my head and met Jonathan's gaze. His eyes were glassy.

"Three men violated my little girl. *My little girl.* They stole her innocence, and they stole more than that, which I'll get to in a minute."

"Three? Where the fuck *are* they? Rotting in prison? I'll have them killed. I have money. Money."

"They're not in prison, Brad." He took a drink. "They were never caught."

"What?" I pounded my fist onto the bar.

"Easy. I spent a year pounding things. It doesn't help."

"Just finish," I said, pulling at my hair. "Tell me everything. It can't get any worse."

"Oh, it can. They were both in ICU for a couple of days, lucky to be alive. Daphne fared better than Sage. Sage was nearly dead when she was found, and to save her life, the doctors had to perform a complete hysterectomy."

I stared at him, frozen. I couldn't feel anything. I just wanted to get through this.

"You can't imagine the happiness I felt when you told me Daphne was pregnant. It's a shitty time for both of you, but it means the doctors were right. She *can* have children."

I said nothing. Still stared at him.

"They both suffered severe concussions, with only one difference. Sage remembered everything. Daphne, though, suffered from retrograde amnesia. When she woke up, she'd lost all her memories from the incident and from the entire seventy-two hours prior."

"Wait a minute? You let her think—"

"Don't judge us too harshly, Brad. Her mother and I had the chance to spare her from the horror of that night. We talked to doctors and therapists. Some advised us against keeping it from her, but in the end, it was our decision as she was a minor." He cleared his throat. "I don't regret it."

"But it *did* affect her. She spent a year locked up."

"First of all, she wasn't locked up. She was hospitalized."

"You know what I mean."

"Do you consider that your own mother was locked up?"

"No. I ... I don't know what the hell I think."

"I'd say that's normal under the current circumstances."

Memories flooded me. Taking Daphne's virginity. No blood and no pain.

Because I *hadn't* taken her virginity.

It had been stolen in a horrific and violent way by three strangers.

Only she didn't know that.

My God. My poor baby.

Jonathan cleared his throat again and continued, "Because Daphne didn't remember anything and there were no other witnesses, only Sage could tell us what happened. She told us there were three men, all wearing masks. They took turns raping and beating both of them. They said they'd

be harder on Sage, because she was ugly and deserved worse."
Jonathan shook his head, his eyes sunken and sad. "Sage
was not unattractive, but as you know, no one can compare
to Daphne. Even now, I feel the guilt. The guilt over feeling
happy that my daughter was the prettier of the two. It might
have saved her life."

I gulped. "What else?"

"That's it. That's all Sage ever said. A week after she was
discharged from the hospital, she hanged herself while her
mother ran an errand to the grocery store."

My head fell into my hands again.

"We couldn't bear to tell Daphne what had happened to
Sage, so we told her the Peterson family moved. Sage's parents
did move. They needed a new start, and who could blame
them?"

His words registered, even with my face buried. They
were only words, devoid of emotion.

I couldn't let myself feel anything.

If I did, I'd lose it.

I couldn't lose it. Daphne needed my strength.

"Daphne came home and remembered nothing of the
attack due to her amnesia, so we had to tell her *something*."

I raised my head. "What? What did you tell her?"

"That she was attacked by a gang of girls who were jealous
of her."

"She told me that. Some girls bullied and hit her a few
times and she went into anxiety and depression. What about
spending the night with Sage?"

"She didn't remember any of that. She lost the previous
seventy-two hours."

I nodded. This wasn't real. Couldn't be real.

"There's more," Jonathan said.

More?

Fucking more?

"God, please. Just tell me. Get it over with."

He opened his mouth but closed it when the bartender appeared in front of us.

"Jonathan Wade?" the bartender asked.

"Yeah, that's me."

He heaved a phone onto the bar. "You have a phone call."

CHAPTER SIX

Daphne

"Hello?"

My father's voice. My father's deep and comforting voice.

"Daddy? You've got to come home."

"Daphne? What is it? Are you all right?"

Sirens blared in the distance. The ambulance. Finally.

"I have to go. The ambulance is here."

"Daphne, what happened? Are you all right?"

"It's Mom. She's ... I have to let them in, Daddy."

"Stay on the line, sweetie."

I put down the phone and ran to the front door. Paramedics carried a stretcher and rushed inside.

"Where's your mother?" one of them asked.

"Upstairs. Come on."

I raced up the stairway and led them to the bedroom.

"Is she okay? Will she be okay?"

"We don't know yet. Give us some space, please."

"But it's my mother. She needs me."

"Ma'am, please."

I stepped away and stood in the doorway to the bedroom. Then—

Daddy! I bolted back downstairs to the phone. "Daddy? Daddy, are you still there?"

Dial tone.

How far away was McFall's? My father and Brad would be home soon.

Then everything would be okay.

It had to be.

A few seconds later, the paramedics carried my mother downstairs on a stretcher. An oxygen mask covered her face, and other wires and things stuck out of her.

"Is she okay?" I asked frantically.

"We're doing all we can, ma'am."

"Where are you taking her?"

"The hospital. You can ride with us if you want."

"Yes, yes." Then I changed my mind. "No. My dad's on his way home. I need to be here to tell him where to go. Which hospital?"

"St. Joe's. It's closest. Go to the ER."

I trembled as I nodded. "Thank you. Thank you. Please, help her. Please."

They left and loaded my unconscious mother into the ambulance.

I fell to the floor and cried.

★ ★ ★

"Daphne, baby."

Brad's voice.

"What happened, sweetheart? Where did they take your mother?"

My father's voice.

"S-St. Joe's," I said. "She . . . She took some pills. Valium. After she was drinking."

"God," my father said. "I have to get to the hospital."

"I'm coming with you," I said.

"No, sweetheart. It's late. I want you to stay here. I'll call with news."

"But what if—"

"She won't. I won't let her."

I nodded. My father never broke a promise to me.

"You two stay here. I'll call as soon as I know anything."

Guilt pulsed through me—guilt because I was almost happy to stay here. Even though I wanted to be with my mother, I hated hospitals. Hated them with a purple passion.

My father left.

Brad lifted me off the floor and held me.

I cried into his hard shoulder, completely messing up his shirt, but I didn't care. I couldn't stop the heaving sobs that racked my body.

This was me at my worst, and Brad was witnessing it.

What would he think?

He didn't say anything, just held me and rubbed circles on my back. He was trying to comfort me, but I couldn't be comforted. Not until I knew my mom was okay.

Why? Why had she done this?

Had I upset her that much by getting pregnant? It had been an accident. A true accident. We'd used a condom.

"It's okay," Brad whispered.

I pulled away then. "That's not true. It's not okay. My mother OD'd on Valium. Nothing about this is okay."

He met my gaze. "You're right. I'm sorry." Then he stared at me.

I couldn't bear it. I couldn't see myself, but I could imagine. My face would be red and puffy, my eyes swollen and bloodshot.

I turned away.

"Daphne." He touched my shoulder. "Look at me."

"I'm ugly."

"You're beautiful."

"Crying makes me ugly. I hate crying. I've vowed never to let anyone see me cry."

"Your mother is in an ambulance. Of course you're crying. It's okay." He kissed the top of my head. "And I'm not anyone."

I sniffled.

"Hey." He lifted my chin. "You're not alone."

I sniffled again.

"I'm here, and I'll never leave you, baby. I swear on my life."

His words were sweet, and even though they rang true, they made me fall into sobs again.

I cried and I cried and I cried.

In Brad's arms, I cried.

Until finally, over an hour later, the phone rang.

CHAPTER SEVEN

Brad

I loved her. So damned much.

How could I not?

Learning the truth about Daphne had frightened me, unnerved me, enraged me, but never had I considered leaving her. I loved her, and we'd made a child together.

I would never turn my back on that.

Her father had described her as ethereal, and she was. My Daphne was too perfect for this fucked-up world. Too damned perfect. She didn't deserve the horrors that had fallen onto her. Maybe her parents were right. It was a blessing that she didn't remember it.

Would it stay buried forever?

Would I someday have to tell her what had truly occurred before her junior year? What she'd gone through? What had happened to her best friend?

Thoughts whirred through my mind with the sound of a buzz saw—jumbled thoughts that had no bearing on what was happening now.

Daphne's mother had overdosed. Daphne's mother might die.

No.

Daphne was strong, but could she handle this now? She

was young, she was damaged—she didn't even know *how* damaged—and she was pregnant.

She needed her mother.

What if—

The phone rang.

Daphne jerked away from me and picked it up. "Daddy?"

Then a pause. A pause that seemed to last for hours as Daphne presumably listened to what her father was saying.

Her red and swollen face turned white.

No. God, no. That meant bad news.

No. Just no.

Not on top of everything else.

"I understand. Thank you, Daddy." She hung up the phone and turned to me. "She's going to be all right. They pumped her stomach. She's going to be all right."

I held her when she fell back into my arms.

"See? Everything's going to be fine."

She pulled back and sniffed. "Everything's not fine, Brad. Everything's so far from fine. My mother just tried to end her life. Because of me."

"Baby, this wasn't because of you."

"Of course it was. I came home pregnant after a month in college. She expected more from me. I promised her I'd be okay."

"You *are* okay. It was an accident. A true accident. We took precautions."

"I know." She dabbed at her eyes. "Crap. I need a tissue."

"Okay." I stood. "Where's the bathroom?"

"Upstairs, to your right."

I went up, grabbed the box of tissues out of the bathroom, and brought them to Daphne. "Here you go."

She took several and blew her nose. "I must look atrocious."

"You look beautiful."

"You're such a liar."

"Baby, you'll always be beautiful to me."

"What about when I'm nine months pregnant and big as a house?"

"Especially then."

That got a chuckle out of her—a tiny one, but a chuckle nonetheless.

"Why?"

"Because the baby we made is in there." I touched her belly tenderly. "He's in there now."

"He?"

"Yeah, I think it's a boy. What do you think?"

"I *know* it's a boy. I'm not sure how, but I do."

I smiled at her. She was so beautiful. So innocent. Yet her innocence had been stolen, though she didn't know.

Now, more than ever, I renewed my vow to look after her always. She needed my protection, and I'd never waver.

Had I bitten off more than I could chew? Maybe, but it didn't matter. I was all-in now. All-in for this sweet and wonderful young woman and the baby she carried. My baby. Mine and hers.

Daphne grabbed more tissues, dabbed at her eyes, and then blew her nose again. "Brad?"

"Hmm?"

"Daddy won't be home tonight. He's staying at the hospital."

"I figured as much."

"That means we're alone. Here. In the house."

The fact hadn't escaped me, but I wasn't going to—

"Make love to me, Brad."

"Baby, this is your father's house."

"I don't care. I need you."

"You're upset. You're worried about your mother. That doesn't mean you need sex."

"It's not the sex I need. It's *you*. I need to feel something beautiful, and you and I together, that's beautiful."

I touched her cheek. It was red and puffy but still like silk beneath my calloused fingertips.

"Are you sure?"

"Of course I'm sure. Don't treat me like a child, Brad."

"But—"

She placed two fingers over my lips. "Please. We're in love. I'm pregnant. There's no going back now. I want to make love with you tonight. I need to."

Trying to be a gentleman while this goddess begged me to make love to her was more difficult than I ever imagined.

"Please," she said again.

Already my cock was responding. I wanted her. I always wanted her. But more than my desire to satiate myself in her body was my desire to take care of her, to do what was best for her. I wasn't sure lovemaking fit into that category tonight.

"Daphne, I don't think—"

"This is what I want. Show me what's truly important."

I'd made love to her before. But now . . . Now that I knew what she'd been through, how could I do this to her? She was so innocent. So damaged.

But so wonderful. And so fucking beautiful. And I loved her. I loved her so damned much.

Despite my name, I wasn't made of steel. "All right, baby. Take me to your bedroom."

CHAPTER EIGHT

Daphne

My bedroom wasn't decorated in pink. Wasn't overly girlie. The only problem was the twin bed, but we'd make do.

Puppy still sat where I'd left him earlier. I wasn't embarrassed by my stuffed dog. I picked him up and moved him to a chair.

Brad looked around. My room was so small compared to his bedroom at the townhome, and especially compared to the room at his ranch house outside Snow Creek. He was so big and broad that this room seemed to swallow him up.

He acted hesitant, so I did something I'd never done. I took the lead. I walked to him, wrapped my arms around his neck, and pulled his head downward until his lips met mine.

I kissed him softly at first, and then I opened my mouth and let my tongue wander out to meet his. He tasted of liquor and woods, of cinnamon and strength, of everything that was important in the world. Then I deepened the kiss, kissed him the way he'd taught me. I wanted to take from him while giving to him. I wanted a raw and feral kiss.

He responded slowly, gently easing into it.

I pulled away. "Don't hold back," I demanded. "Kiss me like you mean it."

"I always mean it, baby."

"Then show me."

He eased away from me. "I ... I'm not sure I can."

"Why? Don't you want me?"

"I always want you."

"Then why—?"

He grabbed the back of my head and planted his mouth on mine. This time he dived in, taking my tongue with his, snaking it over my teeth and gums.

A kiss. A real kiss. Brad had taught me what a real kiss was. It could be soft and sweet, and those kisses were wonderful. But right now? I wanted a kiss of passion. A raw kiss of need.

Because I needed Brad. I needed him so badly.

Our mouths melded together. Heat swept over me, through me, around me, landing between my legs. If anything, I felt it more intensely now that I was pregnant. Was it my imagination? Maybe. Or maybe it was the pure emotion of knowing the product of our love was growing inside me.

My little dove.

Brad broke the kiss and inhaled sharply. "I want you. I want you so much, Daphne."

"I want you too. Now." I lifted my shirt over my head.

He sucked in a breath. "Every time I look at you, you're even more beautiful than before."

His words warmed me, settled over me like warm chocolate syrup. He took his own shirt off and discarded it. I touched him, trailed my fingertips over his broad shoulders, his muscular arms, his chiseled chest and abdomen. Traced his nipples that hardened under my touch.

"I love how you touch me," he said. "How it makes me feel." He removed his boots and unbuckled his belt. "Will you touch me, Daphne?"

"Yes," I murmured.

"I mean…"

"I'll touch you anywhere you want me to."

He lowered his jeans and underwear, sliding them down his legs and kicking them off.

His cock was hard and ready. That was what he wanted. For me to touch him there.

I wanted to. It was part of him, and I loved every part of him. It had been inside me, helped me have such pleasure.

Guys loved to be touched there, loved to be sucked there. It was all new to me, but I wanted to please Brad more than anything in the world.

I tentatively reached forward—

"Wait." He unclasped my bra and set it on the chair next to Puppy.

I had to close my eyes for a moment. Puppy wasn't real. He couldn't see what we were doing. But he was a symbol of my childhood, and I was no longer a child.

No longer a child.

In fact, before long, I'd *have* a child.

But that was my last thought of a child. No more while my body was responding to Brad's eyes on me. I was hot. So hot. Burning in flames.

He unzipped my jeans and helped me out of them. He pulled my panties down my hips until I was as naked as he was.

He was beautiful. So beautiful.

"Tell me what you want," I said.

"I need your touch, baby."

I nodded. "Show me what to do. I want to please you."

"You always please me." He took my hand and led it to his penis.

My fingers trembled as I touched him. It was warm, so warm, as if it were made of burning embers underneath the smooth skin. Yes, it was smooth. Smooth and hot and perfect, two blue veins running over it like the marbling on his countertops in the townhome.

"Show me," I said again.

"Grasp it. Like you're shaking someone's hand."

I gripped him as he instructed.

A low groan left his throat. "God."

"Is that good?"

"You have no idea." He closed his eyes. "Do whatever you want, baby."

"But I—"

He opened his eyes, meeting my gaze. "It feels good just to have you touch me."

"Do . . . you want my mouth?"

"Only if you want to."

"I want whatever you want."

"That works perfectly, because I want whatever you want. If you want to put your mouth on me, then I want that too. But if you don't, I don't."

"Except that you do." I warmed all over. "I may be inexperienced, but I'm not naïve. I know what men like."

"Baby . . . "

"Please, Brad. We're going to be together for a long time. I need to know how to please you."

He nodded. "Start as slowly as you need to."

"You mean I don't have to deep throat you this time?"

His eyes shot into circles.

I couldn't help a laugh. "See? I know a few things. Not that I've ever done any of it." Looking at Brad, I wasn't sure any woman could ever deep throat him. He was massive.

I fell to my knees and let his dick dangle in front of me. I touched my tongue to him and swirled it over the head. Salty. And rather pleasant. When he shuddered, I knew I was okay. I could do this. I could do anything for Brad Steel.

I puckered my lips and kissed the head. He shuddered again.

Then I gripped it as he'd shown me and kissed it again.

"Fuck, baby."

I looked up at him. His dark eyes were burning.

"Okay?" I said.

"Perfect. Except now I need to be inside you. Right fucking now." He pulled me to my feet and set me on the bed. "Do you have any idea what you do to me, Daphne? Any idea?"

I quaked beneath him. "I imagine it's along the same lines as what you do to me."

"Maybe. I don't know. All I know is if I don't get inside you right now, I'll go insane." He touched his fingertips to my vagina. "Thank God. You're ready. More than ready." He shoved his erection into me.

"Oh!" I cried as he filled me, completed me.

"I love you," he gritted out against my ear. "I love you so damned much. No matter what, baby, I'll always love you."

No matter what? But I didn't think any more about his words.

"I love you too," I panted.

His thrusts were hard. Hard and fast. Hard and fast and perfect. For this was what I needed. This raw taking. Later, we could make slow, sweet love. Later, maybe I'd be able to give him a real blowjob. Now? I wanted to be fucked.

Yeah, fucked. I never used that word, but I understood it

now. Fucking was raw. Fucking was hot. Fucking was an escape.

An escape I craved.

As he fucked me, I closed my eyes and let him take me to a new place—a happy place, a place where I didn't have to think. Only feel.

And I felt everything.

When Brad filled that aching emptiness inside me, all the problems went away, floated off on the waves of our passion.

When he pushed into me with his final thrust, I reveled in the completeness, the joining of our bodies, the love we shared. Everything. Everything was okay when we were together.

Everything would always be okay.

CHAPTER NINE

Brad

Had I given her what she needed? She hadn't come, and I felt bad about that. I also felt like a heel for wanting a blowjob from her after all she'd been through. All she didn't *know* she'd been through.

"I'll take care of you," I whispered against her ear after I'd rolled off her.

"You did. It was perfect."

"But you didn't—"

"I don't need to. I wanted the closeness tonight. I wanted you inside me. I don't need anything else."

"Maybe you don't need it, but do you *want* it?"

She smiled. "Maybe, but my mind is back with my mom now. I'm not sure I could have a climax tonight. You gave me what I needed."

"Are you sure? I'm happy to . . . "

"I know you are. You gave me what I asked for."

"You asked me to make love to you."

"I did, but I found out what I really needed was a good fucking. Just the two of us joined, forgetting about real life for a blissful moment. You gave me that. Now I'm back, and I need to think about where we go from here."

"What do you mean? We go where we were always

going. We get married and we have the baby. Surely you're not reconsidering."

"No. No, I'm not. But I didn't think about my parents' needs in all this, and I'm paying for that now."

"Daphne, your mother didn't take those pills because of you."

She bit her lip. "Yeah, she did. She was fine until now."

"I don't think she was ever fine."

"But—"

"Shh. I've been around depression. I told you my mother struggles as well. Don't blame yourself for this. You have enough on your plate. You don't deserve it."

"I can't help it."

"Then blame me as well. I contributed to your condition as much as you did."

"But we didn't do it on purpose. You used a condom."

I smiled and shoved a stray hair away from her eye. "That's my point. It happened anyway. It was fate."

"Fate," she said softly.

Daphne had first used the word to describe our meeting, and I'd grown to believe her. Fate had a hand in it. A big hand. Any other time, a condom would have prevented pregnancy. We'd beaten the odds.

As far as I was concerned, this child was meant to be.

I kissed her forehead. "You've had a rough night. Go to sleep. I'll find the guest room."

"I'm not sure Mom put it together yet."

"Doesn't matter."

"No. Stay with me."

"I'd love nothing more, but this bed is tiny."

"I'll lie on top of you."

"Then neither of us will get any sleep. Besides, if your father comes home early and finds me in bed with you—"

"I'm already pregnant, Brad. What else does he think could happen?"

She had a point, but I'd come to respect Jonathan Wade. He loved his daughter and would take care of her forever if he had to.

He didn't have to.

It was my job now.

"It would be disrespectful for me to sleep in here with you, baby. You know that."

"Yeah, I know," she relented. "The guest room is right next to this one. I hope there are sheets on the bed."

"If there aren't, I'll find something. Don't worry about me." I rolled off the bed and grabbed my clothes. "Come on. Get under the covers."

"I should put some pajamas on."

"Yeah, good idea. I'll get them. Where are they?"

"Top drawer of my dresser."

I opened the drawer and pulled out what appeared to be a nightgown. "This?"

"That'll do."

I gave it to her. Once her beautiful body was covered, I gently tucked her into bed. "Holler if you need anything. Try to get some sleep. Your mom is in good hands."

She nodded and closed her eyes.

I walked out, flipping the light switch.

I found the guest room, and there were sheets on the bed. I put my underwear back on along with a T-shirt and slid under the covers.

★ ★ ★

"Brad."

A low voice.

I jerked upward.

"It's me. Jonathan."

My eyes adjusted to the dark. Jonathan Wade stood in the guest room.

"Is everything okay? Lucy?"

"She's going to be fine," he said. "Come downstairs. We need to finish our talk."

"What time is it?"

"Six a.m."

I got out of bed. "No problem. I get up at five on the ranch."

"I've already brewed a pot of coffee and checked on Daphne. She's sleeping soundly."

I pulled on my jeans and followed Jonathan downstairs to the kitchen. He'd already poured two cups of coffee.

"Black, right?"

I nodded.

"I thought that's how you took it last night. I wasn't sure, though. Seems like a lifetime has gone by since then."

"Yeah, I know what you mean." I swirled the coffee in my cup to cool it and then took a sip.

"I haven't had a chance to talk at length with a doctor about Lucy."

"Of course not. It was the middle of the night."

"Yeah, and today is Sunday. I'll make an appointment first thing tomorrow."

I nodded. "What exactly happened? Daphne said they pumped her stomach."

"Yeah. Just to get the drugs out of her, but most of it had gotten into her bloodstream by that time. Turns out it's nearly impossible to die from overdosing on Valium. You'd have to take way more pills than Lucy had."

"Thank God."

"Still, she's not out of the woods. She had a lot of alcohol in her system as well as some barbiturate sleeping pills. I don't know what she was thinking."

I didn't know what to say to that, so I said nothing.

"Honestly, Brad, I had no idea she was suffering so much."

"If it helps, I don't think Daphne did either."

"Daphne hasn't been here for the last month. I have been. I should have seen the signs."

"Not if they weren't there." I cleared my throat. "Daphne is blaming herself."

Jonathan's eyebrows shot up. "Why would she do that?"

"She thinks her pregnancy sent Lucy over the edge."

"I hope you told her that's not true."

"I did. Whether she believes me is another story."

Jonathan shook his head. "Daphne doesn't need this. She has enough to deal with."

I nodded. She did, even if she didn't know part of what she was dealing with.

"I've been thinking," Jonathan said. "Lucy had to be so strong after what happened to Daphne. She could never falter, never let our daughter see the pain she was carrying. Now, with Daphne gone, Lucy's had time to dwell on things. In retrospect, I could see her declining. I should have been more attentive."

"Hindsight is always twenty-twenty." How well I knew. "Don't blame yourself. You didn't force those pills down her throat." I winced at my own words. Had I gone too far?

46

Jonathan seemed okay, though. "I understand that. But I could have prevented this, and I didn't. I don't know how I'm supposed to live with that. Not after everything else."

I had no words of wisdom for the man across from me. I was twenty-two years old. Twenty-two! Jonathan needed advice from someone more experienced than I.

He continued, "I need to focus on Lucy."

"Of course."

"I've been distracted. Distracted by work. By Daphne."

"She's your daughter, and she's been through a lot. Of course you've been concerned."

"I have been. Maybe more than I should be, or maybe not enough. I never expected her to . . . "

"Get pregnant?"

"Get involved in a relationship so soon. I believe that the pregnancy was an accident. I've told you that."

"I know. Trust me, I wasn't looking for a lifetime commitment either when I met Daphne. But she's the one. I knew it before the pregnancy. I can't explain it."

"I hope you're right. I hope you truly do love my daughter."

"I do."

He nodded. "Because I'm counting on you, Brad. I'm counting on you to take care of her now."

CHAPTER TEN

Daphne

Running.

Fear pulsed through me as I ran.

Panting. Can't catch breath. Running. Got to get away. Away, away, away ....

I jerked up in bed, my heart racing.

The dream.

The damned dream.

Again.

I didn't scream. Why?

A moment passed before I realized I was home in my own bed. I'd come home for the weekend. Brad had come with me. We'd told my parents about our child.

And my mom had overdosed on Valium.

I didn't scream because I was home. I'd trained myself not to scream when I woke up. I didn't want to upset my mother.

But my mother wasn't here. She was at St. Joseph's hospital being treated for a drug overdose—a drug overdose that I'd likely caused.

Dawn was breaking. I eased the chills on my arms, rose from my bed, and walked to my window.

I could watch the sunrise this morning.

That would chase the nightmares away. I loved the

sunrise—the beginning of a brand-new day. The aurora. The beauty that told me anything was possible.

I put on my slippers and padded out of my room. The door to the guest room was open. I peered in. "Brad?"

His bed was rumpled, but he wasn't there.

I looked down the stairs. "Brad?" I called.

"Down here," came his voice. "Your dad and I are having coffee."

I raced down the stairs. "Daddy? How's Mom?"

Brad and my father sat at the dining room table. Our galley kitchen wasn't big enough for a kitchen table.

"You want some coffee, sweetie?" Dad asked.

I poured myself a cup. "Please. Tell me how Mom is."

"She's okay," he said. "She'll be gone a few days."

At the hospital. I hated hospitals. But I'd suck it up. "I want to see her."

"You will. It's so early. What are you doing up?"

"I want to watch the sunrise."

That got a smile from both Brad and my father.

"That's a spectacular idea, sweetheart," Dad said. "Let's all watch the sunrise. The view is great from the deck."

Brad took my hand as we walked outside onto the deck. The mountains were purple and crisp in the distance to the west, but we looked the other way. Toward the east, where the sun would rise in its pink-and-gold glory.

I had the nightmare.

My mom's in the hospital.

Brad and I have a hard road ahead of us.

None of that mattered when I let the beauty of the dawn consume me.

And oh, it was so beautiful. Was anything in the world

more beautiful than a Colorado sunrise?

"Next time you're on the ranch, we'll watch the sunrise," Brad said. "The mountains are to the east there, and I tell you, there's nothing more amazing than watching the sun rise over them."

"I'd like that," I said.

My father perked up. "Wait a minute. What do you mean 'next time'?"

Uh-oh. I hadn't told my parents about my trip to Brad's ranch a few weeks ago. I smiled. When our baby was conceived.

"I've been there," I said.

"I had to take care of some business, so I took Daphne home with me for the weekend."

My father pursed his lips, but he didn't say anything. What could he say? We were both adults, and what was done was done.

"I met Brad's father," I said.

"And his mother?"

"She was out of town," Brad offered. "We'll go there next weekend when she's home. You know, to give them our news."

"How do you think your parents will feel about all of this?" my father asked.

"Probably the same way you felt," Brad said. "It's not the optimal situation, but it happened despite precautions. We'll get their blessing."

My heart raced. I'd wanted to enjoy the sunrise, and now I had to think about telling Brad's parents about our situation.

And of course my mind slammed back to my poor mother in the hospital.

I stood. "Let's go in."

"But the sunrise," Brad said.

"It's over. We were too busy talking to notice."

"I'm sorry, sweetheart," my father said. "It's my fault. I was a little taken aback that you'd already been to the ranch."

"It's no big deal." But it was a big deal. It was one less sunrise I'd see in my lifetime. One fewer thing of beauty I'd witness.

I patted my belly. *You and I will watch all the sunrises, little dove. You'll get me up early anyway, and we'll mark each new day together.*

"I'm going in," I said.

"We'll come with you," Dad said.

"Sure. I could use another cup of coffee," Brad agreed.

"Don't bother." I sighed. "I'm going to take a shower."

I left them on the deck and went upstairs to the bathroom. One bathroom for all three bedrooms. Certainly different from what Brad was used to. In the ranch house, all the bedrooms had their own private bath. Plus, this one bathroom was tiny. We had a small powder room on the main level, but it only housed a toilet and a sink. If you wanted a bath or shower in this house, the bathroom upstairs was your only choice. I turned on the shower and shed my gown.

Soon I'd go to the hospital to see my mother, and then Brad and I would drive back to campus.

Where I'd have to act like nothing was the matter.

I could do that. I was used to it.

CHAPTER ELEVEN

Brad

"Is she okay?" I asked Jonathan.

He nodded. "She gets a little distant sometimes. Surely you've noticed that."

"Honestly, I haven't. She's always happy at school, always looking on the bright side of things."

"Oh? That's good to hear." Jonathan smiled. "She's probably worried about her mother, then."

"Of course. That makes sense."

"When Daphne's done in the shower, I'll take mine."

"Yeah, I should do that as well."

"Sure. After I'm done."

"Oh. Yeah, of course," I said. They only had one shower in the house? It was a small suburban residence, but surely . . .

Daphne and I had certainly grown up differently. I had taken so much for granted in my own life.

"Daphne will want to go to the hospital to see her mom. Then we'll head back to campus."

Jonathan nodded. "I hope you were serious about wanting to take care of Daphne and the baby."

"You know I am."

"Good. It's important. Especially now."

"Especially now?"

"I've neglected Lucy. I see that now. I should have seen this coming and prevented it. I've been so focused on Daphne that I didn't see what was right in front of my face. Lucy needs me."

"She's going to be fine, Jonathan," I said. "She'll need some therapy, but—"

"Yes, and I'll see that she gets everything she needs. She will be my primary focus. That's where you come in."

I lifted my eyebrows.

"I meant it when I said Lucy and I would take care of Daphne and the child, but right now, I must see to Lucy's needs. I'm depending on you, Brad. I'm depending on you to take care of my daughter."

His blue eyes held emotion I couldn't identify. Was he abandoning his daughter? I couldn't believe it, but that seemed to be what his words indicated.

"Of course I'll take care of her."

"She's your responsibility now," he said. "Yours. Just like Lucy is mine."

"She's a grown woman," I said.

"I know that. So is Lucy. But my wife needs me. She deserves my undivided attention. I haven't been giving it to her, and that's changing as of today."

"I understand."

"I've told you Daphne's history," he said, "but I haven't told you everything."

Right. We'd been interrupted at the bar last night when Daphne had called about her mother.

Did I want to hear this?

Didn't really matter. I needed to hear it. I'd just promised this man I'd take care of his daughter. I would, anyway, but it would be better to know everything I was dealing with.

"Go ahead."

"It's not pretty."

"Can it possibly be any worse than what you've already told me?"

"Nothing is worse than the incident itself, but you need to know how Daphne ended up in the hospital for so long."

I nodded. "I need more coffee. And won't Daphne be down soon?"

"Are you kidding? It takes her an hour to get ready."

"Really? She doesn't wear much makeup."

"No, but her hair takes a long time to dry, even here in Colorado, because it's so long and thick."

"Oh. Okay." I drew in a breath. "Let me have it, then."

"Daphne was partially right when she told you she had severe anxiety and depression. When she was released from the hospital and came home, the school year was about to begin. Daphne had always loved school and done well. She was a straight-A student, so when the first day of her junior year rolled around, Lucy and I were surprised when she froze."

"Froze?"

"Yeah. She completely froze. Wouldn't get out of bed. Wouldn't speak. Nothing."

"What happened then?"

"We called the doctor, of course. We originally thought she was missing Sage, but it was more than that. She'd had a psychiatric evaluation in the hospital, and the doctor warned us to watch for symptoms of PTSD."

"PTSD? But she didn't remember what happened."

"That's what I said. Turns out that doesn't matter. Being in the hospital with her injuries was traumatic enough, and though her mind didn't recall the actual trauma, her body did. The symptoms showed up with a vengeance on that first day of school. We literally had to pick her up and take her to see a doctor that day. She wouldn't move. He diagnosed her with severe PTSD and suggested a brief hospitalization so experts could figure out how to treat her. What else could we do? We agreed."

I nodded.

"She was hospitalized for evaluation and remained catatonic for several more days. When she finally came out of it, she still didn't want to go back to school. Lucy decided she could homeschool Daphne until she was ready to go back, so she quit her job and we brought Daphne home."

I nodded again.

"Neither Lucy nor Daphne took to homeschooling. It was a bad fit all around, so the psychiatrist suggested we admit Daphne to a psychiatric treatment center where she'd get her schooling and also receive treatment."

"And..."

"Daphne didn't want to go, of course. Who would? But we insisted, and she went under a lot of duress. She got used to it after a few days."

"She says she doesn't remember most of that time. Did they keep her drugged up?"

"No, they didn't. She had *some* medications, of course, to help with the severe anxiety and depression, but mostly she *chooses* not to remember, Brad."

"Wait. What do you mean she *chooses* not to remember?"

"Simply what I said. Part of her therapy required her to keep a journal while she was there."

"She never mentioned that."

"Because the therapist has the journal. He hasn't let her read it because he doesn't want to traumatize her. Dr. Payne said it's important that she ask for it. When she does, he'll give it to her."

I cleared my throat. "Have you read it?"

"No, I haven't. Dr. Payne offered, but Lucy and I haven't been able to bring ourselves to. Besides, it may be highly personal, never meant for our eyes."

"So she kept a journal. What else did she do at the hospital?"

"Therapy, of course, and studies. And she learned to play a musical instrument."

My mind whirled back to our time in the guesthouse. She'd sat down at the baby grand piano in the living room...

"Was it the piano?"

"Yes. Why do you ask?"

"We have a piano at the guesthouse on the ranch. When I took her there, she said she didn't play, but she sat right down and played some notes and chords. When I asked her where she learned, she said music class."

"I suppose you could call it music class. It was one-on-one piano instruction at the facility."

I cleared my throat. I needed to ask the next question, even though I didn't necessarily want to hear the answer. "Did anything traumatic happen to Daphne at the hospital itself?"

"No. Not that we know of. It's a good facility. If I had any doubts about it, I would have pulled her right out of there, Brad."

"I know that. I'm just trying to understand why she doesn't remember so much of it."

"Dr. Payne says she's blocking it out. It's a time in her

life when she didn't have any control, and she doesn't want to remember it."

"This is the same Dr. Payne who said she was ready to go away to college, right?"

"Yes. He's a good man and an excellent therapist. She got through her senior year with excellent grades, and she didn't have any issues with memory. She had some recurring nightmares, but they eventually subsided."

"Jonathan," I said, "they haven't subsided."

He wrinkled his forehead. "Oh, no."

"They're not interfering with her daily life. She's doing well in classes and enjoys college. I know she's had the dream twice since she's been at college, though. Once was while we were at my ranch."

"Did she tell you about it?"

"Briefly. She doesn't remember it. She only knows she's afraid, but she wakes up and can't remember why."

"Dr. Payne thinks it's her subconscious remembering the assault," Jonathan said quietly.

"Could I talk to Dr. Payne? If Daphne's my responsibility now—"

Jonathan stopped me. "You can't. Daphne's over eighteen now. You'd need her permission to talk to her doctors or access her records. Even Lucy and I can't at this point."

"What about after we're married?"

"Still no, unless you get Daphne's written consent. Adult medical files are private."

Damn.

Damn, damn, damn.

"Is it possible that she'll remember the incident?"

"Memory can come back, but Dr. Payne doubts it."

"What if she *needs* to remember? What if the only way she'll be able to stop the nightmares is to deal with what happened to her?"

"Lucy and I talked to Dr. Payne at length about that before Daphne turned eighteen. It's a tough call. Would you want to tell your daughter she'd been beaten and raped by three men? That her best friend committed suicide because of it?" He shook his head. "I can't do it. I just can't."

"I understand. I'm not sure I could either."

"Dr. Payne feels the nightmares will eventually go away. In fact, we thought they had."

"Like I said, it's only been twice in the last month." Twice that I knew of, anyway.

He nodded. "I can't tell Lucy about the nightmares. Not right now."

"I get it."

"Daphne is still on our health insurance, but once you two get married . . . "

"She'll be covered. My father has an excellent policy for everyone at the ranch. She'll be covered as my wife."

He nodded. "Good. Daphne needs coverage."

"Coverage for what?"

Daphne stood in the doorway.

CHAPTER TWELVE

Daphne

"Hi, sweetheart," my father said.

"Hey, baby." From Brad.

"Coverage for what?" I repeated.

Dad cleared his throat. "Brad and I were just discussing his health plan at the ranch. Once you're married, you'll be covered."

"Oh." Of course I needed coverage. Who knew when I might go crazy again? That was what my father was thinking. He would never say it, but that was where his mind was. What he didn't know was that I'd never lose it again. I was determined. I'd fainted twice in the last month at school. When I got anxious, I tended to hyperventilate. I was also determined that wouldn't happen again. I needed to keep my health. I couldn't let my little dove be deprived of oxygen.

I'd be okay.

I knew it.

For my little dove.

I had to be.

My father stood. "I'm going to take a quick shower. Then we'll go see your mom."

I nodded. I wanted to see my mother, but I hated the idea of going to the hospital. Would she end up in the same facility where I'd spent most of my junior year? And then I'd have to visit her there?

Ugh. I couldn't deal with that thought at the moment.

Brad smiled and patted the spot beside him. "Sit down, baby."

I returned his smile, even though I wasn't feeling it, and sat next to him. The warmth from his body seeped into me, comforting me.

"Do you want me to go with you to see your mom?"

"You don't have to."

"I want to do what you need me to do. If it's easier if I'm not there, I understand."

I sighed. This wouldn't be easy no matter what. My father would be there, but my father was no longer the most important man in my life.

The man sitting next to me was.

And always would be.

"I can handle it on my own," I said.

He took my hand. "That's not what I'm asking. I don't doubt that you can handle it. Do you want me there?"

"Yes. Yes, I want you there."

"Then I'll be there." He stood. "I need to take a quick shower as soon as your dad is out. We won't be long."

I nodded as he walked back into the house.

Alone on the deck.

I'd spent hours out here last year. God knew I didn't have any friends to hang out with. That was the great thing about college. I'd chosen a small and very exclusive school in Denver where no one else from my senior class went. I'd gotten in on a full scholarship due to my test scores and GPA, but no doubt also in large part because of the essay I'd written about my rise from mental illness.

I liked to write.

Maybe Brad was right. I should pursue a career in writing. But what would I write? A personal statement about the horrors of my mental illness might impress college admissions staff, but no one would pay money to read it.

And would I even pursue a career? I'd be lucky to finish my second semester. What if the baby came early? Once I had the baby, would I go back to school in Grand Junction? Or would I do what most students in my situation did—never finish?

I'd promised myself I'd live life to the fullest now. I'd find joy in every moment. That goal had become easier once senior year was over. Senior year without close friends and with your classmates whispering behind your back didn't lend itself well to joy. So I'd thrown myself into my studies. Prepared for my SAT and ACT and gotten near perfect scores. No clubs, no sports, no prom for me. Just the books, and it had paid off with the scholarship.

The scholarship to the college Brad Steel attended.

Fate.

Always fate.

And now...our baby. My little dove. It had to be fate. We'd tried to prevent his conception, but he was determined to come anyway.

Fate.

Fate always found a way.

Fate had led me to Brad Steel.

In a way, that horrid year of my life had led me where I was today. Before, I always assumed I'd attend CU with Sage and everyone else. I never would have tried to get into Stilton.

My parents certainly couldn't have afforded it without the scholarship for tuition.

Everything happens for a reason.

Dr. Payne used that phrase a lot.

"Why do some things have to be so painful?" I'd asked once.

"What doesn't kill us makes us stronger."

I liked Dr. Payne, but he was the master of the cliché.

Of course, clichés were clichés for a reason. They made a lot of sense.

For the first time, I was thankful for my junior year.

It had led me to Brad.

I laughed out loud. My life sure was heading in a different direction from where I'd assumed it would head. Married at eighteen? Who did that anymore? Mother at nineteen?

This was my life now.

No time to plan any kind of wedding, and my parents couldn't afford it. Brad and I would probably be married at city hall. I could live with that. Not like I had a choice.

Still, what girl doesn't dream of being a princess in white for a day?

I'd had those dreams once, when I was younger. Before I had other more important things to think about—like keeping my memory intact.

Now silly girlhood dreams seemed like exactly that—silly girlhood dreams.

I'd been forced to grow up quickly, and now I was doubling down. Soon I'd be responsible for another person—my little dove who I already adored.

I'd rise to the challenge.

Continue to find the joy in everything.

Because my little dove needed me.

"Daphne?" Dad opened the screen door leading to the deck. "You ready, sweetheart?"

I nodded.

Whether I was ready didn't matter. I'd go see my mother. I'd set foot in the hospital. I'd be strong.

I had no other choice.

CHAPTER THIRTEEN

Brad

Lucy was asleep the whole time we were at the hospital. Daphne sat with her for a half hour, holding her hand. I didn't pressure her.

Finally she said to me, "We need to get back to campus."

I nodded. We said goodbye to Jonathan, and I gave him my address and phone number in case he wanted to reach me. Then we drove back to college. Daphne was quiet, but she seemed okay.

"Do you want to stay with me tonight?" I asked.

"No, I need to talk to Patty. Tell her what's going on. I guess tomorrow after classes I'll go talk to the registrar and the campus housing person. Patty will probably be thrilled to have a single room for the rest of the year."

"Probably only the rest of the semester," I said. "They'll most likely fill the room with a transfer student in January."

She nodded. "Well, she can have her fun for a few months, anyway. The girl gets around."

"She does?"

"You know she slept with Sean the first night we were on campus. She also slept with her first nighter—who's a pig, by the way—and still sees him. Whatever happened between her and Sean?"

"Murph likes to play the field," I said. "I love him like a brother, but I don't agree with everything he does."

"Patty seems okay with it. I think she likes playing the field too. She's not actually dating Rex, the other guy. Just screwing him when they both feel like it."

"A lot of people do that in college," I said. "It was never my thing. Not long term, anyway."

"I suppose you were always with … "

"She's gone now," I said. "Wendy and I are over. She won't be bothering either of us for a long time."

"How can I be sure?"

"Trust me."

Wendy had been committed for psychiatric evaluation and treatment after she pulled a gun on Murphy a few weeks ago. I owed my dad for this one. When the Madigans had refused to take charge of their daughter, my father stepped in, found a psychiatrist willing to sign the documents, and then paid the Madigans to sign affidavits testifying to what Wendy had done. Murph also signed an affidavit. No one had to lie. They just told the truth, and the psychiatrist took care of the rest. He guaranteed that Wendy would be hospitalized for at least a year.

In a year, Daphne and I could finish the school year. I would graduate, we'd get married, have our baby, and settle on the ranch.

The timing worked perfectly.

And Wendy would be gone for more than a year. I'd manage it somehow, even if I had to get my father involved again.

My father …

How would he feel when he found out I was getting

married and having a baby? He'd met Daphne and seemed to like her okay, though my dad was difficult to read. He was an asshole, had treated my mother like crap for years. At least he didn't hit her anymore.

My mom would love Daphne. They had a lot in common. Daphne had loved Mom's greenhouse. I felt like she and Mom were similar souls. They'd be close, and my mom would adore our baby.

Yeah, we were young. It wasn't what either of us had planned or what our parents had planned.

But we'd do it.

We'd bring our child into this world, and we'd thrive.

I'd see to it.

"Brad, are you listening to me?"

I jerked out of my thoughts. "I'm sorry. What did you say?"

"I said, 'How can you be sure Wendy won't bother us?'"

"She's going out of town."

Not exactly a lie. The Madigans and the psychiatrist had arranged for Wendy to be hospitalized in Grand Junction so they could visit her easily. So yeah, she was out of town.

I didn't like lying to Daphne. It left an acidic taste in my mouth—a taste I'd never grow used to, which meant I needed to keep lies to a minimum.

But how could I keep lies to a minimum? Already I was lying by omission on the daily because of what Jonathan had told me. I had to compartmentalize—had to—because just thinking about what Daphne went through sent me into a tense rage.

Yes, compartmentalize. It was the only way. I had to grow accustomed to the lies.

Besides, it was better Daphne didn't know where Wendy

was or why. Otherwise, I'd have to explain what Wendy was capable of, and that might scare Daphne.

Hell, it scared *me.*

"Oh. Where's she going?"

"I'm not sure." God, I hated lying. "I don't really care, as long as she stays away from us, and she'll be away from us."

Daphne nodded. "Yeah. That's good."

I pulled up to Daphne's dorm. "You want me to go in with you?"

She smiled. "You don't have to."

"Maybe I want to."

"Okay."

I opened the door of the truck for her, and we walked into the dormitory.

"Hey there, you two." Daphne's friend Ennis Ainsley, a British exchange student, stood at the reception desk.

"Hi, Ennis," Daphne said.

"You've been scarce."

"I took Brad home to meet my parents for the weekend."

"Sounds fun."

Ennis and I didn't exactly see eye to eye. That was mostly my fault. I'd punched him the night I met him because I thought he'd gotten Daphne drunk. In reality, he was a nice guy and I'd been a jerk.

But he also had the hots for Daphne, which I didn't like.

Of course, most guys who met Daphne got the hots for her. She was the most beautiful woman on campus.

And she was mine. Especially now.

"Want to grab a bite later?" Ennis asked.

"I don't know . . . "

"I meant both of you," he said.

"Yeah, sure," I said. "Okay with you, baby?"

Daphne's face split into a wide grin. "Yeah. I'd like that."

"Have you been off campus yet?" I asked Ennis.

"Not really."

"We'll go for pizza. Ask Patty if she wants to go along. I'll be by around six to pick you up."

"Sounds great," she said.

"I'll be here," Ennis agreed.

Good. I didn't much like the guy, but Daphne did. He was important to her, so I'd get to know him. Even if he did look and talk like Prince Charles.

CHAPTER FOURTEEN

Daphne

Brad took us to the same place we'd eaten the first day we'd met. The second-best pizza in Colorado. I'd called Brad earlier and told him I wanted to tell Patty and Ennis about our situation at dinner. They were my two closest friends here at school—other than Brad himself—and I didn't want to hide this from them, especially since things would be moving quickly. I told him not to mention my mother's suicide attempt, though. I couldn't go there yet, even with friends.

We ordered our drinks and pizza, and then the table got quiet.

Which was unusual, since Patty was there.

Did they know something was up?

"How's Sean?" Patty finally asked Brad.

"He's good. Likes his new place," Brad replied.

"I hardly see him around anymore," Patty said. "He's always with that new girlfriend of his."

"Lorraine? Yeah. But Murph isn't serious about her. She's just his flavor of the week."

I winced. Patty had been Sean's flavor of the week, except only for two days. Patty stayed her bubbly self, though, and didn't seem to mind talking about Sean. "Tell him I said hi if you see him."

"Will do," Brad said.

He didn't say much more. He was giving me time to bring up our news. I loved him for it, but I wished he'd talk. The silence was deafening, and it made my mind wander to my mom. I had to call Dad later.

"How did you like Daph's parents?" Patty finally asked.

"I like them a lot. They're both very nice."

"Were they surprised that you guys got together so soon?" Patty asked again.

Brad looked at me.

Now or never.

"They were surprised about that, yeah," I said. "They were surprised about a lot of things."

So surprised my mother had a mental breakdown, but no . . . not going there.

I cleared my throat. "So . . . Brad and I . . . We have some news."

"What's that?" Ennis asked.

Brad picked up the pitcher of cola the server set down and poured us each a glass. I took a long drink, letting the sweetness flow over my tongue and down my throat. I was suddenly parched. I took another drink.

"We . . . Well . . . We're going to get married."

Patty, in the middle of bringing her glass to her mouth, stopped it in midair. Ennis's eyebrows nearly flew off his forehead.

"Big surprise, huh?" Brad said.

I got the impression he was trying to sound jovial, but instead he sounded a little nuts.

"We know it's really soon, but the thing is . . ." I took another drink of Coke. "I'm pregnant."

This time Patty's glass had made it to her mouth, and she spat soda all over Ennis. "Oh, God," she said, grabbing a napkin. "I'm so sorry."

"No problem," Ennis said. "I'm used to beautiful women ruining my shirts."

He was alluding to the first night in the dorm, when I'd gotten sick all over him. My cheeks warmed.

"Obviously, we didn't plan this," Brad continued. "We used protection, but sometimes it doesn't work."

"So when you went to the health center last week..." Patty said.

"Yeah. That's when I found out."

"Do you feel okay?" she asked.

"So far, but the nurse practitioner said I'm too early for morning sickness yet."

"Maybe you won't get it," she said. "My mom says she didn't have it for my brother at all. With me only a little."

"My mum said she was sick the whole nine months," Ennis said. "But maybe it's a British thing."

I adored Ennis, but I wished he'd kept that to himself. I didn't want to think about nine months of nausea.

Patty swatted Ennis on the arm. "What a thing to say! That won't happen to you, Daph."

"I sure hope not."

"You're really getting hitched, huh?" Patty said. "So you've discussed all the...you know...options?"

I nodded. "We have. This is what we both want. Right, Brad?"

Brad had been so quiet, letting me take the lead. "Yeah. We're going to the ranch next weekend to tell my parents."

"What kind of wedding are you going to have?"

"We haven't discussed it," I said. "I can't think about that until we tell Brad's folks. But there isn't a lot of time for a wedding anyway. Plus, my parents can't afford anything big."

"Mine can," Brad said. "If you want a big wedding, you'll have it."

I shook my head. "I don't."

"Sure you do," Patty said. "I'll help you. This should be your day to shine."

"I try to shine every day," I said. No truer words. I was determined to get the most out of life. "I don't need a big wedding for that."

"Come on," she urged. "I want to see you get married."

"Well, you can come, then. You and Ennis. And Sean. Our parents. And whoever else you want, Brad. But it doesn't have to be anything big."

"I'll help you plan it," Patty said. "We'll have— Oh, no!"

"What?" I asked.

"You won't be living in our room anymore, will you?"

"No," Brad said. "After we're married, she'll move into the townhome with me, and we'll finish the school year. Then we'll move to the ranch."

"I'll miss you," Patty said.

"I'll miss you too, but you'll probably get your own room, at least for the rest of this semester."

Her green eyes gleamed. "That could be fun."

Ennis turned and met Patty's gaze.

Was that a spark that just shot between them? Ennis wasn't dating anyone that I knew of. He'd made out with a blonde during orientation week, but other than that, I hadn't seen him with a woman.

Patty and Ennis . . .

I liked the idea.

I hoped they would too.

Quiet descended on the table again when the server delivered our pizza. Now that our news was out in the open, I was happy not to talk.

I bit into a slice of Colorado's second-best pizza with mushrooms and peppers. No pepperoni unless I knew it had come from humanely raised animals.

My mother never left my mind.

I couldn't help thinking I was the cause of her suicide attempt. I wanted to press "pause" on this whole thing and wait until my mother recuperated.

But I couldn't.

My little dove wouldn't stop growing just because my mother had done the unthinkable.

Thank God she hadn't succeeded.

I needed my mother, now more than ever.

CHAPTER FIFTEEN

Brad

The week went by without incident. Knowing Wendy couldn't show up at my place unannounced put my mind at ease. Daphne had made arrangements with the school to live off campus, but she didn't want to move in until we told my parents.

Which we would do shortly.

I drove up the long driveway to the ranch house. My home.

I'd called earlier to tell my mother we were coming. She was excited to meet Daphne. I hoped she'd continue her excitement after we told her our news.

Daphne was biting her lower lip, and her rosy cheeks were paler than normal.

"Nervous?" I asked.

She nodded. "Aren't you?"

"No. Not really. We're both over eighteen. What can they do?"

"Cut you off?"

I laughed. "Is that what you're worried about? Listen, I'm their only child plus the only person who knows how to run this operation as well as my father does. But even if they did cut us off, I'd find a way to support you and our baby."

She smiled. "I know you would."

"So no worries, okay?"

She nodded again.

"Come on." I got out of the truck and opened the passenger door for her. Then I pulled our bags out and carried them to the door.

Ebony and Brandy jumped on me when I entered.

"Hey, girls." I petted them both.

Daphne dropped to her knees, letting both of them pepper her with licks and kisses. The smile on her face as she hugged my dogs was worth every dollar of the Steel fortune.

To me, at least.

Belinda, our housekeeper and cook, walked out from the country kitchen. "Mr. Brad! Your mother's in the greenhouse and your father's at the office. They'll both be here in about a half hour for dinner. That gives you and Miss Daphne time to settle in."

"Thanks, Belinda." I led Daphne to the room she used a few weeks ago. "Do you need to . . . I don't know. Change or anything?"

"I'll just run a brush through my hair."

"Okay. I'll come get you when it's time for dinner."

"Brad?"

"Yeah?"

"Could you stay with me for a few minutes?"

"Sure." I sat down on the bed and patted the spot next to me. "Everything okay?"

She nodded. "My mother . . . What should we tell your parents?"

"Whatever you want to tell them."

"I'm not sure it's a good idea to get into all that. Not yet, anyway. I don't want to talk about it. I want to be happy about our news, and talking about what's going on with my mother isn't going to make me happy."

I touched her soft cheek. "I want you to be happy, Daphne."

"I know. I want you to be happy too."

"You make me happy."

She smiled, turned into my hand, and kissed my palm. The warmth of her kiss surged through me. Yeah, it turned me on, but more than that, it made me feel loved—more loved than I'd ever felt in my life.

This woman loved me. She'd love our baby with the same feverish intensity.

When Daphne Wade loved, she loved with everything she had.

That was how I'd love her and our child.

With everything I was and with everything I had.

"Your mother will be okay," I said. "She'll get through this. Your father loves her very much."

"I know he does."

"He'll make sure she gets everything she needs."

"But—"

I placed two fingers over her lips. "If you're worried about money, you don't have to be."

"My father's not a rich man."

"Your husband-to-be is."

"No." She shook her head. "I can't let you—"

"Baby, listen to me. Your father will take care of her. He has health insurance. And if he needs a little help along the way, we—you and I—will be here for him."

"You're very sweet, but the money isn't yours, Brad. It's your parents'."

"The majority of the fortune is, but I have a trust fund. I

took control of it when I turned twenty-one. I can take care of whatever your mother needs."

"Still, I don't want—"

"Shh. We'll do what we have to do to get your mother well. If we need to contribute, I'm happy to do it."

She choked back a sob. "I didn't want our life together to begin like this. I never expected my mother . . . "

"I know."

"She was always so strong for me."

"She's still strong. Look at you. You're one of the strongest people I know, and you've been through a lot of mental and emotional turmoil." More than she even knew. My heart hurt just thinking about it, and I absently clenched my hands into fists, aching to pummel the men who'd violated her.

"I never tried to take my own life," she said.

True. She'd told me that the last time we were at the ranch. Thank God. I couldn't bear to think of my beautiful Daphne in that much pain.

"Your mother will get the help she needs."

"I feel like we should postpone everything until she's better." She touched her abdomen. "But we can't. We need to get everything settled."

"We can wait a few weeks if you'd like. Technically we don't need to get married until right before the baby's born for me to be considered the father."

"You *are* the father."

"I mean legally. To keep the child from being illegitimate."

She clasped her hand over her mouth. "My baby isn't going to be a bastard."

"Of course not. He's mine, and I want him. I want you both."

She nodded. "Thanks."

"For what?"

"For talking. Let's not say anything to your parents about my mother."

"Okay. I'll just say I met them last weekend and they're okay with the situation."

"They are. I think."

"Your father is. He and I talked quite a lot."

"True. What all did you talk about, Brad?"

Brick in gut. I didn't want to lie to Daphne, but I couldn't go into any detail about what her dad and I talked about.

My poor baby.

Every time I looked at her now, I imagined what those three degenerates had done to her and her friend.

Keeping secrets, though, always took a toll on everyone involved. Again, my hands clenched into fists, and every muscle in my body tensed.

How? How could anyone harm this beautiful and innocent woman? This woman I loved so damned much?

Daphne's body had healed, but her mind... Her mind didn't know anything had happened.

Best to keep it that way, as Jonathan said.

I had a feeling that toll was going to be steep.

Daphne's mother's suicide attempt was only the beginning.

CHAPTER SIXTEEN

Daphne

Brad's mother was one of the most beautiful women I'd ever seen. She was striking, with dark hair and eyes much like her son's. Her hair was cut short in a new-fashioned pixie style, and it worked on her because her facial features were so soft and feminine. From her straight nose and high cheekbones to her full lips and only slightly prominent chin, Mazie Steel was nearly perfect to look at.

She wore bell-bottom jeans and a peasant blouse, and silver hoops dangled from her ears. When she shook my hand, I noticed dirt beneath her unpolished fingernails. The only part of her that wasn't perfect.

Of course. She'd been working in the greenhouse.

She gave me a hug. "It's so nice to meet you, Daphne. I'm sorry I missed your last visit." She let go of me. "Let me look at you. My, but you're a beautiful thing. So tall, too."

I warmed with embarrassment. "Thank you."

Then she grabbed Brad in a hug as well. "I've missed you."

"I've missed you too, Mom. Where's Dad?"

"I have no idea," Mazie said. "He'll be here in a few. He's never late for dinner, as you know."

Brad and I had decided to wait until after dinner to share our news, as we had with my parents.

I suppressed a shiver as I regarded Mazie Steel. She'd been hospitalized before. What if the news drove her over the edge as it had my mother?

No.

No, no, no.

I would not go there.

Brad had told me she'd found solace in her greenhouse and other activities. She looked and acted fine.

No reason to worry.

I hoped, anyway.

Clomp. Clomp.

Footsteps that could only mean George Steel.

He marched into the kitchen, trailing bits of dirt from his boots. I felt sorry for Belinda. She'd have to clean up his mess. But I guessed that was what they paid her for.

He didn't speak to his wife or son. He nodded at me. "Daphne."

"Hi, Mr. Steel. Nice to see you again."

"You too. What's for dinner, Belinda?"

"Filet mignon wrapped in humanely raised bacon." Belinda winked at me.

"Say what?" Mr. Steel said.

"Mr. Brad's request. We're also having twice-baked potatoes, broccoli with almonds, and fresh peaches from the orchard."

He nodded and sat down at the kitchen table. "Table's not set."

"We're eating in the dining room."

"Just for four of us?"

"Mr. Brad's requ—"

"Yeah, yeah. I guess I should change." He stood and left

80

the kitchen, clomping down the hallway.

Mrs. Steel smiled at me. "Don't mind him, Daphne. He's just being himself."

Was I supposed to laugh at that? I wasn't sure.

"Daphne knows how he is, Mom," Brad said. "I've warned her."

"At least he remembered me," I said. "Is there anything I can do to help, Mrs. Steel?"

"Honey, call me Mazie. Belinda has everything under control, don't you?"

"Yes, Miss Mazie. Potatoes and veggies are already on the table. How do you like your steak, Miss Daphne?"

"Medium rare. And please just call me Daphne."

"Try it rare," Brad said. "A Steel filet is best served rare. It'll melt in your mouth."

"He's right," Mazie agreed. "Make them all rare, Belinda."

"You got it," Belinda said. "Go ahead in. These filets won't take long on the grill, and I'll bring them in. Salad's already tossed and plated."

"Thanks, Belinda," Mazie said, "but I suppose we should wait for George."

"We can at least sit down, Mom," Brad said. "Come on."

Brad took my hand and led me back toward the front door. Across from the formal living room sat the formal dining room. I hadn't noticed it when I came into the house because it hid behind two ornate swinging doors.

My eyes went round.

First, it was huge. The dark wood table could easily seat a party of twenty or more. Did the Steels ever have that many people over for a formal dinner? Second, it was wallpapered in a white and gold paisley pattern. No wonder Mr. Steel didn't want to eat in here. It really wasn't him. It was Mazie, though.

"This is beautiful," I said to her. "Did you decorate it?"

"I did," she said and then chuckled. "George hates it."

"If your dad hates it in here," I said to Brad, "why did you insist we eat in here?"

"Because my mom likes it, and I knew you would too." He grinned.

"Yeah, but if your dad—"

"Forget about him," Mazie said. "We deserve to eat in a nice room every once in a while." She walked to the head of the table. "This is George's spot. Brad, hand me the place setting at my spot."

Brad grabbed the plate and utensils and handed them to his mother. She set them down next to one of the settings on either side of George's place.

"I don't particularly want to scream down the table to be heard," she said. "This is much nicer. Daphne, you sit here, between George and me, and Brad, take the place on your father's other side."

We sat at our designated places and waited for Mr. Steel. Belinda came in and poured us each a glass of ice water and a glass of red wine.

Then we waited.

And waited.

"For God's sake, Mom," Brad said. "What's taking him so long?"

"You know your father. He's on his own time schedule."

"He's never late for dinner," Brad said.

"Except when we screw up his routine and insist that he eat in this room. He's having a silent temper tantrum."

"But we have a guest."

"It's okay, Brad," I said. "I don't mind waiting."

Brad stood. "Well, I do. Everything'll get cold."

Belinda brought in the platter of steaks as Brad walked out of the room.

Mazie smiled at me. "Brad is nothing like his father, thank goodness. He's a gem."

I warmed. "I think so."

"He's my first and only, and he's my life. I couldn't be prouder of the man he's become. You never love anything the way you love your child. You'll understand what I mean when you have a child of your own someday." She patted my hand.

I simply nodded.

That day would come sooner than she imagined.

A few minutes later, Brad walked back in, followed by his father.

George Steel sat down at the head of the table and said nothing. Simply began passing dishes around. We filled our plates in silence.

"Daphne," Mazie finally said, "tell me a little bit about you and your family."

I took a serving spoonful of broccoli, placed it on my plate, and handed her the bowl. "I'm a freshman, though Brad probably told you that. My parents live in Westminster, a suburb of Denver. I got a full scholarship to Stilton based on my grades in high school."

"How wonderful! We value intelligence, don't we, George?"

Mr. Steel nodded but still said nothing.

"What do you want to study?"

"I haven't chosen a major yet, but I'm leaning toward English and creative writing."

"What do you plan to do with that major?" Mr. Steel said, his voice gruff.

I suppressed a shiver. My cheeks were so hot, they must have been the color of a red delicious apple. It was a valid question, and I had no idea how to answer it.

"She's been in college a month, Dad," Brad said.

"So? You knew what you were going to do at that time."

"Yeah, but not too many people grow up on a ranch they'll someday own."

"He's right, George," Mazie agreed. "Don't let him put you on the spot, honey."

I took another bite of broccoli and chewed. He *had* put me on the spot, but the fact was, I wouldn't finish that major anyway. I'd be living here, raising a child. Their grandchild. Only they didn't know that.

By the end of this meal, they would.

And George Steel was not going to be happy.

CHAPTER SEVENTEEN

Brad

My father was in asshole mode. He didn't push Daphne any further on her major, though, thank God.

When I'd gone to his bedroom to prod him into dinner, I'd thanked him profusely once again for helping me with Wendy, which hadn't helped his mood.

Yeah, he was glad I was done with Wendy, but he wished I'd been able to accomplish it on my own.

Indeed, I wished the same.

But that wasn't what he was pissed about.

He wasn't pissed about eating in the dining room, either.

A major contract had fallen through this afternoon, and he had a migraine.

Not a good combination.

Still, I'd promised Daphne we'd tell my parents our news tonight.

I wasn't sure that was a great idea now. At least Belinda had put some wine on the table. A glass of wine might not help my father's headache, but it would at least calm him down a little.

Maybe.

I took the initiative, brought my goblet to my lips, and took a sip of wine, hoping he'd get the idea. Why he'd decided to grill

Daphne on her major was beyond me. She was eighteen.

When he didn't take a drink of his wine, I took another.

Finally, he picked up his glass and took a sip.

Finally.

Daphne cut into her filet and took a bite. Her eyes widened. She swallowed. "Wow, Brad. You were right. This is perfect. I don't think I've ever tasted anything so smooth and savory and delicious."

I smiled.

"Best beef in the country," my father said, this time offering Daphne a small smile.

"It is," my mother agreed. "It was like discovering meat for the first time when I had my first taste of Steel beef."

Dinner went smoothly after that. Daphne didn't realize how much of an impact she'd had on my father. Compliment his beef, his livelihood, and he calmed down.

My Daphne. Here I was, trying to get my father to drink and relax, when all I needed was the beautiful girl across from me. Daphne could bring any man to his knees, including my asshole father. Maybe this would work out tonight after all. I smiled at Daphne.

She looked away shyly.

And I loved her even more.

I was hers. Forever. She had me under her spell, and I didn't ever want to be released. This beautiful, ethereal creature, who had been through so much, had no idea of the power she wielded over me.

I vowed to be worthy of it.

Worthy of *her*.

★ ★ ★

My father had loosened up—two glasses of wine helped—by the time Belinda brought in dessert and coffee. He'd even had a few kind words to say to my mother.

Daphne met my gaze, her eyes questioning.

I nodded.

It was time.

"Mom, Dad," I began.

"What is it, honey?" my mom replied.

I cleared my throat. "Daphne and I have some news."

Daphne looked down at her lap, her cheeks flushed.

"Oh my." My mother regarded her.

She knows.

The words flew into my mind.

"It will be all right," Mom said.

"What the hell are you talking about, Mazie?" my father boomed.

"I'm not talking about anything. Your son is trying to talk to you."

My father harrumphed and turned back to me. "What is it?"

"Daphne, we … We're going to get married."

"For God's sake," my father said. "Why the hell—" He stopped, looking sternly at Daphne. "There's only one reason a twenty-two-year-old and an eighteen-year-old get married."

My mother nodded. "Do you feel okay, honey?" she asked Daphne.

"Yes. I feel fine."

"How the hell did this happen?" my father roared.

"Probably the same way it happened when Brad was conceived," Mom said.

"I'm not talking to you, Mazie. And we were already married."

Daphne still looked at her lap, and her head trembled a bit. *God, no. Please don't cry.* I'd personally deck my father if he made Daphne cry.

"We were careful," I said.

"Apparently not careful enough."

Daphne's head jerked up. "He used a condom. I witnessed it. We *were* careful."

My mother patted Daphne's hand. "We believe you, sweetheart."

My father gazed at Daphne, and—I couldn't believe it myself—his eyes softened.

Fucking softened.

"A grandchild," he said, his voice still gruff.

"Yes, George, a grandchild." My mother smiled. "But are you two in love?"

"We are, Mom," I said. "I know it's soon, but I knew as soon as I saw her."

"Love at first sight doesn't exist, Brad," my mom said.

"Maybe not," Daphne said. "But fate does."

My father regarded Daphne again, his gaze still soft. "A grandchild."

"It's wonderful news," Mom said. "Perhaps Daphne is right. Perhaps it's fate." She looked over to Dad. "George? What do you think?"

"I think I'm happy to have a grandchild." He met Daphne's gaze. "Thank you, my dear. Thank you for giving me a grandchild."

Daphne looked down. I couldn't tell, but I believed she was touching her belly. "I haven't done anything yet."

"The first of many, I hope," Dad said.

My mother frowned then.

Of course. He couldn't resist giving her a metaphorical punch in the stomach. My father was being kind to Daphne, to the woman I loved. Why couldn't he save a tiny sliver of kindness for his wife, the mother of his child? That she couldn't have any more children after me was not her fault.

Still, though, Daphne . . .

She was a magical creature. She'd softened my father.

No one else could do that. No one.

Only Daphne.

She was too perfect for this world, as her father had said.

Too fucking perfect.

I vowed, then, to give her the perfect world she belonged in. She and our child would want for nothing as long as I lived and breathed.

I'd create a legacy for my wife and children—a legacy bigger and grander than my father's.

A legacy worthy of the woman across from me.

CHAPTER EIGHTEEN

Daphne

"I don't need anything fancy," I told Mazie in the greenhouse later. "My parents can't afford a big wedding."

"We can afford it. I want you to have everything." She shook her head. "I can't believe the effect this has had on George. He actually smiled at dinner."

"I certainly didn't expect that," I said. "Not after Brad told me how gruff he is."

"He is. He's usually a jerk." Mazie cut one of her pale-green tulips. "You're probably wondering why I'm still with him."

"No. It's not my place to wonder anything like that. No one can know what goes on between a husband and wife."

"You're wise, Daphne. Believe me, I thought many times about leaving, but I stayed for one reason and one reason only."

"Brad," I said.

"You got it. He's everything to me, and George would have fought with everything he had to take him from me. So I stayed, and I think Brad is a better man for it."

"Brad is a wonderful man. If you had something to do with that, I owe you a lot."

"He got his work ethic and knowledge of the business from his father, of course. I'd like to think I'm the one who taught him the finer things in life, like how to love. And he loves you, Daphne. I can see it in his eyes."

"I love him too," I said shyly.

"I know. I see it in your eyes as well."

"I know we're really young..."

"You are. But at least you won't have to worry about money. That's something."

I cleared my throat. "I hope you don't think—"

"That you're with Brad because of his money?"

"I'm not. Not at all. We used a condom."

"I believe you. I believe in my son. He knows how to prevent pregnancy. George and I both made sure of that."

"Sometimes I feel like I should have done more. Like be on the pill or use a spermicide or something. But I can't bring myself to be unhappy about the baby. Yeah, it wasn't in my immediate plans, but it's mine. Mine and Brad's. That's pretty special."

"It's very special," Mazie said. "I know you're young, but I'll help you. I'm sure your own mother will be happy to help you as well."

I smiled but didn't reply. My own mother was a mess at the moment. Maybe a grandchild would help to bring her out of it. I didn't know. I had to depend on my father to take care of her. I'd do what I could, but my first priority was my own baby. I touched my belly.

"Do you want a boy or a girl?" Mazie asked.

"Either is fine with me, but this is a boy."

She smiled. "You're sure?"

"I know it sounds silly, but I know it's a he."

"We'll find out in May," she said. "Now let's talk about this wedding."

"I really don't want—"

"Please, don't worry about the cost."

"I'm not worried about the cost." How could I tell her I couldn't have any kind of wedding if my mother couldn't be there?

Mazie rambled on and on about decorations and flowers and guests.

I simply stared at the pale-green tulips she was cutting into a bouquet.

I'd sworn never to be a colorless flower again. So I wouldn't be.

"Mazie..."

"Yes?" She looked up from her flowers.

"I don't want a big wedding. It's not me. Please."

"Oh." She smiled weakly. "Whatever you want, Daphne."

"Brad and I have talked. It's just easier to get married at the courthouse."

"I understand." She went back to work on her tulips and said nothing more.

And I felt like the colorless flower.

CHAPTER NINETEEN

Brad

I sat in my father's study, in one of the comfortable chairs across from his desk.

"Thank you, Dad," I said, "for being so kind to Daphne."

"She seems like a nice young woman."

"She is. And I do love her."

"I know you do."

I arched my eyebrows.

"Don't forget, I was in love once," he said. "Your mother was nearly as beautiful as your Daphne."

"I know. I've seen the pictures."

"You look a lot like her. It used to bother me. It doesn't anymore. I know you're mine."

I cocked my head. Had he once thought I might *not* be his? Could that have been the catalyst for how he treated my mother?

"She and I ... Well, you know all that."

"Why, Dad? Why couldn't you ... " I shook my head.

His countenance grew stern, and he looked down at his desk. "I'm not going to talk to you about this. A man's relationship with his wife is his own business, and certainly not his child's."

I nodded. I'd remember that if he ever tried to get involved in my relationship with Daphne. I'd throw his own words back at him.

"I'm not proud of everything I did," he said.

I nodded again. What could I say? I'd wanted to murder him on more than one occasion.

"I'm glad you stopped me, son."

"I'm glad I did too."

"I don't know if I could have stopped on my own. It became kind of a sickness, but you made me see what I was doing. Your mother and I, though, we could never be close again. Not after everything."

"I see." Though I didn't. I didn't at all. I could never treat Daphne the way he'd treated my mother. No way.

"I hope you never do see. I want better for you. You can be the man I never was. Take care of that girl of yours. Take care of that baby."

"I plan to." No truer words.

"Good." He shuffled some papers on his desk. "In that vein, take a look at this."

I took the document he handed me. A warranty deed. For the house. Signed by my father.

"I'm deeding this house to you."

My eyebrows nearly shot to space. "Excuse me?"

"A house like this is made for a large family. I want you to fill it with children. Fill it with the laughter it was built for."

"But you and Mom . . ."

"We'll move into the guesthouse, of course. Your mother will want to be near the baby."

For the first time since I could remember, my father had rendered me speechless.

"It'll all be yours one day anyway, Brad. You can start your family here. It's yours now."

"I don't know what to say."

"Thank you is usually appropriate."

"Of course. Thank you, Dad. I never imagined . . ."

"I haven't been the most loving father or husband. I can't change that now. But I can challenge you to do better than I did. You can begin by giving your wife-to-be the perfect house to raise your children in."

I perused the document.

"I loved her once, you know."

"I'm sorry. What?"

My father gazed at me. "Your mother. I loved her once. She was my world."

"What happened, then?"

I knew what had happened. She couldn't have any more children. But I wanted to hear him say it.

As if he were reading my mind, he continued, "You may think it was the accident, but there was more to it than that."

My mind darted back to his previous words. *You look a lot like her. It used to bother me. It doesn't anymore. I know you're mine.*

"What?"

"I already told you I won't go there. It's between your mother and me, Brad."

"How am I supposed to understand if—"

"I said it's between your mother and me. I have my reasons."

I nodded. No use fighting George Steel once he dug in his heels. Perhaps he was right. A relationship between a man and his wife was no one's business except theirs. In fact, I agreed.

But his comment edged its way into my head once more.

I know you're mine.

As if he'd once questioned whether he'd actually fathered me. But that would mean . . .

No. Not my mother. She wouldn't do such a thing.

"Mazie was a good mother," my father offered. "But you already know that."

She'd also been a damned good wife, but he didn't say that. He was almost blatant in *not* saying that.

"She's the best," I said.

He didn't reply. Was he waiting for me to tell him he was a good father? He'd be waiting a long time. He was an excellent rancher, an excellent businessman. He'd taught me well in those areas.

But a good father? A good all-around father?

Yeah, he'd just given me this house, but I couldn't make myself say it. I could say something else, though.

"Thank you, Dad. For everything."

"No need to thank me."

"Yeah, there is. I'm not just talking about the house. I'm talking about being nice to Daphne."

"She's a lovely girl."

"She is. And also for . . . helping me deal with Wendy."

"I was glad to do that. I never wanted her anywhere near your life."

"You were right. I should have listened to you."

"Hell, you were young. You had a hard-on for a pretty girl. We've all been there. You had no way of knowing what a bad seed she was. Not then, anyhow."

"I made some bad choices."

"You did, but who hasn't?" He shook his head, chuckling but not smiling. "Like I said, we've all been there. Maybe someday I'll tell you about my own experiences."

I wrinkled my forehead. I knew so little about my father. Was it possible we had more in common than I thought?

"I'd like that."

"Not today, though. Go spend some time with Daphne."

"That's a great idea," I said. "Thanks, Dad."

I left the office, walked to Daphne's guest room, and knocked.

"Come in."

I walked in. Daphne sat on the bed, her eyes forlorn.

"What's wrong?"

"Nothing. I think I disappointed your mother, though. She wanted to plan a wedding for us, and I told her I didn't want a big wedding."

"Why not?"

"Brad, you know why. I can't have any kind of wedding if my mother can't attend."

Of course. I'd been obtuse. Lucy Wade had attempted suicide. She had to recover, which could take a long time.

"I'm sorry, baby. I wasn't thinking."

"It's not your fault."

"I should have told my mother—"

"No! Brad, no. Please don't tell your mother what's going on. She'll wonder why my mother did it, and then everything about me and my junior year will come out. I just can't."

"Honey, my mother has been through some of the same." *Some* being the operative word. Every time I thought about what had truly happened to my Daphne, I wanted to pummel someone and throw up at the same time.

"I know, but please. I can't have your parents looking at me like that. I want them to like me."

"They do like you. I've never seen my father take to anyone the way he took to you."

"It's because of the baby."

"That's part of it, but he thinks you're special. He told me."

"He did?"

"He did. And you know what? He's right." I smiled and kissed her gently on the lips.

We lay together on her bed and fell asleep that way, secure in each other's arms.

CHAPTER TWENTY

Daphne

My mother came home two weeks later.

She seemed okay when I visited, and she told me she wanted me to have a real wedding.

"I don't want one," I said.

"Daphne, come on. We can afford to give you a little wedding. Let me get in touch with Mrs. Steel."

A day later, my mother called. "Mazie has invited you and me to the ranch this weekend to make plans."

"Mom, how am I supposed to keep up with my studies when I'm nauseated all the time and I'm running around all weekend?"

Yeah, morning sickness had arrived. Only I didn't have it in the morning. I had it most of the day. Brad kept the townhome—I had already moved in—stocked with saltine crackers, the only food that didn't make me want to puke.

"Daphne, you're only going to get married once. Mazie and I want to do this for you."

So Mom and Mazie were on a first-name basis already after only one phone call. That was good. I guessed, anyway. One great thing about the wedding—it gave my mother a project to focus on. Anything that kept her mind out of dark places was a plus in my book.

As luck would have it, Brad and his father were on a business trip this weekend. It would be just us girls. Mazie was lovely, so everything would work out.

Right?

I kept telling myself that.

"I should come along," my father said. "I want to meet these people."

"Mazie says George won't be there," my mom said.

"Lucy, shouldn't we meet our daughter's in-laws before the wedding?"

"In a perfect world, yes," Mom said.

Which meant this situation *wasn't* perfect.

I knew that, but still, Mom's words hit me in the belly.

I absently rubbed my abdomen. *It's okay, little dove. Everything's okay.*

"I'm coming."

"No," Mom said. "Let me do this, Jonathan. I need to do this. By myself. I want to show you and our daughter that I'm okay."

Finally, Dad agreed. Mom had used the magic words. She wanted to be strong. He had to let her, just like both of them had to let me be strong.

I believed in my mother. She'd apologized all over the place for her actions, had promised she'd never do it again. In fact, she hadn't had a drink or a Valium since then. She was seeing a therapist and was determined to remain sober.

She was going to be okay.

★ ★ ★

"Daphne!" Mazie hugged me tight. Then she turned to my

mother. "You must be Lucy. Welcome to Steel Acres!"

I missed Ebony and Brandy. One of the hands was taking care of them for the weekend because of my mother's allergy to dogs. Mazie had promised the house would be dog-dander-free while we were there.

I looked around. The house seemed empty without Brad.

I was just as glad George wasn't around, though. He'd been kind to me about the baby, but still, I didn't want my mother to deal with him just yet.

"I've been making some plans," Mazie went on. "I don't want to step on your toes, though. You're the mother of the bride, after all."

"Whatever Daphne wants is fine with me," Mom said.

"Of course, Daphne will have the final say in everything."

"I just want something small," I said. "Just Mom and Dad, a few friends from school."

"What about family?" Mazie asked.

"Maybe my half brother, though I barely know him."

"Yes, Larry," Mazie said. "Brad mentioned him. They went to high school together. He's a nice kid." Then she laughed. "Oh, but he's not a kid anymore. None of you are."

"Yeah." I nodded.

"Brad has a few other friends from high school he'll want to include," Mazie said. "And Sean Murphy and a few others from college. We don't have any family. George and I are both only children."

I lifted my eyebrows. Interesting. No wonder George had wanted a big family.

"I'll do the flowers myself," Mazie was saying. "I love horticulture. Daphne wants yellow, and I have the perfect blooms."

"Mom, you have to see her greenhouse. It's amazing."

"I'd love to take a look."

"Then there's the food. Belinda is a wonderful cook, or we can have a small meal catered. What do you think, Lucy?"

"Whatever Daphne wants," Mom said again.

"Come out back," Mazie said. "We have the perfect little alcove for a small wedding."

My mother followed Mazie, but I stayed inside and joined Belinda in the kitchen.

"Hi, Belinda."

"Hi, honey. Great to have you back. Are you hungry? I can fix you something."

"No. I'm feeling kind of icky."

"Morning sickness?"

"Try all-day sickness."

"I'm sorry, honey."

"It's okay. I'm getting used to it. Sort of."

"Spaghetti tonight," she said. "One of Miss Mazie's favorites. Her mother was Italian."

"Spaghetti's my favorite too, when I'm not pregnant, at least. Homemade meatballs?"

"You bet. Made with our own beef."

"Yum." I rubbed my belly, hoping I'd have a break in nausea to enjoy it. "Hear that, little dove?"

"What, honey?"

"Oh. Sorry. I was ..." I laughed. "You'll think it's silly. I was talking to the baby."

"That's not silly at all." She smiled.

"I suppose I should join my mom and Mazie outside."

"All right."

I walked out the ornate French doors. Mazie had taken

my mother across the yard to where a redwood gazebo stood.

I had to admit that it was perfect for a small wedding.

"We'll set up chairs here," Mazie was saying. "No more than fifty. There's plenty of room for tables and a sit-down meal. Open bar of course, and a champagne toast. I know the most wonderful baker in Grand Junction for the cake, too. I've already contacted the minister in town, and Brad and Daphne have chosen their attendants."

"Sounds like you've planned it all out," my mother said.

"I welcome your input, Lucy. If you want to make any changes..."

"Daphne, does it all sound good to you?" Mom asked.

"I think it sounds lovely."

"Then it sounds lovely to me. Thank you, Mazie, for putting together such a perfect little event."

"It's no problem. I'm thrilled to do it. I don't have a daughter of my own, so I never thought I'd get to do anything like this."

My mother nodded, smiling. It was her forced smile. Was she feeling left out?

I squeezed her arm.

She gave me a reassuring nod. "I'll need a breakdown of the cost. Jonathan and I want to pay for everything."

"I wouldn't hear of it," Mazie said. "It was all my idea. We'll foot the entire bill."

"Mom..." I hedged.

"Daphne, please. Mazie, she's *our* daughter. It's our job to pay for the wedding. She's getting married so young, and this is the last thing we'll be able to do for her while she's our daughter and not someone's wife. You understand, don't you?"

I stood, rigid. Would Mazie understand? And why was

Mom pushing this? She and Dad didn't have the money, and the Steels did. She knew that.

Seconds that seemed like hours passed with no one speaking. Finally, Mazie broke the silence.

"Of course, Lucy. I understand."

★ ★ ★

After a rather tense dinner—though I was able to choke down some spaghetti and meatballs for my little dove—I retired to my room. My mom was using a different guest room on the opposite wing of the house.

I lay in bed, not tired yet, which surprised me. During the past week, fatigue had overwhelmed me—part of the first trimester, my gynecologist had said.

Yes, I now had an obstetrician-gynecologist. Brad had found one in Denver for me—tops in his field, of course. He had me on a strict regimen of prenatal vitamins and extra folate. Lots of green vegetables—which truly made me gag—and a calcium supplement.

Thoughts of Brad consumed me. I missed him.

Hmm. His bedroom was right next door. I got up, walked into the next room, and closed the door. I lay down on his bed.

I inhaled. Woodsy, musky Brad. I could smell him as if he were lying next to me. Yeah, the sense of smell got more intense with pregnancy too. But at least this smell didn't make me want to vomit. The opposite, actually. It made me feel at home. Comfortable. Loved.

Oh, Brad. I wish you were here.

I walked into his bathroom and looked around. Inside the shower were two bottles of Mane 'n Tail. Horse shampoo! I opened the bottle and took a sniff. Not much scent at all. Just lemony fresh.

The smell of Brad's hair. His silky dark hair. Perfect.

I walked back into the room. It was larger than the one I stayed in and boasted a little alcove with a bay window decorated with two chairs and a small desk. A perfect place to study or read when he wasn't at school. I switched on the lamp on the small desk. A few textbooks sat on the desk along with some manila folders.

My eyes zeroed in on the one word written on the top folder.

Wendy.

CHAPTER TWENTY-ONE

Brad

My weekend of business with my father was definitely business—just not ranch business.

Dad and I met with Dr. Devin Pelletier, the psychiatrist who'd signed the papers to have Wendy committed. We both wanted to make sure she was locked up and out of our lives for at least the year that he'd promised.

I sat in his office with my father during a quickly arranged evening meeting.

"I assure you she'll be gone for a year," Dr. Pelletier promised.

"I know that, and I appreciate it," I said, "but you don't know Wendy."

"I know enough from talking to the two of you, her parents, and Mr. Murphy."

"That's not what I mean." I rubbed my jawline. "She finds a way out of everything."

"This is beyond her control."

"I understand you *think* it is," I said. "But she finds ways that others can't conceive. The woman's a genius."

"I'm aware of her IQ tests. That doesn't mean she can get out of a locked door or past guards. She's not Harry Houdini."

Except that she kind of was. How to explain?

"I've only seen Wendy completely freak out once, and it was when she had no control over the situation."

"When was that?" Dr. Pelletier asked.

I looked toward my father. His eyes were questioning as well. Wendy and I hadn't told our parents about the unplanned pregnancy in high school. She'd gone to the doctor, had the test, gotten the positive result, and we'd been deciding what to do when she miscarried a few days later. I wasn't excited at the thought of admitting this in front of my father, but I had no choice.

"When she miscarried our baby."

"Excuse me?" My father wrinkled his forehead.

Hmm. Not the reaction I expected. This was something that should have made George Steel furious.

"Sorry, Dad. It was stupid, and we didn't use protection. We were horny teenagers. What can I say?"

"This isn't a joking matter, Brad."

"I know it's not. But she miscarried, so there was no reason to tell anyone. It was a blessing at that point."

Dr. Pelletier cleared his throat. "What do you mean she was out of control?"

"She finds a way out of everything, like I said. She wanted this baby because it was mine. She was—and is—obsessed with me. When she miscarried, she freaked out because she couldn't stop it. She couldn't control the situation."

"How exactly did she freak out?" the doctor asked.

"She went crazy. Screaming, yelling, pulling out a few chunks of her hair."

"Brad," my father said, "she acted like this and still you stayed with her?"

Yeah, not my finest moment.

"We hadn't been together that long," I said. "What should I have done? Abandoned her after she lost a baby? That's not my style."

My father harrumphed.

"Of course you shouldn't have abandoned her," Dr. Pelletier said. "But perhaps you should have seen that she got help."

"I was seventeen. I didn't realize she needed help. It wasn't until later that I realized why she'd cracked. She hadn't been able to manipulate the situation the way she wanted."

"And you fear she'll manipulate her way out of the mental health facility?"

"I know she will, if given the chance."

"We don't routinely strap our patients down unless they're a danger to themselves or others."

"Isn't that why you were able to put her away in the first place?"

"Yes, of course. She can't be in society in her current condition, but under supervision, there's no reason to strap her down."

"What about electroshock treatment?" my father asked.

I widened my eyes. Had I just heard him correctly?

"For what, exactly?" Dr. Pelletier asked.

"To keep her docile."

"Mr. Steel, that's not what ECT is used for, and frankly, its use is declining. It's contraindicated in this case."

"How much would it cost?" Dad asked.

I remained wide-eyed.

"I don't think you're hearing me." Dr. Pelletier raised an eyebrow. "If your wish is to make her docile so she won't be in control and finagle her way out of the facility, ECT will not have the desired effect. Even though it's a stigmatized treatment, it works well for stubborn depression. It doesn't make a patient catatonic."

"What about that movie? *One Flew Over the Cuckoo's Nest*?"

"It's called fiction for a reason, Mr. Steel."

"What *will* have the desired effect, then?"

"Well . . . medication would be the way to go."

"Perfect," Dad said. "Drug her."

"Mr. Steel, I'm a doctor. Unless Ms. Madigan shows symptoms of—"

"I'm not a patient man, Dr. Pelletier," Dad said. "How much is this going to cost me?"

"Putting away a young woman who is stalking a young man and who pulled a gun on another is one thing. I may have overstepped my bounds a little there, but I can live with myself. Drugging her is another thing altogether."

"You were paid very well for overstepping your bounds. You'll be paid even better to do what I ask."

"I'm sorry, Mr. Steel. I cannot in good conscience—"

"In good conscience? You took my money in the first place." My father cleared his throat. "Brad, step out of the room, please. I'd like to talk to the doctor alone."

Seriously? "Dad, I'm an adult."

"Brad." He said only my name, but it was a command.

However, I was no longer a little kid who did everything his father said without question. I hadn't been that person since I hit the age of ten.

"No, Dad. If this concerns Wendy, it concerns me. I'm the reason she's a nutcase."

Dr. Pelletier spoke then. "You're not the reason for

anything, Mr. Steel. If it weren't you, it would be something or someone else."

"What's wrong with her?" I asked.

"I haven't made an official diagnosis yet," he said, "but even if I had, I couldn't tell you. Doctor-patient confidentiality."

"Brad, I'll ask again. Please give me a moment with the doctor."

"No," I said again.

"All right." My father cleared his throat. "You may as well know how this is done. You'll have to do it one day yourself. More than once, I'd bet. Doctor, I appreciate everything you've done so far. I'm willing to offer you a million dollars in cash to make sure Wendy Madigan stays drugged up and out of my son's life for the next year. We'll renegotiate at that time."

My mouth dropped open.

My father offered a bribe. A big-ass bribe. I'd known he was no saint, but this . . .

Still, I couldn't bring myself to say anything. Wendy drugged out of her gourd was A-okay with me.

"Mr. Steel, I'm sorry. I can't—"

Quicker than a flash, my father pulled a pistol from a hidden waist holster and pointed it at Dr. Pelletier's head.

"What do you say now?"

CHAPTER TWENTY-TWO

Daphne

Walk away, Daphne. Just walk away.

Whatever was inside this envelope was no business of mine.

Or was it?

I was Brad's fiancée, after all—the future mother of his child.

And Wendy was his ex.

My hands trembled as I picked up the envelope.

Crap. It was sealed.

Walk away, I told myself again. *You shouldn't be in here anyway.*

No, a better way to ask about Wendy existed. Brad's mother was here. She seemed to like me. I'd ask her.

I found Mazie in the family room. "Where's my mom?" I asked.

"She said she wanted to read. She's in her room."

"Oh."

"Is there something you need?"

I paused a moment. "Yes, actually."

"What is it?"

"I want to know," I said, "all about Brad and Wendy."

Mazie's smile dropped. "I'm sure I can't tell you anything

more than Brad can himself."

"He's only told me that they were high school sweethearts and were on-again, off-again until he met me."

"That's about the extent of it."

"If they were together that long, surely you've met her."

"Of course I have. Many times."

"I'm just curious. What's she like?"

"She's very intelligent. Very personable."

I cleared my throat. "I should tell you. She came to my dorm room a few weeks ago and told me Brad would break my heart. Basically told me I should stay away from him."

"Clearly you gave her warning no credence."

"No. Not after I talked to Brad. But all he told me was the same old thing—that they were over."

"My son is trustworthy. You should believe him."

I want to believe him, but I just found a thick manila envelope with her name on it in his bedroom.

I couldn't say that though. I couldn't admit to snooping.

"It just seems like they were together for a long time," I said. "He and I have only been together for a couple months, and now we're getting married and having a baby. So naturally, I'm curious about her and the effect she's had on his life."

"My son adores you, Daphne."

"I'm not questioning that."

"Then why dredge up the past? Wendy's gone."

"Is she, though?"

"Didn't Brad tell you?"

"Yeah, he told me she wouldn't bother us anymore."

"She won't. That facility is the best place for her."

I widened my eyes. "Facility?"

"Oh, he *didn't* tell you, then."

"What kind of facility?"

"A mental health facility, dear. Wendy pulled a gun on one of Brad's friends. I think you know him. Sean Murphy."

"She *what*?" I gulped. Goosebumps erupted all over me. "Is Sean all right?"

"Yes, he's fine."

"Oh my God, that's why he moved out of Brad's place."

"That's right. Brad didn't tell you any of this?"

"No. He said Sean had to move because he could no longer pay the rent."

"Brad didn't charge him rent. Well, just a nominal amount."

Why didn't Brad tell me any of this? Silly question. I knew why. He was afraid it might send me over the edge, now that he knew about my past.

"Where is Wendy?"

"The facility is in Grand Junction."

"That's close to here."

"It is, because her parents live here in town. But you have nothing to be concerned about, Daphne. She's locked away, and she's getting the help she needs. She'll no longer be a threat to anyone."

"Maybe she should be in a prison cell."

"I can't disagree with you," Mazie said. "I never liked her much. Something about her always seemed a little ... off."

A little off.

How many times had students at my high school said that about me? Oh, they whispered it behind my back, but I heard them. I always knew.

"What seemed off about her?" I asked, not sure if I truly wanted to know.

"In some ways, she tried too hard to please George and me. I was actually gone for a while ... "

Right. She'd been in a facility herself for a while. I wouldn't bring that up, though. I didn't want to break Brad's confidence.

"Anyway," Mazie continued, "she seemed almost obsessed with Brad sometimes. She hung on him all the time. I'm pretty sure they were having sex in high school."

I knew this, but still, I hated hearing it, since the only person I'd ever had sex with was Brad, and he'd clearly had sex with many.

"Lots of people have sex in high school," I said, trying to sound nonchalant about the whole thing.

"But you didn't."

"No, I didn't."

How did she know?

"Brad told me," she said in answer to my silent question. "I hope that's okay."

"I have nothing to hide."

Wow. What a big damned lie. I had a lot to hide. What would Mazie think if she knew about my junior year?

She'd been through something similar, so she probably wouldn't judge me. Still, though, was *I* what a mother wanted for her son? An eighteen-year-old girl who'd been hospitalized and who didn't remember much of it?

"I think it's wonderful that you waited, Daphne. I waited as well. George was my first."

"Oh?"

"He was. Of course back then it was much more common to wait. Now, it seems everyone's in such a hurry."

"Brad and I didn't wait very long," I said.

"True. But he says you're special, and he's right. I knew as soon as I met you."

My cheeks warmed. "Thank you."

"I know neither of you planned this baby, but I couldn't be happier. To have a child around again will be so good for me. For George too." She sighed. "We always wanted a houseful of kids. But it wasn't to be."

"I know. I'm sorry about that."

"Maybe you and Brad will give us a houseful of grandkids."

I stroked my belly. Had she forgotten I was only eighteen? "One, at least. We're both so young."

"Oh, take all the time you want and need. We'll have one to dote on in the meantime."

She was sweet, and she would have been a wonderful mother to a gaggle of kids. My heart hurt for her. She was going to be a wonderful grandma.

And I had to hand it to her. She'd effectively steered the conversation away from Wendy.

But I wasn't done yet. I opened my mouth to say as much, when the phone rang.

CHAPTER TWENTY-THREE

Brad

"Dad!" I stood, my heart a mass of movement in my chest. "What the hell are you doing?"

"Sit down, Brad."

I dropped back into my chair. What else could I do? I wasn't going to try to take the gun away from him. We both knew how to handle weapons, but accidents could happen. I was going to be a father. I couldn't take the chance.

Dr. Pelletier's face went white, and he gripped the edge of his desk. "Mr. Steel, please. Put that down before someone gets hurt. You and I both know—".

"Save it," my father said. "I know how to use this and can have a bullet inside your brain before you take your next breath. Tell him, son."

"Leave me out of this."

"Tell him!"

"He's right. My dad's a crack shot." How well I knew. He'd taught me everything I knew, and I was as good as he was now. I'd proved it at the range.

Again, I reiterated my promise to myself never to teach another person how to shoot a gun. No way. I would not be party to any of this.

"No one's here at your office this evening. I don't even need a silencer."

"Mr. Steel . . . "

"You're going to make arrangements to keep Wendy Madigan so doped up that her brain can barely function. You got it? I don't want to hear that she finagled her way out of that place. She's a danger to my family, and I won't allow it."

"Mr. Steel—"

"If you don't do it, I *will* put a bullet in your head. Not tonight, of course. But soon. I'll put a bullet in yours and Wendy's both."

"You won't get away with it."

"Doctor, I assure you I've gotten away with worse."

My heart dropped to my stomach.

He'd gotten away with *worse*?

"I tried to do this the nice way," my father said, "with money. Now that offer's off the table. You give her the medication, or you don't live to see your next birthday. Your choice."

"Fine," Dr. Pelletier relented. "Only because I have a family and they need me."

"Understood," Dad said. "I have a family as well, and I'm going to make sure they're protected from Wendy Madigan. That's where you come in. You know she's a dangerous person. I get that you think she can't escape from the facility. You'll have to trust my son and me on this. Wendy is capable of just about anything."

"No one's that smart."

"She's not just smart," I said, finally adding to the conversation. "She's shrewd and she's cunning. I've had my lock changed half a dozen times, and she's gotten into my home."

Dr. Pelletier widened his eyes, shuddering. "Could you put the gun down now, Mr. Steel?"

"Fine." Dad lowered his gun but didn't replace it in the holster. "Don't think we don't appreciate this. You'll be well compensated, once I see that you've upheld your part of the bargain, and no one will be hurt."

"Except for the patient."

"The needs of my family outweigh the needs of one mentally ill person," Dad said. "She's a bad seed. You're doing a good thing, Doctor. Believe it or not, I don't like pulling out my gun."

Dr. Pelletier nodded weakly, saying nothing.

"Ready to go, Brad?" Dad said.

God, yes. I was more than ready. I still couldn't quite wrap my head around what had taken place here.

"Good night, Doctor," I said. "And thank you."

Again Dr. Pelletier nodded.

"We'll be in touch." Dad walked toward the door. "Come on, Brad."

★ ★ ★

I sat in a dive bar with my father. "I come here to think," he said.

I never imagined my dad in a place like this. It was pretty quiet, though, situated in a seedy part of the city. A few regulars sat at the wooden bar. Dad ordered two whiskeys.

"Rotgut at its finest." Dad took a drink. "Burns. In a good way."

I took a sip. He wasn't kidding. For a minute I thought I'd taken a drink of battery acid.

"I'm sorry you had to see that, son."

I was still numb. "That's not the first time you've done

that." A statement, not a question. I already knew the answer. My father had been way too comfortable to have never before been in a similar situation.

"Nope. And it probably won't be the last."

"So it's true, then? Money *can't* buy everything?"

"I won't lie to you, Brad. Money can buy a damned lot of things. But when it can't, a threat to a person's life will get the job done."

"You wouldn't have . . . killed him. Would you have?"

"I haven't had to take a life yet."

I haven't had to take a life yet.

Interesting words. They seemed to imply that he *would* take a life if he had to. I hoped like hell I was wrong in my interpretation.

"I meant what I said. I *am* sorry you had to see that, but you did have to see it. Do you know why?"

I shook my head. "I can't even begin to imagine."

"I won't be around forever, son. You know my health situation. When I'm gone, you'll be responsible for this family. Not just for your wife and kids, but for your mother also. My legacy will become yours."

"I know that. I'm prepared to take all of that on."

"I believe you are, which is why you had to see what happened at the good doctor's office."

I gulped down another drink of the burning liquor. It clawed down my throat, scorching a trail of ash in its wake. My father's use of the words "good doctor" was blazingly sardonic. A good doctor wouldn't have pulled strings with Wendy in the first place. When you've already sacrificed your integrity, it's easier to do it again.

And again.

I regarded my father.

How far had George Steel gone? *Doctor, I assure you I've gotten away with worse.* Yet he said he'd never taken a life. What was worse than taking a life?

I suppressed a shudder.

"Are you saying I'll have to do that someday?"

"Why do you think I taught you how to handle a gun?"

"Because it's a good skill to have."

"You're right about that. I think I just proved it."

"I want to be able to defend myself. Defend my family. I don't plan to use a gun to threaten someone."

"Don't think of it as threatening," Dad said. "Think of it as protecting your loved ones. That's what I did. Wendy is a threat, and I protected you, Daphne, and your unborn child from that threat by making sure she's kept drugged. You know as well as I do that she'd find a way out of that place if left to her own devices."

I nodded. In a warped way, my father was making sense, which was scary as shit. What was scarier was that I could totally see his point—especially where Wendy Madigan was concerned.

She was volatile, and she was skilled with weapons—thanks to me.

I might have to defend my father's legacy the way he did, but I'd do better for my own children. I'd teach them the way to make a living honorably, without the need for guns.

This fucked-up situation would end with me. I'd bury all my father's ghosts once he died, and I'd leave a life of peace for my wife and family.

I'd succeed, no matter what I had to do.

Which meant I had to put an end to the Future Lawmakers once and for all.

CHAPTER TWENTY-FOUR

Daphne

"Excuse me," Mazie said. "I need to get that."

I left the family room. I didn't want to intrude on her phone call.

"Daphne," she called me back in a few minutes later. "It's for you, dear. It's Brad."

A smile split my face. "Doesn't he want to talk to you as well?"

"Goodness, he told me that he and his father are fine and then asked for you." She smiled. "Makes perfect sense to me."

I took the receiver from her, and then she walked out of the room.

"Hello."

"Hi, baby."

"I miss you."

"I miss you too. Is Mom treating you and your mom okay?"

"Of course. She's great. She's already put together an amazing little wedding for us."

"That's Mom, all right."

"I think she's really happy about all this, Brad. I know our timing kind of sucks, but it seems to have made your mom happy. She's already talking about us having a houseful of grandkids."

"We will."

"I'll tell you what I told her. I'm only eighteen. There's no hurry."

"Oh, Daphne," he said, "I forgot to tell you."

"What?"

"The house. It's ours."

My mouth dropped open. "What house? This one?"

"Yeah, the ranch house. My father deeded it to me. We'll live there. With that houseful of kids my mom wants."

I looked around the vast family room. This was *ours*?

"Think about how you want to decorate it," he said. "You can have it any way you want."

"Brad, that's silly. It's beautiful the way it is. I wouldn't change a thing."

"Like I said, whatever you want. If that's what you want, we won't change a thing."

"Good. My parents are paying for the wedding, by the way."

"Daphne . . ."

"My mom insisted. Your mom offered to foot the bill, but my mom gets pretty stubborn sometimes."

"I can't imagine that," he said sarcastically. "Her daughter is *nothing* like that."

I couldn't help giggling. "Brad, they don't have the kind of money—"

"I'll take care of it," he said.

"Thanks." I had no idea what he thought he would do, but I trusted Brad. He'd take care of it.

Damn.

I *did* trust him.

Which meant I had to tell him what I'd found.

"Brad..."

"Yeah?"

"I went into your room today."

"Oh?"

"Yeah. I wanted to lie on your bed. It smells like you."

He laughed. "That's sweet."

"If it's sweet, why are you laughing?"

"I don't know. It's cute."

"I saw something."

"What?"

"A stack of manila envelopes on your desk. The top one had *Wendy* written on it."

Silence.

"I didn't open it. I would never do that."

"I know that, Daphne."

"But I did ask your mother about Wendy. Why didn't you tell me you had her committed?"

"I didn't want to upset you. You know... because of your history."

"I'm not upset. I'm glad she's gone."

"Good. So am I. She won't bother either one of us again."

"Promise?"

"I promise, baby."

I heaved a sigh of relief. "What's in the envelope?"

"Just some documents about the facility where she is. It's in Grand Junction."

"That's what your mom said. I wish she were farther away."

"I do too, but her parents want to be able to visit her."

I patted my belly, thinking of my little dove. I hadn't even met him yet, and already I knew I'd treasure him and would always want to be able to see him, no matter what. "I guess I understand that."

"But don't worry, baby. She won't be a problem. I've taken care of it. I'll always take care of you and our baby."

I warmed all over. "I know you will. Thank you for that. I love you so much, Brad."

"I love you too. I'll see you back home on Sunday."

"I can't wait. I miss you."

"Miss you too. I have to run. Bye."

"Bye." I replaced the receiver and walked to the kitchen.

Mazie sat at the table, sipping a cup of tea. "Everything okay with Brad?"

"Yeah, he says they're both fine." I sighed. "I miss him."

"So do I, honey."

I kissed her on the cheek. The action was out of the blue. I was never that forward, but I'd grown to love Mazie in a short time. "Thank you for everything," I said.

"You're most welcome. Thank you for giving me a grandchild."

"It'll be a while yet." I smiled down at my belly. "But he'll be wonderful. I know it."

CHAPTER TWENTY-FIVE

Brad

Tom Simpson lived in Boulder with his new wife, Evelyn. He was a first-year student at the University of Colorado Law School.

I didn't tell my father where I was going. Just said I had some stuff to take care of. He'd nodded and told me to take his car. I'd taken my truck instead.

I pulled up at the small house Tom rented near the school. He should be home on a Sunday.

We needed to talk.

After Tom, I'd contact Larry.

Then Theo, if I could find him. He moved around a lot and was always a question mark.

I walked up to the door and knocked.

His wife answered the door. "Brad. Hi." She looked a little pale.

"Hey, Evie. Are you okay?"

"Not in the slightest. Come on in."

"If you're sick, I don't want to bother you."

"You won't bother me. I'm sure you're here to see Tom."

"Yeah, I am."

"I'll get him for you. Have a seat."

I sat down on the green couch and waited. Tom came in a

few minutes later, followed by his wife.

"Did you tell Brad the good news, Evie?"

"Oh. No, I didn't."

Tom smiled. "We're pregnant!"

Oh. That explained why she looked like she was going to lose her breakfast. "Congratulations!"

"Ugh," Evie said. "I'll be happy when the first trimester is over. I feel completely awful."

"I know what you mean," I said.

"How could you possibly know?" she said.

"Oh, sorry. Not me, of course. My girlfriend. Er... fiancée."

"You're fucking kidding me," Tom said. "Wendy's pregnant?"

"God, no. Not Wendy. I'm sorry I've left you out of the loop. Daphne Wade."

"Not Larry's kid sister?"

"Yeah. We met at school, and well... you can guess the rest."

"Are you going to marry her?"

"I am."

"Marriage isn't for the faint of heart, dude."

"You think I don't know that? I watched my parents' shitty marriage."

Evelyn swatted Tom's arm. "Don't give marriage a bad name. We're very happy," she said to me.

She didn't look happy. She looked like—

"Excuse me!" She clamped her hand over her mouth and ran out of the room.

"Poor thing," Tom said. "She's sick as a dog. I don't have to tell you that this came as a surprise. We weren't planning to start a family until after I finished law school."

"I hear that one. Ours was a major surprise, especially since I used a condom."

"No shit?"

"No shit."

"Do you at least like her?"

"More than that. I love her, man."

"So you and Wendy are over for good this time."

"Yeah. It's been a long time coming, but I'm glad. She was becoming... hard to control."

He guffawed. "No one will ever be able to control Wendy. She's hot as hell, but damn, I'm glad you were the one saddled with her. Theo and I talk about that all the time."

"You do?"

"Oh, hell, yeah. She's nuts."

"Thanks for letting me in on that."

"Seriously, how did you *not* know?"

"I did. Eventually. She's gone now. Committed."

"Fuck. Seriously?"

"I'm surprised you didn't know. It happened a few weeks ago."

"She and I haven't been in touch. The three of us guys have been working on something by ourselves."

"Yeah, Theo told me. What is it?"

"Still in the planning stages," he said. "Keep your voice down. Evie doesn't know anything about my dealings with the club."

"Yeah. Okay."

"So where's Wendy?"

"Piney Oaks, in Grand Junction."

"Right. Good. Can't say I'm sad to have her out of our hair.

She's brilliant, but she's a loose cannon."

"You're telling me."

"Still, she was the brains behind getting us going. She figured out the business strategies and then took our profits and invested them in all kinds of shit. We made a mint, as you know."

Yeah, I knew. I hadn't minded pocketing the profits.

"That's kind of what I'm here to talk about," I said. "I'm out. As of now."

"Steel, we need your cash."

"Not anymore you don't. I gave Theo some money a month ago, and that's the last time. I'll be taking over my dad's business soon, and I'm getting married. You're invited, by the way. You and Evie. It's in two weeks, at the ranch."

"Great. We'll be there."

"Tell Theo. I have no idea where he is."

"I'll do it." He pulled something out of his pocket. "Ever smoked marijuana, Steel?"

My eyebrows shot off my forehead. "What the fuck? Put that away!"

"This is el primo weed."

"Since when do you smoke dope, Simpson? Your wife is pregnant, for God's sake."

"Theo and I got a great deal on a huge stash."

Fuck it all. No way. I grabbed Tom's collar. "Tell me you did *not* use my money to buy drugs."

"For God's sake, pipe down. Of course we didn't."

"You're in fucking law school, Tom. Pot is illegal."

"Did I say we were going to sell it?"

"You said you got a huge stash. What the fuck am I supposed to think?"

"Maybe think that being a full-time law student and running the business with Theo and Larry is a lot on my plate. I need to relax every now and then. Enter, this joint. Besides, this is Boulder, man."

"What about Evie?"

"Evie knows. She indulges herself. Not since she got pregnant, of course."

"Evie?"

"Don't act so shocked. It's not a narcotic, Steel. It's a little weed."

"Yeah, well, no thanks."

"Your loss." He shoved the joint back in his pocket. "You're really out, huh?"

"Yeah, and don't tell me again that you need me. You're all millionaires."

"Shh!" he said again. "Evie."

"Why the hell are you letting her work when she doesn't need to? Especially now that she's pregnant?"

"Because I don't want to tell her about the biz. Not yet."

"Why—" I stopped, closing my mouth.

Why wouldn't he want his wife to know about his side business? That he was rich?

Only one reason.

They were getting into . . .

God, I couldn't think about it.

"Be careful, man," I said.

"Everything's under control."

"It's drugs."

"Do you think I'm lying to you, Steel? Come on."

I said no more. If I did, our friendship would end. Not that I cared a lot about the friendship anymore, but something held me back.

Because, yes, he was lying to me.

My father had taught me long ago how to spot a liar.

A liar didn't look you in the eye. He averted his gaze.

A liar blinked a lot.

A liar shifted his stance.

A liar smiled to hide the lie.

The only problem?

Tom Simpson did none of these things.

But he was lying. I felt it in my bones.

Tom was an enigma—different from both Theo and Larry in a way I could never quite pinpoint.

I pinpointed it now.

He was a master at hiding his emotions.

It would serve him well as a lawyer.

"Watch your back," I said to him. "Don't bite off more than you can chew."

"Steel," he said, his blue gaze icy, "you know me much better than that."

I did.

I'd watched him, Theo, and Larry grow from awkward teens into men. I'd seen the subtle changes take place.

And I was never gladder to be walking away from the Future Lawmakers.

CHAPTER TWENTY-SIX

Daphne

Two weeks later...

I wore white.

Yeah, I was pregnant, and I wore white. But I'd always dreamed of being married in a white flowing dress. I gave up the flowing, since our little wedding wasn't a truly formal affair, but I kept the white.

My mom and Mazie fluttered around me, helping me don the white sundress. It was a beautiful autumn day, and the Indian summer held out. I wouldn't be cold today.

Morning sickness hadn't eased at all, and today I had the added bonus of nervous butterflies.

I didn't have any friends other than Patty and Ennis, so I'd asked Patty to act as my maid of honor. Sean was to be Brad's best man.

Other than my parents and Patty, Ennis was the only other person in attendance for me.

Everyone else was someone Brad knew, including my half brother, Larry.

I'd met them all the prior evening at our rehearsal dinner, but honestly, other than Theo, who I'd already met once before—his eyes were a normal brown this time—I couldn't tell you who any of them were.

I'd meet them all again after the wedding, when I wasn't as nervous.

My father approached us, wearing a white tuxedo with a black bow tie. White tuxedos were in right now, Mazie had said.

I'd okayed it, even though I thought black was classier.

"Daphne"—he cupped my cheek—"you look radiant."

"That's probably sweat, Daddy." I tried to smile. I'd thrown up fifteen minutes earlier in the powder room.

"Nonsense. It's that glow of being a bride, plus the glow of impending motherhood."

I didn't respond. My heart was in my throat.

Was I ready for this?

Didn't really matter. The little dove was coming. According to my doctor, the pregnancy was progressing perfectly. Plus, I couldn't love Brad Steel any more than I already did. He was my destiny. I knew it without question.

I just never thought part of my destiny would be to be pregnant and getting married at eighteen.

I'd wanted a few years to be independent, to prove to myself that I could exist in the real world and not succumb to anxiety and depression.

Too late now. I had to be strong, not just for myself, but for Brad and little dove.

Someone knocked on the door.

"Come in," I said.

Patty entered. She wore vibrant yellow, a color I'd insisted on. Mazie had wanted me to carry her pale-green tulips. I held out for yellow. Nothing about this day was going to be drab and colorless.

Nothing.

"It's time, Daph." She smiled. "You look *amazing*."

"I feel like I'm going to hurl."

"Need some crackers?"

"God, no. Nothing. Please. I can't even think about food." The elaborate spread Mazie had ordered for the reception—complete with roast baron of Steel beef—would be lost on me.

"Honey, if you can't do this right now, it's okay," Dad said.

I swallowed. "It's not that. I want to do this. I just feel . . ." Nausea crept up my throat. I ran into the bathroom.

Dry heaves were the worst. Of course they were dry heaves. I hadn't eaten anything. Between morning sickness and nerves, I couldn't.

At least I wouldn't screw up my hair and makeup. I wiped the last of the saliva from my lips and left the bathroom.

"Daph?" Patty said.

My father took my hands. "Okay?"

"Nothing different from every other day," I said. "It will pass. Let's just do this."

"Are you sure?" Dad asked.

Why did people keep asking me that? Of course I was sure. I'd never been surer.

"Yes, for the last time, I'm sure. This is what I want, Daddy."

"Okay, honey. Let's go."

★ ★ ★

"Dearly beloved," the minister began, "we're here on this beautiful day to witness the joining in marriage of Bradford Raymond Steel and Daphne Kay Wade. If anyone present knows why these two people should not be joined in holy matrimony, let him speak now, or forever hold his peace."

Brad went slightly rigid beside me. The seconds stretched into what seemed like hours.

But no one spoke.

Had he been expecting Wendy? How could he be, when she was locked in a mental health facility? They didn't just let you walk out of places like that. I should know.

Finally, the minister continued. "Do you, Bradford, take Daphne to be your wife, to have and to hold, from this day forward, for better, for worse, for richer, for poorer, in sickness and in health, to love and to cherish, till death do you part?"

Brad smiled at me. "I do."

"And do you, Daphne, take Bradford to be your husband, to have and to hold, from this day forward, for better, for worse, for richer, for poorer, in sickness and in health, to love and to cherish, till death do you part?"

"I do," I said, willing my voice not to shake.

"The rings, please."

Rings? We had rings. Of course we had to have rings. With everything else going on, I hadn't thought of any of that. Brad— or at least Mazie—apparently had, thank goodness.

I lost track of the words as Brad placed a ring on my left finger. Diamonds sparkled in the sunlight. It was beautiful.

Patty then handed me a simple gold band. I trembled as I placed it on his finger, repeating the words the minister said.

"With this ring, I thee wed."

"By the power invested in me by the state of Colorado," the minister said, "I now pronounce you husband and wife. Brad, you may kiss the bride."

Brad grabbed me and pulled me to him. He crushed his

lips to mine in a powerful kiss.

Our first kiss as husband and wife.

And it was a doozy.

I was already light-headed from nausea and nerves.

This kiss took me over the top.

My body wavered, and if Brad hadn't been holding me, I no doubt would have fallen.

The sun seemed to cloud over, and the happy voices surrounding us became a cloudy din.

Happy, I was happy.

So why...

Why did I feel so...?

Then...nothing.

CHAPTER TWENTY-SEVEN

Brad

Daphne went limp in my arms.

I broke the kiss, holding her. "Baby?"

The string quartet began to play. We were supposed to walk back down the makeshift aisle now, as man and wife.

But my wife had passed out.

What was I supposed to do?

Murph nudged me. "Everything okay, bro?"

"She fainted," I said.

"Oh. Shit. What should we do?"

"I don't know." I made a quick decision. I lifted her in my arms and carried her down the aisle like a child.

Lucy and Jonathan, along with my mother, raced behind me.

"Is she okay?" Lucy asked.

"She passed out," I said. "I need to get her to a bed."

"Poor thing," Mom said. "This is just all too much for her. She's so young, and she's been sick with the pregnancy."

I hoped Mom was right. That was all it was.

I took Daphne to the room she stayed in and laid her on the bed. I softly patted her cheek. "Baby? Baby, are you all right?"

Her eyes fluttered open. "Brad?"

"Yeah, it's me."

"Are we married?"

"We are. What happened, honey?"

"I'm not sure. I just got really light-headed."

"Are you better now? Can you sit up?"

"I haven't eaten anything today."

"Oh, Daphne, no wonder you fainted. You need to eat. Your body is working hard right now, nourishing our baby."

"If I need to eat, why does my body make me feel so horrible?"

"I don't know, but that's the way pregnancy is. You know that."

She sat up. "I can't go back out there."

"Why?"

"Why? Because I'm completely embarrassed, Brad. I fainted at my own wedding. Now they're all going to know why we got married."

"Most of them know anyway. Besides, everyone knows why a couple gets married as young as we are and as early as we are in our relationship. There's nothing to be ashamed of." I touched her soft hair. "You're still . . . happy about this, right?"

She cupped my cheek. "Of course I am. I just wish my body hadn't betrayed me like this. I feel like such a fool."

"You can't help what happened. But Daphne, you have to eat. Even when you feel sick, you have to force yourself to eat. For the baby's sake."

She nodded. "You're right. I'm sorry."

"Don't be sorry. Just take care of yourself. I love you."

"I love you too."

"Are you strong enough to come out?"

"I will be. Could you get me some crackers and water?

And maybe some protein? I'll force it all down."

I kissed her forehead. "Of course. I'll be right back. I'll send your parents in. They're worried about you."

"Okay."

"Go ahead in," I told Lucy and Jonathan when I left the room. "She's awake. She needs something to eat. I'm going to get it for her."

On my way to the kitchen, I was waylaid by my father. "How is she?"

"She's okay. She just hasn't eaten."

"I'll have Belinda fix her a tray."

"It's okay. I've got it, Dad."

My father gripped my shoulder. "She's your responsibility now."

"I know that."

"Do better than I did, son."

I plan to.

I didn't say the words, though. This was my wedding day, and I wasn't going to pick a fight with my father.

He continued, "You have your hands full with this one."

"I know what I'm getting into."

"Do you?" He cocked his head.

"Damn." I shook my head, scoffing. "You had her checked out, didn't you?"

"Did you think I wouldn't?"

"Dad, I've had a few other things on my mind lately." Including things he didn't even know about. "But I can't say I'm surprised."

"You shouldn't be."

"Why didn't you come to me with what you knew before we were married?"

"I thought about it. I did. But there was the issue of the child."

"For God's sake. You thought I'd back out, and you want the baby. Of all the—"

"Keep your voice down, Brad."

I looked around. He was right. The wedding and reception were outside, but stragglers were milling around inside the house. Still, I couldn't deny the anger whirring through me like the blade of a buzz saw.

"You were afraid you wouldn't get your grandchild," I hissed.

"What do my motives matter at this point? You know everything anyway."

"I do, but Daphne doesn't."

"I know."

"Her father told me everything. Does that surprise you?"

"A little, but I don't know the man. I will, though. I've got my best men looking into him."

"You're checking Jonathan out? Seriously?"

"Yes, seriously."

"He's a man who loves his daughter. He wanted to make sure I was serious about marrying her, and he told me point blank that if I wanted to back out, he and Lucy would take care of her and the baby."

"Lucy is another matter."

"You know about that too?"

"Of course. Do you think there's anything I don't know about concerning you?"

I stopped myself from gulping. Did he know about the Future Lawmakers? Did he know that Theo, Tom, and Larry were most likely getting into drugs? Did he know I'd fronted them money out of my own accounts?

Of course he did.

He knew about Wendy, then, too.

About the miscarriage. No wonder his reaction to that news in Dr. Pelletier's office had seemed off.

He knew about . . . *everything*.

Nothing I could do about it now, no matter how livid I was. I forcefully unclenched my fists. "I'm married now, Dad. I'm going to be a father. Stop spying on me."

"I can't do that."

"Why the fuck not?"

"You'll understand when your child is born." He turned and walked away.

As angry as I was, I had to give him credit. He'd never interfered in my life. He hadn't interfered with Wendy until I asked him to. He spied, he knew everything, and then he let me deal with the fallout.

I'd do better for my own children.

I'd be there for them.

Always.

Count on it, I said silently to the child resting in Daphne's belly. *I'll always be there for you.*

CHAPTER TWENTY-EIGHT

Daphne

Brad sat next to me as I forced down the crackers and mild cheddar he'd brought me. Once I ate, I had to admit I felt a little better.

"Ready to go out and meet your public?" he asked.

"My public?"

"Sure. You're queen for a day. It's your wedding day, Daphne. Everyone wants to see you."

"I don't know anyone except my parents and Patty and Ennis."

"You'll meet them. I'll introduce you."

I stood finally and felt a lot less weak than I had previously. "Let me make sure I'm presentable." I walked to the bathroom. Not bad. My makeup was fine and my hair okay. I walked back out. Now or never. "I'm ready."

Brad and I walked through the house and out into the backyard, where people were talking in groups and Belinda was helping the caterers set up.

Brad's friend Theo approached us. "There you are," he said. "Feeling better?"

"Yeah, I am. Thanks."

"She just needed to eat something," Brad said.

"I like you better this way," I said.

"What?" Theo's eyes widened.

"Without the blue contacts," I said.

"Oh, right. I forgot I was wearing them that day we met in town. They're kind of uncomfortable."

"You look much better with your own natural eyes." In fact, Theo was incredibly handsome in a dark and Mediterranean way.

"I'll remember that. Congratulations, you two."

"Thanks, Theo," Brad said.

My half brother, Larry, was next to approach. "Hey," he said.

"Hi."

We had no idea what to say to each other because our contact had been so minimal over the years. I always wondered why, but Dad and Mom never talked about it much. Dad saw Larry one weekend per month in Grand Junction. He never came to Westminster to visit us.

Larry didn't look like my brother at all, though he did bear a resemblance to my father. Larry was blond, though, and his hairline was receding. He seemed pretty young to be going bald.

"Hey, Larry," Brad said. "Thanks for coming."

"Wouldn't have missed it. When you have a minute, I need to talk to you."

"Sure. Maybe later," Brad said.

"Can you spare a few now?" Larry asked.

"Go ahead," I said. "I'm fine."

"Are you sure?"

"Yeah, now that I've eaten something, I feel a lot better."

"All right." Brad left with my half brother.

Ennis approached me then. "Feeling better, love?"

"Yeah. This pregnancy thing isn't all it's cracked up to be."

"I don't think it was ever cracked up to be fun."

"How are things with you and Pat?" I asked.

"Good. We're taking it slow."

"I'm glad to hear that."

He chuckled. "Why is that? Don't want me to get any?"

"No, no, that's not what I mean." I'd put my foot in my mouth. Patty wasn't known to be discriminating. She'd slept with two different guys our first week at college. Ennis was a nice guy, and I wanted this to work out between them.

"What *do* you mean, then?"

"I just hope it works out for you. You two are my only friends at college."

"Only because you and your husband have been inseparable since day one."

I smiled. He was right. Brad and I had met, and fate took its course. "I like seeing you and Patty together. You're a nice guy, Ennis."

He feigned a heart attack. "Ah! The worst thing to say."

"What's wrong with being a nice guy?"

"Nice guys finish last, as you Yanks like to say."

"I've never said that."

Ennis gestured toward Patty, who was talking to Sean Murphy. "Do I have anything to worry about there?"

How did I answer that? Patty had slept with Sean our first night at college and then again the second night. They hadn't been together since, though. That I knew of, anyway.

"No, of course not. They're over. In fact, they never really began."

"She told me about it."

"Good. I'm glad. If it's going to work with you guys, there

143

shouldn't be any secrets hanging over you."

"What about the other one?"

"Rex? Please. Sean's at least a nice guy. Rex is a jerk."

"But he's better looking than I am."

"That's a matter of opinion."

I couldn't fault Ennis's observation. He was handsome in a decidedly English way. Rex, Patty's first nighter, was gorgeous. But an asshole, which in my book made him ugly.

"She was still seeing him when we got together."

"Is she still seeing him now?"

"She says she isn't."

"Then what's the issue?"

"He's pursuing her. Big-time."

"Is she interested?"

"She says she isn't, but..."

"Trust her, Ennis. So she likes sex. She's not the only girl in the world who does."

"Are you saying I should be doing it with her?"

"Only if it's something you both want."

"Fuck, yeah, I want it. She's the holdup."

"Really?" I tried to hide my surprise.

"Yeah. Says she wants to do it right this time. Take it slow, like I said."

"That's very mature of her."

"I suppose."

Patty ran up to us then and tugged on Ennis's arm. "Come on, I want you to meet some people."

Who could Patty want Ennis to meet? She didn't know anyone here other than Sean, Brad, and me. But that was Patty. I'd only known her a couple of months, but she was so perky and outgoing, she made friends within minutes wherever she went.

I was so *not* like that.

I swallowed down my rising nausea, pasted a smile on my face, and walked farther into the courtyard where the tables were set up. We'd be sitting down to dinner soon.

CHAPTER TWENTY-NINE

Brad

"In private," Larry whispered.

I sighed and led him into the house and then my bedroom, closing the door behind us. "What is it?"

"Tom and Theo," he said. "They're up to something."

"Theo's always up to something," I said. "That's not exactly news."

"They bought a bunch of marijuana."

"I know."

"You do? And you're okay with this?"

"I'm out, man. I told Tom before he told me about the pot. I'm no longer investing in this mess. Now that Wendy's locked up, I can get on with my life."

"You're already in, Steel."

"The fuck I am."

"Your money started all this."

"And my money is cut off as of now."

"Doesn't matter."

"The hell it doesn't. You three keep me out of it from now on. Keep my name out of all your dealings, or you'll be sorry."

"What exactly do you think you can do to us?" he asked.

"Trust me"—the image of my father threatening Dr. Pelletier raced into my head—"you don't want to know."

Larry's already fair face went whiter. "You don't know what those two are capable of."

"Tom and Theo? Sure I do."

Theo was capable of just about anything, and Tom? His icy demeanor would get him through the worst shit in the world, and no one who met him would have a clue.

It was fucking scary.

"I don't want to get into drugs, man," he said. "You've got to help me."

"Then don't get into drugs. You don't have to go along with them. Just get out, like I did."

"It's not that simple."

"Sure it is. It's *exactly* that simple."

"It's not, Brad, and here's why—"

Someone pounded on the door.

"Shit," I said. "What is it?"

"Dinner is being served." My mother's voice. "We need you out here now."

Damn. I wanted to hear what Larry had to say, but I couldn't disappoint Daphne and the rest of our guests.

"Coming." I met Larry's gaze. "This isn't over."

★ ★ ★

Daphne managed to eat a decent amount of dinner at my urging. At least she didn't look green anymore, and she seemed happy. She was worried about her mother, though. I could tell.

The servers began filling champagne flutes at the table— sparkling cider for Daphne and Evie Simpson, of course. Murph then stood up to make his best man's toast.

He clinked his spoon on his flute until he had everyone's attention.

"Hey, everyone, thanks so much for being here today," Murph began. "I've known Brad Steel for nearly four years. We met freshman year of college and became fast friends. He's the only guy who can outdrink me!"

Laughter rang throughout the yard.

"I was lucky enough to be his roommate for a little over a year as well. We sure had our fun, and there was no better guy to go out with. The ladies flocked to us when Brad was around. He's a chick magnet."

More laughter. Daphne eyed me.

Geez, Murph. You could have left that out. This is my wedding toast, for God's sake.

"But his skirt-chasing days were over the first day of orientation a few months ago when he locked eyes with Daphne Wade."

Okay, Murph. You're forgiven.

"I've never seen anyone fall that hard that fast." He shook his head, smiling. "Brad finally found the woman who brought him to his knees, and Daphne, I never thought it could happen, but you're the one."

She smiled.

I'm the luckiest man in the world. Yeah, she comes with baggage. A lot of it. But so do I. Together we'll conquer it all.

"Though I may never forgive you for taking away my best girl-chasing buddy!"

Laughter again, even from Daphne this time.

"So everyone, please raise your glasses to Brad and Daphne! They deserve all the happiness in the world, and I—" Murph stumbled a little. "Sorry, got a little woozy there. I know I haven't had that much to drink yet."

More laughter.

But not from me.

No matter how much he drank, Murph never stumbled. He was a master at hiding his inebriation. What was going on?

"So please raise your glasses—" He stumbled again.

I stood. "Murph, are you—"

"Yeah. Not feeling great," he said. "Steel, I'm sorry, man." The flute fell from his grasp and landed with a soft plop on the grass underneath his feet.

His body followed.

Damn! First the bride fainted at the end of the ceremony, and now the best man passed out in a drunken stupor? What the hell kind of wedding was this? My heart raced.

"Brad," Daphne said frantically. "Is he all right?"

"Of course he's not all right. He's shitfaced. At our wedding. For God's sake, Murph!"

Patty reached him before I did. "Should I do my toast now?" she asked.

"I don't know. Fuck." I smacked Murph in the cheek a couple times. "Murph, Murph. Wake up!"

My father came forward as well. "Should we call an ambulance?"

"For what? He's just toasted."

"Sozzled," Ennis said, who had come to join Patty. "Though I didn't see him drink a lot."

"He didn't," Patty agreed. "He had a beer after the ceremony, no wine with dinner, and he hasn't taken a sip of champagne yet."

"Watching him that closely, eh?" Ennis said.

"Ennis, Sean and I are over. I've told you that. This is a little bit more important than your jealousy."

"You're right, love. I'm sorry." Then, to me, "I don't think he's drunk, mate. Something else is going on."

I'd been dealing with Larry, so I had no idea how much Murph had drunk. Both Patty and Ennis hadn't seen him drink a lot. What the hell was going on?

"Could be anything," my father said. "He might be ill. Or . . ."

"Or what?"

"He might have been drugged."

"Who the hell would—"

I looked up and met Theo's gaze. He was frowning. Then I met Tom's. His expression was stoic. Icy as usual.

They were getting into pot. Not anything that could take down a grown man after one beer. Besides, what did they have against Murph? They didn't have any reason to screw up my wedding.

No, this could only be the work of one person—and that person was locked up at Piney Oaks.

I met my father's gaze.

He shook his head slightly.

Good. It wasn't Wendy. The good doctor had drugged her as my father commanded.

What was going on, then?

"Murph! Come on!" I tried once again to rouse him.

"Get him inside," Dad said. "I'll brew some coffee. Put him under a cold shower. If that doesn't wake him up, nothing will."

I grabbed Murph's dead weight and slung him over my shoulder. "Come on, dude."

My mother stood. "Please, enjoy your champagne. When Brad gets back, he and Daphne will cut this beautiful cake."

I carried my friend into the house and to one of the spare bedrooms that wasn't being used. With my father's help, we got him stripped down to his boxers and under a cold stream of water.

My heart had been beating double time since he passed out, but when he didn't come to in the shower, my apprehension turned to icy fear.

Dad pressed his fingers to Murph's neck. "He still has a pulse. That's good. We need to get him to an emergency room. Get your truck."

"Dad, it's my wedding day."

"All right. I'll take him. We can call the squad, but by the time they get here, I'll have him to the city."

Murph was my best friend. I should go along.

But I'd just gotten married. Hell, my guests were still here.

We hadn't cut the damned cake yet.

And Daphne . . .

My Daphne, who was finally feeling stronger after her fainting spell.

What would this do to *her*?

"All right, Dad. Thank you. Take good care of him."

Dad got Murph wrapped in a giant bath towel and picked him up like a baby. My father's lungs weren't in great shape, but still he was strong as an ox.

"I'll call when I have news. Get back to your party."

CHAPTER THIRTY

Daphne

I gulped down a sob that threatened to come hurtling out of my throat.

Some wedding.

First I fainted.

Then the best man fainted.

Who'd be next?

Was this all foreshadowing of something horrible to come?

I didn't want to entertain the thought.

Brad returned to the party, the front of his white tux shirt wet. He'd removed his jacket and bow tie, and his shirt was unbuttoned.

Even as fatigued and sick as I felt, he looked yummy to me.

"How is he?" I asked frantically.

"I don't know. Dad's taking him to the ER."

I gulped. "You couldn't wake him up?"

He shook his head somberly. "No. I couldn't."

I said nothing more. What was there to say? Sean was one of Brad's best friends.

"I'm so sorry for the disruption," Mazie was saying, standing by the cake. "Brad, Daphne, if you'd like to come on up, I know everyone is anxious to try this gorgeous cake."

I was hardly anxious. At least the cake didn't have a smell I had to deal with, like the roast beef had. I couldn't tell Brad the smell of his family's beef made me want to toss my cookies.

I joined him next to the cake. Mazie handed me the cake knife. "Go ahead and slice into it, Daphne. Brad, put your hand over hers."

The photographer clicked in our faces as we sliced a piece of the white cake with raspberry filling.

We fed each other a small bite to thundering applause and then walked back to our seats while the caterers cut and served.

My belly churned—and not just from pregnancy nausea.

Worry consumed me. Patty was right. Sean hadn't drunk a lot, so something else was going on. But what?

I wandered inside the house after everyone was served. I needed some time alone. I walked past the bustling servers in the kitchen to my guest room.

I was Mrs. Bradford Steel now, and this was my home.

Surreal.

I patted my tummy. *I'll make it through, little dove. I swear to you.*

I jerked when someone knocked softly. "Yeah?" I said.

Patty opened the door, followed by Ennis.

"Are you okay, Daph?" she asked.

I nodded. Sort of.

"Sorry, love," Ennis said. "We're not convinced."

"I'm married to the man I love. But I'm so worried."

"We are too," Patty said. "I've never seen Sean like that."

"Brad said his dad will call when there's any news. Leave it to me to have a wedding like this." I sighed.

"What do you mean?" Patty asked.

I'd said too much. Patty and Ennis, though they were my closest friends at school, didn't know anything about my junior year of high school or about my mother's suicide attempt. Now wasn't exactly the optimal time to fill them in. Weddings were supposed to be happy occasions.

Right?

What a mess.

Brad appeared in the doorway then, his face somber.

"Everyone's leaving," he said.

"Have you heard anything?" Patty asked.

"No, not yet. Once everyone's gone, I'm heading to the hospital."

"I'll go with you," I said.

"No, baby. You stay here with my mom and your parents. Get the rest you need. There's nothing you can do there anyway."

"There's nothing you can do there either," I said. "I want to be there. For you."

He kissed my forehead. "Please. Do this for me. You've already fainted once today."

"Because I was hungry. I ate my dinner, Brad."

"I know, but it'll be dark by the time I get there, and you need your rest. I don't want you sitting up all night in a hospital waiting room."

"But I—"

He gently placed two fingers over my lips. "No arguments. Both of our mothers agree with me. You need to stay here and take care of yourself and the baby. I'd stay as well, except Sean—"

"Is your best friend. I get it." I sighed. "I'm sorry, Brad."

"About what?"

"About today. About fainting. About Sean."

"None of that is your fault, baby." He smiled. "Except maybe the fainting. Don't go without eating again, okay?"

"I won't. I promise." I'd keep that promise, no matter what. The baby inside me was my first priority.

"I guess we should shove off," Ennis said. "We have a hotel room in town."

"You can stay here," Brad said. "We still have a couple spare rooms."

Patty smiled. "Thank you for the offer, but... we kind of want to be alone."

"Got it," Brad said.

I smiled at both of them. Tonight would apparently be the night.

At least someone should get some on my wedding night. I wouldn't be because my husband would be at the hospital.

Oh, well. I was nauseated anyway, and Brad and I had a lifetime of sleeping together.

A lifetime with our little dove.

After Patty and Ennis left, Brad gave me a searing kiss on the lips.

"I love you, Daphne."

"I love you too, Brad. Come home to me soon."

CHAPTER THIRTY-ONE

Brad

I sat with my father, drinking really bad coffee, in the ICU waiting room.

Yeah, Murph had been transferred to ICU. A blood test showed heroin in his system—heroin!—and even after the doctors had pumped everything out of his stomach, he still hadn't come to.

Murph's parents sat at the other end of the waiting room. I'd called them when I got to the hospital. They, of course, were blaming me, and though I hadn't drugged him, I couldn't fault their logic.

He'd been at my wedding.

Someone at my wedding had drugged my best man.

At this point, the only person I knew for sure was innocent was Daphne.

My father, sitting beside me, had been a rock, had taken my best friend to the ER when I had other responsibilities, namely to my wife and our guests. Did I think he was behind this? No, I didn't, but I couldn't unsee him pulling a gun on an innocent psychiatrist who'd already done him a massive favor.

George Steel was capable of so much more than I ever gave him credit for—and not in a good way.

Why should I be so surprised? This was a man who'd

knocked his wife around simply because she couldn't give him more children.

He seemed to regret those actions now.

Did he regret threatening Dr. Pelletier?

Not that I could see.

Still, what would he have to gain by drugging my best friend?

Then there were Theo and Tom. They both knew Murph, had partied with Murph. As far as I knew, they liked Murph. At least they'd never let on they didn't.

Of course, Larry had all but admitted the two of them were getting into the drug business. Pot, though. Marijuana was a long way from heroin. How would they even know how to get heroin?

My mother... She liked Murph. Would she do such a thing? No.

Daphne's parents. Of course not. Lucy was recovering from an overdose herself, and neither of them had any sort of motive.

Patty and Ennis? No way.

The few other guests were friends of my parents from Snow Creek. Good people who had no reason to drug a person they didn't even know.

That left one person.

Larry.

Larry, who had tried to tell me something before we got interrupted in my bedroom.

Larry, who was technically family now that I'd married Daphne, his half sister.

Family wouldn't do that.

Besides, of the three Future Lawmakers, Larry was the

one who actually had a semblance of a conscience. Not a whole conscience, mind you, but at least the semblance of one.

He had something to tell me, and I needed to find out what it was.

Could I call him now? It was the middle of the night. He probably wouldn't answer. He might not even be home. He could be staying at a hotel.

Damn!

Larry had nothing against Murph that I knew of, but he knew something—something about Theo and Tom.

I had the feeling he wanted out.

And for some reason, he didn't think he could get out.

Who would want to hurt—

Hurting Murph would hurt *me*, and the only person who wanted to hurt me was . . .

But she was locked up and medicated.

Locked doors didn't stop Wendy. I knew that firsthand. But medication would. First thing in the morning, I'd call Piney Oaks to make sure she was still docile and inside her room.

Better idea, I'd have my father do it. Money talked.

I quickly asked him.

"They have someone at the switchboard twenty-four-seven," he said. "I already called them. She's medicated and in her room."

"Thanks," I said. "I don't know why I didn't think of it first thing."

"It's your wedding day, son. You've had a few other things on your mind."

"Yeah. I guess so. I should be with my wife right now."

"Go if you want. I'll take care of Sean. He'll have everything he needs. You have my word."

"Daphne's asleep by now," I said, "and it's the best thing for her. I'll stay."

"As you wish." Dad rubbed his chin. "You and Daphne are so young to be saddled with all of this."

"We can handle it." I prayed my words were true. "I just don't understand who would want to hurt Murphy."

"Have you considered that he did it himself?"

"OD'd? Hell, no. Murph doesn't do drugs. Plus he's the happiest guy on the planet. At least he was, until Wendy pulled that freaking gun on him."

"Being held at gunpoint can fuck you up, Brad."

"Do you think it fucked Dr. Pelletier up?" I couldn't help asking, albeit quietly.

My comment didn't faze him. "It may well have, but it was a move I had to make. You weigh all the pros and cons, son, and when the benefit outweighs the cost, you do what you have to do. Besides, we're not talking about Dr. Pelletier. We're talking about a college senior with no psychological training who might not know how to deal with such a trauma."

I considered his words. "I don't think so. I can't see Murph doing something like that."

"We have to consider every angle."

"I get that, but no. Murph didn't do this. I'm certain. Even if he'd been thinking about it, he wouldn't fuck up my wedding."

"All right. I won't leave any stone unturned, son. I'll get to the bottom of this for you."

"Thanks, Dad."

My father was such an enigma. I both loved and hated him. Right now, I was thankful for him and his money. I had no doubt he'd figure out what had happened to Murph.

"Shit. There's a doctor talking to Murph's parents." I stood.

"Leave them be. Let them deal with this."

Perhaps I should have listened to my father, but I was missing my wedding night for their son. I walked over.

"How is he, Doctor?" I asked.

"And you are?"

"Bradford Steel. Sean's best friend. My father is the one who brought him to the ER."

"I see." He looked to Murph's parents.

"It's okay," his father said.

The doctor cleared his throat. "We got the rest of your son's blood work back. The amount of heroin wasn't enough for him to overdose. Just enough for him to get dizzy and pass out. The problem is the other thing the screening showed. He has botulinum toxin in his system."

"Botulism?" his mother said.

"The toxin that causes it, yes."

"And ... ?" his mother said.

"And ... I'm so sorry to have to say this. We've administered antitoxins, but they're not having any effect. He's not awake, and his organs are failing. I've told the nurses to let you spend his last hours with him in the ICU."

His father glared at me, and his mother seemed to look past all of us.

It hadn't registered yet.

Hell, it hadn't registered with me yet.

"How ...? Where would he ...?" I wasn't sure whether the words came from me or someone else.

Someone had thought out every detail. I clenched my hands into fists.

"He most likely ingested it," the doctor said.

"From the food at your wedding?" Mr. Murphy glared at me once more.

"No! Of course not. No one else is sick." That I knew of, anyway.

"Someone drugged and poisoned our son." From his father. A statement, not a question.

"It appears that way. I'm so sorry. Please, follow me. I'll take you to him."

I gulped. "I want to see him."

"No," his father said. "You've done enough."

"I assure you my son has done nothing." When had my father walked over? "He'd like to see his best friend. To say goodbye."

"No," Mr. Murphy said again flatly. "Our son's last moments are for us."

"Doctor ... " I began.

"I'm sorry. It's his parents' call."

"But he's an adult."

"And they are his next of kin. I'm sorry." The doctor led the Murphys out of the waiting room.

"Wait!" My father walked swiftly through the door.

I sat down in the closest chair, my whole body numb.

Murph.

Murph was dying.

Someone had drugged and poisoned him. Heroin. Botulism. My mind raced. The heroin to make sure this happened at the wedding because no one knew when the botulism would kick in. Then the botulism—enough to take down a healthy and robust twenty-two-year-old.

The only person I knew of who might be capable of such a heinous act was locked up and medicated.

Several minutes later, my father returned. "Go ahead back, son. You can see him."

"How . . . ?"

"Money talks," he said dryly. "They're a hundred grand richer."

"You spent a hundred grand so I could see Murph?"

"Money well spent. Go see him. Tell him goodbye."

I nodded and walked through the door. The doctor and the Murphys stood outside an ICU room.

"Thank you for letting me do this," I said.

"Your father made a strong argument," Mr. Murphy said. "Go in. You have two minutes. The rest of the time is for his mother and me."

I nodded. How could I argue? I walked into the room. Murph was hooked up to all kinds of beeping machines.

His eyes were closed, his skin pale. An oxygen mask covered his face.

"Hey, Murph," I said.

I'd begged for this, and now I had no idea what to say.

"I'm so sorry this happened. I'll find out who did this to you, and they'll pay. I swear to God, they'll pay." I moved to squeeze his hand but held back. An IV line stopped me. "Thank you for being my best man. You've been the greatest friend a guy could ask for. I'm going to miss you."

Crying is for girls.

Words of wisdom from my father. He'd said them for as long as I could remember.

I sniffed back a tear.

I wasn't going to succumb now. I'd be strong. Not just for Daphne and my unborn kid but now for Murph as well. I'd find out how this happened and take care of whoever was responsible.

I'd avenge my friend.

If it was the last thing I did.

CHAPTER THIRTY-TWO

Daphne

Something nudged me.

I jerked upward.

"It's just me, baby."

"Brad!" I melted into his arms. "How's Sean?"

Brad cupped my cheek. "I'm so sorry to have to tell you this. He...didn't make it."

What? Confusion muddled my brain. I hadn't heard him right. That was it. It had to be. "He just had too much to drink. That's all."

"Baby, he had a beer. One beer." Brad kissed the top of my head. "He was drugged. Heroin."

"But he doesn't—"

"Do drugs. No, he doesn't. He was also poisoned. The doctors might have been able to save him if it had only been the drugs, but the poison killed him. His body just shut down."

This wasn't happening. Nothing bad had happened at my wedding. This was a dream.

No, a nightmare. A really bad nightmare.

Except that it wasn't anything like my normal nightmares. I wasn't running from something that scared me only to wake up and not remember who or what was responsible for my torment.

No, this was real-life torment.

Real life . . .

"Who would . . . ? Why would . . . ?" I couldn't grasp the words I wanted.

"I don't know, baby. But I assure you that I'll find out. I'm going to put the best PIs in the business on this. I owe that to Murph."

"Brad, I don't understand."

"I don't either, Daphne."

"Our wedding . . . "

"It was beautiful. We have to remember the beautiful parts."

The beautiful parts? No sooner had we exchanged vows than I had passed out. But that was the least of the problems.

Brad kissed the top of my head again. Then he pulled back from me a bit and met my gaze. His eyes were sunken and sad. He pressed his lips to mine. They were wet. His cheeks were streaked. Had he been crying?

Somehow I'd never thought of Brad crying. He seemed so strong. So very strong.

Of course, he'd literally just lost his best friend.

He needed me to be strong now, and I wouldn't let him down. I'd vowed once never to be a colorless flower again. I'd become one, if only for a moment, on my own wedding day.

That self-indulgence was over.

I'd be strong for my baby. Strong for the man I loved. I pulled his face toward mine and kissed him. Hard.

He pulled away. "I need you so much right now."

"I'm here for you. Take whatever you need from me."

"My God." He slammed his lips back down on mine.

I opened for him, let him take my mouth with his tongue

and teeth. It was a hard kiss. A raw kiss. A kiss of need and ache.

A kiss of life.

He was proving to himself that he was alive because Sean wasn't.

I melted into the kiss, let him take what he wanted, needed, desired.

Was my door locked?

I didn't know. Didn't particularly care at the moment.

The only thing I wanted was to ease Brad's pain.

He moved quickly, nearly tearing my pajamas from my body and then unzipping his trousers. Within seconds he was inside me, thrusting, thrusting, thrusting...

Grunting, grunting, grunting...

Then releasing.

Releasing inside me.

It was that fast.

And I was happy to give him what he so desperately needed.

"God, baby," he rasped against my ear. "I needed that. I needed *you*."

I stroked his hair. "It's okay."

"I'll take care of you in a minute, okay?"

"Don't worry about me."

"I want to. I just needed... I just..."

"It's okay," I said again, still stroking his hair. "I'm here."

"I don't know what I'd do without you, Daphne. You make me whole, and I need to be whole right now."

"You were always whole, Brad."

"I thought I was, but I wasn't. I am now."

His words played in my mind, and I understood.

Fate.

Destiny.

We completed each other.

We were whole with each other.

I smiled against his cheek. "You're still wearing your tux. When does it have to be returned to the rental place?"

"It doesn't," he said. "It's mine. Though it's completely ruined now."

"I'm sorry."

"Are you kidding? This tux is the last thing I'm concerned about. Just let me lie here for a few minutes. I need to hold you in my arms."

"I need that too."

And I did. More than I needed more kisses or an orgasm. I needed to be in Brad's arms, comforting him and getting comfort from him.

In a few seconds, Brad had fallen asleep.

★ ★ ★

I woke up an hour later with Brad still asleep next to me, his trousers still unzipped and his boxers around his hips.

He looked troubled even in sleep.

I ached to take his pain away, but what could I do?

His dick lay flaccid. I tentatively reached toward it. What would it feel like against my fingers?

I touched it. It was smooth and soft, but just my touch made it harden a little. I continued to play with it, rubbing my thumb over the tip, and within a few minutes, it was large and hard in my hand.

We hadn't had a traditional wedding night. That ship had sailed, but perhaps I could give him a gift I'd never given anyone.

I leaned down and took his dick between my lips.

It was hot and smooth against my tongue.

A groan rumbled from his throat and through his body. Was he awake? I wasn't sure.

I trailed kisses over the head and down the shaft.

"Morning, baby."

So he was awake after all.

I swirled my tongue around him and then took him as far into my mouth as I could.

He groaned again.

Now that he was well lubricated, I added my hand for extra stimulation. This was new to me, but I was determined. I loved this man, and I wanted to please him.

Another groan.

Another, "God, baby."

Then—

"Fuck." He pushed me off his dick. "Can't. I won't last long."

"That's okay," I said, a little perplexed.

"You're not ready for me to—"

"I'm ready for whatever you want me to do, Brad. I'm your wife. I love you. Just tell me what you want."

"I want to come in your mouth."

I inhaled sharply. Yes, I could do that for him, for the man I adored. "O-Okay."

"It's all right. We'll work up to that. Right now I need to be inside you one way or the other. Come here." He pulled me onto him. "Get on top of me."

I straddled him as he held his dick. I slipped down onto him and let out a low moan.

He filled me so completely, eased the emptiness I never knew I had.

"You feel so good, baby. God, I need you. Need you to chase the pain away."

"I'm here for you," I said. "Always. I love you, Brad."

"I love you too, baby. So fucking much." He thrust his hips upward, ramming into me.

My own hips seemed to move on their own, meeting Brad's thrusts and creating a rhythm that touched every millimeter inside me. I closed my eyes, and his warm hands found my breasts, my nipples. When he tugged sharply on one, a blast of pleasure hit me.

I came.

I came hard.

I came fast.

I came with a fierceness I'd never known.

Words left my throat—unintelligible words that were a jumble of coiled emotions. I soared above the mountaintops for a few blissful seconds, reveling in Brad's thrusts. When he finally released, I fell onto his chest and pressed our mouths together.

We kissed as our climaxes ended.

Together.

Then a knock on the door.

CHAPTER THIRTY-THREE

Brad

Daphne froze on top of me.

"It's okay, baby," I said.

"But what if someone finds us together? In bed?"

Normally I'd have chuckled, but laughter seemed out of the question given all the circumstances. "We're married. Remember?"

She gasped. "Of course. Still, I'm naked, Brad, and your pants are around your knees."

"Doesn't matter."

I rolled off the bed and adjusted my trousers. Then I threw Daphne her pajamas. She hastily scrambled into them. I walked to the door and opened it.

My mother stood there. "I'm sorry to interrupt, darling, but Daphne's parents are getting ready to leave, and they want to say goodbye."

"Sure. Of course. You ready, Daphne?"

"Yeah."

"I'm so sorry about Sean," Mom said.

I simply nodded. I couldn't think about that right now. I had to put on a brave face for Jonathan and Lucy.

Daphne and I followed Mom to the kitchen. My father was at the head of the table drinking coffee. Jonathan and Lucy sat silently.

I cleared my throat.

Jonathan stood. "I'm sorry about your friend, Brad."

"Thank you." I wasn't sure what else to say.

"Could I speak to you alone for a moment? In private?"

I looked to my father. He nodded slightly at me.

"Of course. Follow me." I led him to my father's office.

We entered, and he and I sat opposite each other in two leather chairs.

"What is it?" I asked.

"I'm concerned. Your father told us that Sean was drugged and poisoned."

I nodded.

"I'm trusting you to take care of my daughter."

"Of course. I already promised I would."

"You didn't take the greatest care of your friend. Someone drugged and poisoned him at your wedding."

A sliver of anger coiled in my belly but quickly dissipated. I didn't have the strength to be angry at the moment. I was too fucking sad. "It could have happened in town," I said. "We just don't know—"

"Brad, listen to me. I'm a patient man. I've had to be, to deal with Daphne's issues and now Lucy's. I've had to be loving and patient when sometimes I didn't want to be. Sometimes I wanted to scream and punch something and run away from it all. It can be a lot to deal with."

"I understand." He had no idea.

"Do you? Because I didn't succumb to those urges to punch walls. To run away. I stayed put, I maintained composure, because my family needed me."

"I'll do the same."

"You're a young man, Brad. So young yet."

"I assure you my father and I—"

"Daphne isn't your father's responsibility, young man. She's yours."

"That's not what I meant." The anger threatened to coil once more. I liked Jonathan, but he was treating me like a child.

"Look. I like you. I do. But a man is dead, Brad. Can you tell me with certainty that my daughter is safe here?"

"With all due respect, Jonathan, she's my wife now. I've told you I'll take care of her, and I'll tell you again. She and the baby are my first priority."

"You're going to see to her needs, then? Not go off avenging your friend?"

I don't see why I can't do both. I didn't voice the words, though. "My father and I will investigate Sean's death, of course. Would you rather we not? I can't believe that of you."

"I expect you to investigate. We all want to know what happened to prevent it from happening again. But you're young. Don't forget. I was young once too, and I know how easy it is to go off half-cocked when you're angry."

"You and I are two different people, Jonathan."

"Maybe. I'm not so sure, though."

I'm not so sure, though.

What the hell did that mean? Was there a side to Jonathan I wasn't seeing? Something my father was looking into?

Maybe, but I couldn't deal with the possibility at the moment.

"This conversation is over, I think." I stood. "I *will* take care of Daphne and the baby. You have my word."

He rose as well and nodded. "You take care of your wife, and I'll take care of mine. Deal?"

"That was always the deal, Jonathan. Nothing has changed."

Except that it had. Murph was gone. Dead.

And I *would* avenge him.

Jonathan was wrong about me.

I could take care of Daphne *and* avenge Murphy.

I could do both.

I could do it all, and I damned well would.

I had a lot to think about.

One thing I knew for sure. I needed to build a legacy for my wife and child, and to do that, I needed all information at my disposal.

Which meant one thing.

Daphne and I weren't going back to college.

CHAPTER THIRTY-FOUR

Daphne

Eight months later...

He was perfect.

My perfect little dove.

He was a boy, as I'd always known, and though I'd gone through the worst pain imaginable to bring him into this world, I'd do it all again in a heartbeat.

I'd chosen his name a few weeks earlier.

Jonah, which meant dove, because he'd always be my little dove. His middle name was Bradford after his father.

Jonah Bradford Steel.

My son.

My beautiful son.

Brad had let me name him, said I'd do a better job than he ever could.

"It's a perfect name," he told me. "For our perfect child."

I held my newborn son and gazed down at his full head of dark hair. His eyes were dark blue, but there wasn't a doubt in my mind that they'd turn dark brown like his father's.

"Are you hungry, little dove?"

The nurses had shown me how to breastfeed him, and though we hadn't had a lot of luck at first, he was finally getting the hang of it. My nipples were sore as all get-out, but they'd toughen up, everyone promised.

Didn't matter. I didn't care. All that mattered was Jonah. If I had to deal with sore nipples for him to get the nutrition to begin his growth into a strong man like his father, that was what I'd do.

I'd been home from the hospital a day now. My mother was visiting, and she and Mazie hovered over me and little Joe like flies milling around honey. I was happy to have them here.

My one regret?

George hadn't lived to see the grandson he'd wanted so badly.

He'd succumbed to a heart attack a month before little Joe's birth.

Now Brad—my sweet husband—owned the Steel ranch.

All of it.

George's legacy was now Brad's legacy.

The doorbell rang. I stood, ready to place little Joe in his bassinet, but Mazie was already sailing toward the door. "Sit down, dear. I'll get that."

Happy to keep my child in my arms a little longer, I sat.

A few minutes later, Mazie bustled back to the family room. "Visitors!"

I smiled. Patty and Ennis descended the small stairway into the family room. They were still together and happy.

"Daph!" Patty exclaimed. "Let me see that baby!"

"He's right here," I said. "Shouldn't you guys be knee-deep in finals right now?"

"We both got done early," Patty said, "and we couldn't wait to come visit."

"All my finals but one were papers," Ennis added, "and Pat

here said if I didn't get them in early so we could come see you, she'd never forgive me."

Patty swatted him. "I didn't say that. You did."

Ennis laughed. "Either way, we both wanted to see you and your new addition. He's gorgeous, love."

"I'm sure I'm biased," I said, "but I think he's the most beautiful baby ever born."

Patty sighed and sat down next to me on the arm of my chair. "I've missed you so much. I was so bummed when you and Brad didn't come back to school after the wedding."

"I know. I was too." I kissed little Joe's forehead. "But Brad was needed here, and my place is with him."

"Do you think you'll go back to college someday?" she asked.

"I plan to. Eventually. Right now I could never leave Jonah."

"A beautiful name," she said.

"Thanks. I like it. It means dove. I called him little dove while I was carrying him."

"It's a shame Brad couldn't finish his last year," Ennis said.

"He did finish," I told them. "He made arrangements to complete his senior year by mail."

"You can do that?" Ennis asked.

"Apparently," I said, "when you're a Steel."

"Why didn't you finish that way?"

"I could have, but I declined. After the wedding, I had some . . . health issues."

"Oh?" Patty said. "And you didn't tell me?"

"I didn't want to worry you guys," I said. "I'm fine. The pregnancy was difficult, though. When the nausea finally ended, I had other issues and ended up on bed rest. I didn't think I could do my best at school being so tired all the time."

It was the truth but only a half truth. The real truth was that I'd lost some time during the pregnancy. I'd had every intention of keeping up with my studies, once Brad and George arranged for the mail option, but my mind went kind of berserk a few times. The episodes didn't last long, and the doctor wasn't overly concerned. He said hormones did funny things to your brain. He called it pregnancy brain.

I knew it was something more, though.

This particular doctor didn't know about my past, and I kept it that way.

"I'd do it again in a heartbeat," I said truthfully, "but I can't deny I'm glad it's over. During the morning sickness phase, I wasn't sure I'd ever get my appetite back, but it's here with a vengeance now that I'm nursing."

"Oh, I bet," Patty said. "You should see how much we have to feed the pigs after they've had a litter."

I burst into laughter.

God, it felt good to laugh. Yeah, Patty had just compared me to a sow nursing a litter, but damned if it wasn't a riot.

A door opened and closed upstairs, and then cowboy boots clomped on the tile of the kitchen floor.

"Must be Brad," I said. "We're down here, honey!"

Brad descended the staircase, clad in a suit and tie.

Funny. Since George had passed, Brad wore a tie almost every day. He spent a lot of time in Grand Junction and also drove to Denver at least once a week on business. I was lucky he'd been in town when I went into labor with little Joe.

"Look who came to visit." I gestured to Patty and Ennis.

"Nice job, Steel," Ennis said. "He's a beautiful boy."

Brad smiled and shook Ennis's hand. They were friends

now, despite the punch to the jaw Brad had given Ennis the first week of college last fall.

Patty gave Brad a hug. "I couldn't be happier for both of you."

"Thanks. I'm sorry I can't be a better host, but I've got a phone call"—he checked his watch—"in five minutes, and I need to go over some papers."

"It's okay," Patty said. "We're staying for a few days. We got a room in town."

"You should stay here," I said. "We have tons of room."

"No, we don't want to impose," Ennis said.

"All right," I said. "If you change your mind, the door's always open. Can you stay for dinner tonight?"

"Actually, we have a romantic dinner planned in town." Patty's eyes sparkled.

I smiled. "Got it. Tomorrow night, then? Belinda's a wonderful cook."

"Tomorrow it is. We'll get out of your hair now." Ennis shook his head. "I can't get over Steel in a tie."

"Are you kidding?" Patty waggled her eyebrows. "He looks amazing."

"That's not what I meant, and you know it. Other than the tux at the wedding—"

Ennis stopped abruptly.

"It's okay," I said soberly, kissing Joe's forehead. "We all know what happened at the wedding."

"I still can't get over it," Patty said wistfully.

"I know. Brad is still trying to piece out what happened. He's had PIs on it for months."

"We were all sitting at the bridal party table with Sean," Patty said. "Ennis and I talk about it all the time. Either of us could have easily picked up whatever ended up drugging and poisoning him."

"*If* it happened at the reception," Ennis added. "It could have happened before."

"The heroin definitely happened at the reception," I said. "Brad checked everything out. But he had to have ingested the toxin that killed him at least twenty-four hours prior, so it's still a mystery."

"Is it possible he got it from tainted food?"

"It's possible, but Sean was young and healthy. He would have been sick as a dog, but he had a good chance of surviving if it was food poisoning. Brad thinks he was poisoned by some*one*, rather than some*thing*, because of the amount of toxin."

"It's still so hard to think about," Patty said.

"I know. Brad still misses him. I do too, even though I didn't know him that well."

Patty nodded. She *had* known him, in the biblical sense. But only twice. "Lorraine is still pretty shaken up," she said.

"After all this time?"

Patty nodded. "Just because Sean was never serious about any woman doesn't mean the woman wasn't. Lorraine has cried on my shoulder many times. Why she chose me, I'll never know."

"Because you knew Sean," Ennis offered.

"Maybe." Patty sighed. "It's so sad. I can't believe Brad hasn't figured out what happened yet."

"Neither can he," I agreed. "He's become consumed with finding the truth."

I used the word consumed on purpose. I didn't want to use the true word.

Obsessed.

Brad was obsessed with finding out what had happened to Sean.

Obsessed to the point that I worried about him.

CHAPTER THIRTY-FIVE

Brad

"Larry," I said into the phone, "you were ready to give me the details on my wedding day to your sister."

"That was a mistake."

"What happened? Who got to you?"

Silence.

Damn. Larry Wade would be a good lawyer. He knew when to shut up. He'd just finished college and would begin law school in the fall.

"I can only say this. Tom, Theo, and I had nothing to do with what happened to your best man."

"I know that. I've cleared all of you, and Wendy was locked up. This phone call isn't about Murphy. It's about what you were going to tell me eight months ago."

"We go through this once a week," he said. "I was mistaken at the time."

"You were freaked out. Majorly. My money was once used to fund your business, so I have a vested interest. What the hell is going on that you felt you had to tell me at the time?"

More silence.

Then, "I got a call from Tom an hour ago. Evie went into labor."

"Oh. That's nice." Not that I gave much of a damn. "Please, Lar."

"All right. I'll level with you."

God. It was about time.

"Great. Go ahead."

"Tom and Theo had been talking to some gangster dude."

"Who?" Not that I'd recognize a gangster name. My father probably would, though. Never had I wished more for my father than I had since he'd passed. None of us had expected it to happen so soon and so quickly. The man was a bastard, but he knew all the bad guys.

There had to be records around here somewhere. He'd died a month ago, and with Daphne's rough pregnancy and regular ranch business, I hadn't had the time to search for anything else.

"*Who* doesn't matter. I talked them out of it, and they got out."

Wait, wait, wait. Larry talked Tom and Theo out of something? Larry was a yes-man. The weak link. Something didn't jibe here.

"Oh? If the who doesn't matter, can you tell me the *what*?"

"I can't. Only that it was some dark stuff."

"Drugs? I mean, other than the pot."

"Drugs and other stuff."

"What other stuff?"

He gulped audibly. I seriously heard it through the phone.

"That's all I can say. Be glad they didn't go through with it. I think I finally appealed to Tom's fatherly instinct. Evie's pregnancy is what finally made him change his mind, and Theo came along with him. They gave up a shit ton of cash, though."

"They already have a shit ton of cash."

"That's what I told them, but it didn't matter. They both see only green. What mattered was Tom's impending fatherhood. He already loves that baby, man."

"Hey, if anyone understands that, I do."

"Right. Yeah. When can I see my new nephew?"

"Next time you're in town. Just let me know before you drop by."

"You got it. I'm seeing someone myself now. I think she may be the one."

"That's nice. I never saw you as the wife and kids type."

"I didn't either, but Greta makes me rethink that. I think I might be a decent dad."

I wasn't sure about that, so I said simply, "I hope it works out."

"Yeah, me too."

"Are you sure that's everything you wanted to tell me the day I got married?"

"It's everything I can say, Brad."

"All right." I'd let it go. For now.

The second line on my phone lit up. "Hey, I've got another call. I'll talk to you later, bro."

"Sure. Ciao."

I pushed the flashing button. "Steel."

"Steel!" Tom Simpson's voice. "I'm a daddy. It's a boy!"

"Yeah? Congratulations, man. Our sons will be roughly the exact same age."

"They will. Cool, huh?"

"What's his name?"

"Bryce. Bryce Thomas Simpson."

"Nice. How's Evie?"

"She's out like a light. She had some issues, and they had to do a C-section. But she and the baby are fine. Unfortunately, it doesn't look like she'll be able to have any more kids."

HELEN HARDT

"Oh, man. I'm sorry."

"It's rough. Yeah. I'm not excited about telling her."

"What happened?"

"Apparently she has something called severe endometriosis. The doc couldn't believe she got pregnant this time after he saw it."

"I'm sorry."

"We'll get through it. Any news on your end?"

"Daphne and the baby are fine."

"Good to hear, but I meant about your best man."

"Nothing. *Nada.* Whoever did this covered their tracks. Not just covered. Eliminated them. I've looked high and low, and Murph didn't seem to have an enemy in the world. I'm flummoxed."

"Sorry, man."

"It's unreal. If my old man couldn't uncover it, I'm not sure anyone can."

"And you're sure about . . . ?"

"Yeah. I have eyewitnesses that say she was locked up and drugged the day of the wedding and the days prior. Even if she was lucid, she didn't have access to a phone or anything."

"Crazy. I've got to go. I should get back to Evie. I want to be there when she wakes up."

"Yeah. Tell her hi from me and congratulations."

"Will do. See you."

I hung up the receiver, grabbed a key from the top desk drawer, stood, and walked to the mahogany cabinet on the adjacent wall.

My father's—now my—gun safe.

I turned the key and opened the door.

George Steel had racked up quite a collection, but I was

183

interested only in the Smith & Wesson forty-five.

This was the firearm my father had used to threaten Dr. Pelletier.

I hated that it had come to this, but I would now use it for the same purpose.

Because Larry *hadn't* told me the truth.

When he said he'd talked Tom and Theo out of the deal with the gangster, he was lying.

No way did Larry have the intelligence or the balls to talk Tom and Theo out of anything.

CHAPTER THIRTY-SIX

Daphne

"I'm sorry, baby," Brad said.

"But I invited Patty and Ennis for dinner. I want you here."

I kissed her forehead. "I know. But I can't miss this meeting. Now that my father is gone—"

"I know, I know. The ranch is your responsibility. I've heard it a zillion times, Brad."

"Then you understand."

"I do. But for God's sake, I just had your baby. Little Joe and I need you too."

"I'm doing all of this for you and little Joe. I thought you understood that."

I sighed. "I do. It's just . . . I miss you."

"I miss you too," he said.

"Your kid isn't even going to know you."

He chuckled. "My kid is five days old."

"So? He needs to be held. Cuddled. Fed."

"I'm afraid the feeding is all you, sweetheart. I don't have the equipment."

"It's a lot of work."

"Get a nanny, then."

He caught me. The baby *was* a lot of work, but I had ample help with Mazie living here. Plus my mom would be here for a few more weeks, and Belinda lent a hand sometimes too.

"Brad, I don't want a nanny. I want *you* to be here. To be a part of our lives."

"I will always be a part of your life and Joe's. You know that. The two of you are everything to me."

I nodded. I believed him. Sort of. Now that George was gone, the ranch seemed to be everything to him.

"I'm building a legacy for us," he continued. "For little Joe. One day he'll have everything."

"He *has* everything. He *needs* his father."

"He will always have me, and so will you." He kissed my lips. "I miss you."

"I miss you too."

Then he was out the door.

Again.

I did miss him. I missed his arms around me, his lips on mine. The rest could wait. It had to wait six weeks anyway, until I healed from the birth. I was in so much pain down there, I wasn't sure I'd ever be able to make another baby. But my mother and Mazie had assured me it would heal.

Of course, both of them had only given birth to one baby.

Mazie was looking forward to a houseful of kids. She'd done so much for me, I couldn't let her down. And I adored baby Joe. He was worth all the pain and then some.

My son would never know his grandfather, and I both mourned and was happy about that. George Steel had been kind to me, but I couldn't forget what he'd done to Mazie. She and I didn't talk about that, though. All I knew had come from Brad.

"Hi, sweetie." My mother entered the family room. "When do your guests arrive?"

I looked at my watch. "A half hour. Brad had to leave."

"Oh?"

"Another dinner meeting. I swear, he's out more than he's at home since George died."

"He has a lot of responsibilities."

"He has responsibilities here too."

"He knows that. Would you like me to ask your father to speak with him?"

I shook my head. "That would only make things worse. He'll know I got Dad to talk to him."

She smiled. She'd smiled more since the baby had been born than she had since her overdose eight months prior. This baby was good for my mother.

This baby was good for all of us. Even for Brad, though he didn't seem to realize it yet.

He loved me and little Joe. I had no doubt of that.

He also loved this ranch, though.

I sighed.

Mazie entered then. "Did I hear Brad leave?"

"Yeah. Another meeting."

"Oh, dear." She smiled at me. "That's how this business is sometimes. You get used to it."

"I don't want to get used to it. I want him in our lives."

"I know my son. He'll be in your lives. He loves you so much, Daphne."

"I don't doubt that."

"Bear with him. Running this place is a lot of work, and none of us expected George to die so suddenly."

"But he has people to run this place."

"True. But some things a man wants to do himself. That's what George always said."

"Was George able to teach Brad everything? Before he passed on?"

"Honey, George has been grooming Brad to run this place since he was born. Brad is more than ready."

"But he's so young."

"Young, yes, but smart and determined. You and little Joe have given him even more reason to work his tail off."

"I don't want to be the reason why he's never here."

"You're not. You're the reason he's determined. You'll get used to it, and he'll see that you and little Joe have everything you need."

I nodded. Again, I had no doubt.

The problem was, what Joe and I needed was *him*.

CHAPTER THIRTY-SEVEN

Brad

I knocked on Larry's door in Grand Junction. He'd just finished his last year of college and was moving to Arizona for law school.

No answer.

This time I pounded. My father's—*my*—forty-five was burning a hole through the holster. Or so it seemed. The piece seemed to radiate heat.

Yeah, it was my imagination, but still . . .

Finally the door cracked open.

"Open up, Larry," I said.

"Steel." The door revealed Theo, not Larry.

Great.

"Where's Larry?"

"He's gone."

"Where?"

"Hell if I know. I got here a few hours ago, and he was gone. Probably out with that new chick of his. Gretel."

"You mean Greta."

"Whatever."

"What are you doing here?" I asked.

"Probably same thing as you. Looking for Larry."

"What for?"

"I could ask you the same thing, Steel."

"He has information I need."

"Same here."

"What does he have that you need?"

Theo grinned. "I'll tell if you will."

Right. Not going there. Instead—

I pulled out my pistol. I didn't aim it at Theo, just held it, looking at it.

"What the fuck, man?" Theo inched backward.

"My father's. Well, mine now, I guess. He was always armed. Now that I'm the owner of the ranch, I figured it wasn't a bad idea."

"What the hell kind of shit do you do on that ranch, Steel?"

I blew lightly on the nose of the gun. "I get what I'm after."

"What's this abou— Shit. You came to threaten Larry."

"Why would you say that?"

"Because you're thinking about threatening me. I can see it on your face." Theo's voice didn't waver, but a bead of sweat appeared on his forehead.

Good.

"Why would I want to threaten you, Theo?"

"The drugs. You don't like the drugs."

"I like less that you and Tom lied to me at the beginning. But it's just marijuana. That's what Tom told me. He's a daddy, by the way."

"I heard."

"Don't you think the two of you should get on the straight and narrow? I mean, he's got a kid involved now."

"We're *on* the straight and narrow."

"Not if you're dealing in drugs."

"It's a little weed, Steel. Nothing major."

One thing about Theo—nothing worried him. He'd always been that way. He wasn't an iceman like Tom. No, Theo was more complex. Somewhat sociopathic, even.

Why had I ever hung around these guys in high school?

I blew on the nose of the gun once more and packed it back in the holster. "Think about it. There's a kid involved now."

"We're looking into a new venture, anyway," Theo said, visibly relieved that I'd put the gun away.

"Yeah? Larry didn't talk you out of this one?"

"Talk us out of what? What the hell are you talking about?"

No surprise. I'd already known Larry had been lying to me. "Who are you dealing with?"

"Why do you want to know?"

"Maybe I want in."

Theo guffawed. "Good try. You already told us you wanted out."

"Yeah, that's before my old man died."

"You're saying you got out because of your old man?"

"I'm saying I'm sitting on a fucking shitload of cash, Theo. It's all mine now. To do with as I please."

His eyes widened. Mention a shitload of cash, and Theo always got interested.

"I need something in return," I said.

"What's that?"

"Tell me the truth."

"About what?"

"About what happened to Sean Murphy."

"We've been through that, Steel. I'm clean. You know it. I had nothing against the guy."

"I believe you. I also believe you know what happened."

"I don't. Honest."

I nodded. "Okay, we can play it that way. No cash will be coming your way for your new venture, then."

"Fuck." Theo walked over to Larry's couch and sat down. "Who says we need your cash? Besides, if I knew something, I'd tell you."

"Would you?"

"Of course. How long have we been friends? Six, seven years?"

Friends was a stretch, but I didn't say it. "I've had the best PIs on this for months now, and nothing. Who do you know who's *that* good at hiding something?"

"Only one person."

"And she's locked up." I paced slowly around Larry's small place. "Right?"

"Right. You know that."

"Of course. I have witnesses who claim the same thing. Nurses and orderlies at Piney Oaks. Even her doctor."

"It wasn't her, Steel."

"All the evidence points that way. True."

"You're not convinced."

"When it comes to Wendy Madigan, I'll never be convinced of anything."

"She's out of it. Trust me."

Trust Theo Mathias? Good one. "How do you know?"

"I've visited her. Haven't you?"

"Hell, no."

"Really? You just turned your back on her? After everything?"

"I did. Once I met Daphne, I knew where my future was, and it wasn't with Wendy."

"Well, I've seen her. She's doped up. Doesn't even know where she is half the time."

I nodded. I had no reason to disbelieve Theo, but I'd have to see for myself.

I had to visit Wendy.

The thought repulsed me.

I hadn't come here to interrogate Theo about Murph or Wendy. I'd come to interrogate Larry about the gangster Theo and Tom were allegedly working with. Somehow, though, when I pulled my gun out, I got the distinct impression Theo knew something.

I could be wrong.

But I didn't think so.

"When's the last time you visited Wendy?" I asked.

"Actually, it was yesterday," he said.

My eyebrows shot up. "Did you happen to visit her before my wedding?"

"Fuck it all, Steel. How the hell am I supposed to remember that?"

"You don't have to. I can check the visitors' log at the facility."

"You haven't done that already?"

"The PIs have. They didn't see anything suspicious. But they wouldn't consider you suspicious."

"Do *you*?"

"Do I what?"

"Consider me suspicious?"

"Mathias," I said, "you've been suspicious since the first time I laid eyes on you."

He laughed then. He thought I was joking. I feigned laughter as well. Yeah, best to let him think I was being funny.

That would work in my favor.

"I've got to go," I said. "If Larry comes back, tell him I was here."

"Will do."

I left the apartment. Lucky I had a phone in my truck. I'd call Daphne and tell her I'd be spending the night in the city. I had something important to do come morning.

CHAPTER THIRTY-EIGHT

Daphne

"Miss Daphne," Belinda said. "Phone for you. It's Mr. Brad."

"Please excuse me," I said to Patty, Ennis, Mom, and Mazie. I rose and walked to the family room to take the call.

"Hello, Brad."

"Hi, baby."

"Is everything all right?"

"Everything's fine, but I have to stay in the city tonight."

My heart dropped. "Why?"

"An early morning meeting, but I'll be home after that."

"All right. Patty and Ennis are staying another day. Can you please be home for dinner tomorrow?"

"I will be. I promise."

I smiled. "Okay. Thank you. I'll miss you tonight. I don't sleep very well when your arms aren't around me."

"I don't sleep well without you in my arms either," he said. "Only one night, baby. I promise."

"Okay. I love you."

"I love you too, Daphne. Kiss little Joe for me."

"I will. Bye."

"Bye."

I returned to the table. "He's staying in the city tonight," I said.

"Oh?" Mazie lifted her eyebrows.

"Yeah. Says he has an early meeting." I sighed. "But he promises he'll be home for dinner tomorrow night, so you guys need to come back."

Patty nodded. "Sure. Is that okay with you, Ennis?"

"Yeah, of course, love. This beef is fantastic. Even better than at your wedding."

"It's filet," I said, "and Belinda broils it to perfection."

"It's truly amazing," my mother agreed. "I wish we could get this kind of beef in Denver."

"I'll send a cooler full home with you," I said. "And we'll send you as much as you want after that."

"My daughter, the beef queen!" My mother laughed.

"Mistress of Steel Acres!" Patty raised her wineglass. "Did you ever think, Daph, when we met last fall that you'd be here, with a gorgeous little boy, less than a year later?"

"God, no," I said, "but I wouldn't change a thing."

Except having Brad around more. I'd definitely change that.

"You're so lucky," Patty gushed.

I smiled and opened my mouth to speak, when the doorbell rang.

"I'll get it!" Belinda called.

A few minutes passed as we all continued eating.

"Telegram for you, Miss Daphne." Belinda strode in and handed me a yellow envelope.

"A telegram?" Mazie shook her head. "Do people still send telegrams?"

"My parents got one when I was a kid," Mom said. "That's the last I remember."

I held the yellow envelope from Western Union. "It's already open."

"I thought they stopped sending these a few years ago," Belinda said.

"Who delivered it?" I asked.

"Just a kid. I didn't recognize him."

"Was he wearing anything that said Western Union on it?" Mazie asked.

"No. He looked about sixteen or so."

I pulled out a folded piece of paper. It was plain white and didn't say Western Union anywhere on it. A message was typed.

"It should be yellow," Mom said, "to match the envelope."

"You're right, Lucy," Mazie agreed. "I don't think that's a telegram at all. It's a message using an old Western Union envelope."

I unfolded the paper. It was typewritten.

Keep that baby close. Wouldn't want anything
to happen to him.

My neck went cold.

"Daphne, you're white as a sheet," Mom said. "What is it?" My hands trembled.

"Daphne?" my mother said again.

"What is it, dear?" Mazie this time.

Finally, Patty grabbed the paper from my hand. She glanced at it, and her mouth dropped open. "Who sent this?" she finally said.

I couldn't speak. I didn't know the answer anyway.

"What's it say?" Ennis asked.

Patty handed it to him. His mouth dropped as well.

"What?" Mazie asked. "What is it?"

Ennis handed the paper to her.

"Oh my God. Belinda!" Mazie called.

"Yes, Miss Mazie?"

"Who brought this?"

"I told you. A kid. A boy, teenaged."

"You need to do better than that. This is a threat. A threat against my grandson!"

Belinda went pale. "What?"

Mazie thrust the paper at her. "See? Call the police, Belinda."

"Yes, right away." Belinda left the kitchen. A few minutes later, she returned. "They're on their way."

I couldn't move. I simply froze.

Then I began reciting words to myself.

Remember, Daphne. Remember. Don't lose time. This is too important. Don't lose it. Don't lose it. Remember Jonah. Remember little dove. He needs you. Don't lose it. Don't lose it.

Somehow, I kept it together. Kept it together for my son.

Brad wasn't here for us. He was away on business. Needed to call him. But ... Had he told me where he'd be? How could I get in touch with him?

Yes! His car phone. I knew that number. Frantically I dialed.

And of course he didn't answer.

Why hadn't I asked him where he'd be staying?

Why?

Why?

Why?

My mind turned fuzzy. Muddled.

No, Daphne. No. Hold it together. For your baby.

I breathed in, out, in again. I placed my hand over my mouth and inhaled once more. Hyperventilation. I just needed carbon dioxide so I wouldn't pass out.

Couldn't pass out.

Had to maintain composure.

For my baby.

For me and for my baby.

"Are you okay, honey?" Mom asked.

I nodded, my hand still over my mouth. The light-headedness began to subside.

Thank God.

Patty brought me a glass of water. "Drink," she said.

I nodded again and took a sip. Then another. Mom and Mazie bustled around, checking on Jonah and me intermittently.

I was aware.

I might not be perfect at the moment, but I was staying aware.

Then a cry.

My baby's cry.

I stood, went to him, picked him up from his bassinet, and hugged him to my breast. "Are you hungry, sweetheart?

"I'm taking him to the bedroom to feed him," I told everyone. "Come get me when the police arrive."

CHAPTER THIRTY-NINE

Brad

A couple of fifty-dollar bills to the night watchmen got me into Piney Oaks. Another hundred to the night nurse got me Wendy's file and an escort to her room.

No wonder my old man had chosen this place. Everyone had their hand out. Money surely did talk.

"She has one of our only two single rooms," the nurse said.

"No roommate?"

"No. The doctor insisted she be kept isolated. She's asleep now."

"I won't wake her. I just need to make sure she's medicated as the doctor said."

"I assure you she is. I just administered her meds an hour ago. She gets them every six hours."

"Orally?"

"Yes."

I shook my head. "Are you sure she's taking them?"

"Absolutely, Mr. Steel. I watched her swallow them."

"I see."

Good thing I brought a flashlight. I fully expected to find a stash of spit-out pills somewhere in Wendy's room.

First thing I did was shine the light on Wendy's face. I half expected to see a stranger, but it was Wendy. Definitely Wendy.

I'd seen her asleep enough times to know what she looked like.

I only had a little bit of time with the file, so I fired up the flashlight and began reading.

Wendy Madigan

Sex: female

Age: twenty-one years

Two years of college completed, major in journalism

Intelligence quotient: 165

Yeah, she always was brilliant.

Next of kin: Warren and Marie Madigan, Snow Creek, Colorado

Medication: Valium, ten milligrams four times daily

Wow. That was a lot of Valium. But Valium didn't keep a person so out of it that she couldn't function. Maybe it relaxed her enough that she wasn't thinking about hurting me or anyone else.

But this was Wendy. I wasn't sure I was buying it.

Diagnosis: antisocial personality disorder

What the hell was that? Apparently I had some research to do. Wendy had never struck me as antisocial. Maybe my father had paid Dr. Pelletier for that diagnosis.

I'd have to pay him a visit. The problem? The last time I saw him, my father had pointed a gun at his head.

Oh, well. He had an office here in the city. I'd pay him a

visit tomorrow. I shuffled the files back together.

Time to search the room.

If I were a stash of sucked-on pills, where would I hide? I looked around the room, shining my light. I walked toward the door on the adjacent wall and opened it. Ah. A bathroom. Complete with a toilet—

Shit.

She didn't have to hide her pills. All she needed to do was flush them. Damn! Had my old man arranged for her to have a single room? Having a roommate watching her every move wouldn't have been a bad thing.

Of course...a stash of Valium had its own benefits. She could use it to her advantage. And Wendy would use everything available to her advantage. I checked the bathroom first because I could shut the door and turn on the light. The towels were the size of large washcloths.

This was a mental hospital. Large towels could be used to hang oneself.

No drawers and no cabinet. This was the barest of bathrooms. I pulled the lid off the toilet tank. I half expected to find one of those newfangled zippered plastic bags full of little white pills.

But nothing.

Not a damned thing.

I left the bathroom and turned the flashlight back on. Really, there was nowhere to hide anything. No drawers of any kind. No closet. These people had no freedom at all. Nowhere to stash anything that could potentially hurt them or another.

Which was a good thing.

I picked up Wendy's file, left the room, and returned it to the night nurse's station.

"Thanks," I said.

"It's nice to see you again. I know she appreciates your visits."

"I'm not so sure she— Wait a minute. What do you mean 'it's nice to see me again'?"

"You were here last night, remember?"

"Actually, I wasn't."

"You're Bradford Steel, right?"

"I am, and I was home last night. Most certainly not here."

"Then someone who looked an awful lot like you was here, Mr. Steel, and he also paid me a hundred dollars to see Miss Madigan."

"Did he actually use my name?"

"He did."

"What did he look like?"

"Brown hair and eyes. Like I said, he looked like you."

"Shit." Theo. It had to be. But why use my name?

"Think, please," I said to her. "It wasn't me. I need you to tell me exactly what the guy looked like."

"I didn't look that closely."

"You know it wasn't me."

She regarded me intently. "Now that you mention it, you're right. You're a different man."

"No shit." I didn't have a photo of Theo. If I had, I could have shown it to her and verified it was him. Or maybe not. She'd thought I was the same person at first.

"I'm done here. Thanks for your time." I scribbled my car phone number down on a piece of paper. "If the other guy shows up again, please call me. It'll be worth your while."

"Of course, Mr. Steel. Happy to."

Then I got the hell out of Dodge. This was crazy.

Completely crazy.

My old man might have chosen this place because of the wet palms. The problem? Wendy had her own money. So did Theo.

If a greased palm was all these people needed, it didn't matter who did the greasing.

Any grease would do.

And I had the distinct feeling I hadn't been the first to grease these palms.

CHAPTER FORTY

Daphne

My sweet little Jonah.

He nursed urgently at my breast. Yes, he'd finally gotten the hang of it, and though every tug hurt like hell, I welcomed the pain along with the knowledge that I was giving my child the nourishment nature provided him.

Nursing had quickly become my favorite part of being a mother. It allowed me a closeness with my son that I'd never imagined. I vowed to savor this time while I had it, for soon he'd outgrow his need for breast milk. Time would turn swiftly. Already, in my mind's eye, I saw him as the strong man he'd grow into.

Just like his father.

His father who wasn't here.

While his son's life was being threatened.

Brad, we need you, I pleaded silently. *Please come back to us.*

I looked up when someone rapped softly at the door. I sighed. The police must be here.

"Come in."

My mother entered. "They're here, honey."

I nodded. I pulled Jonah away from my breast, and he let out a howl. "He's still hungry."

"Did you pump anything today? I can feed him for a while so you can talk to the police."

"Yeah. There's a four-ounce bottle in the fridge. You'll have to warm it up."

She took the baby from me and put him against her shoulder, lightly tapping his back. "It's okay, sweetie. Mommy has more milk for you." She turned to me. "They're in the living room talking to Mazie and Belinda."

"All right." I hastily fixed my bra and shirt and walked out.

"I wish I could tell you more," Belinda was saying. "It was a teenager. I think his hair was brown."

"All right," an officer said.

"Here's Daphne now," Mazie said as I entered the living room. "Come sit down, dear."

I nodded and sat down. "I'm Daphne Wa— er . . . Steel."

Weird. I hadn't made that mistake in a long time. Brad and I had been married for nearly eight months.

"Good evening, Mrs. Steel." The officer stood and held out his hand. "I'm Officer Grant and this is Officer Ericson."

"Thank you for coming," I mumbled. I took a seat next to Belinda on the couch.

"I'm sorry about all this turmoil," Officer Grant continued.

I nodded again.

"Do you have any idea who could have sent this note?"

"Not really. I suppose it could be related to the best man's death at our wedding."

"That has never been solved, though."

"No. My husband has had PIs working on it for months."

"Why do you think the two incidents might be related?" Officer Ericson asked.

"I don't know." I sighed. "Just please keep my baby safe."

"We'll do our best," Officer Grant said. "But there must be a reason why you feel the two incidents are related."

"I don't really feel anything. I was just supposing."

"Is there anyone who might have anything against you?" Ericson asked.

"I don't know."

"You and your husband got married quickly."

"We did. But what does that have to do with anything?"

"Did you leave a disgruntled boyfriend behind? Or did your husband—"

"No," I said flatly.

"To which question?"

"Both."

Not exactly true, but Brad's ex was safely in a mental hospital and couldn't harm anyone.

"We can have the type analyzed, find out what kind of typewriter was used," Grant said, "but I don't know if that will help at all."

"What about fingerprints?" Mazie asked.

"We can take a look, but that will only help if we have prints on file to match anything we find on the paper."

"Plus, we've all handled it," I said.

Numb. I was feeling so damned numb.

"When do you expect Mr. Steel home?"

"Tomorrow."

"Where is he now? Can we get a hold of him?"

"I don't know where he's staying," I said, "but he has a phone in his car. I can give you that number, although he didn't answer earlier."

"That would be helpful."

I recited the number while Ericson made some notes on a pad of paper.

"Where's the phone?" Grant said. "I'll try calling him now."

"There's one in the kitchen and one in the family room," Mazie said, standing. "I'll show you."

I followed. If Brad answered his phone, I wanted to hear at least half of the conversation.

Officer Grand dialed. A few seconds passed.

Then, "Mr. Steel?" *Pause.* "This is Officer Will Grant of the Snow Creek Police. I'm here at your home with your wife and mother. Seems there's been an incident."

I half listened as the officer described what had happened.

My mother sat at the kitchen table, feeding Joe from a bottle. Just seeing him drinking made my breasts ache.

Then the tingle. Crap. They were letting down. I was wearing breast pads, but still . . . Wouldn't be long before I was soaked through. I turned to walk out of the kitchen—

"Mrs. Steel?" Officer Grant's voice.

I looked over my shoulder. "Yeah?"

"Your husband wants to talk to you."

I nodded and took the phone from him. "Hi, Brad."

"Baby, are you okay? I'm coming right home."

A heavy sigh blew out of me. Relief. Pure relief.

Brad was coming home.

"Thank God. Please. I need you here."

"I know, baby. I'm so sorry. I won't let anything happen to our baby. Please believe me."

"I believe you."

"I'm on my way."

"What about your meeting tomorrow?"

"I don't give a damn about the meeting. I need to be home."

"I need you here, Brad."

"I'll be home in a half hour. The cops will stay. I already asked."

"All right. Drive safely, okay?"

"I will. I love you, Daphne."

"I love you too."

CHAPTER FORTY-ONE

Brad

Damn.

Damn, damn, damn.

What the hell kind of coward threatened a five-day-old child?

Damn!

Come at me, you fucking son of a bitch. Don't you dare threaten my baby.

Wendy had been asleep in bed. She had no access to a phone or anything else. A typewriter? Maybe, but hospital staff read all incoming and outgoing mail.

And Theo? Theo had visited Wendy and used my name. Why? I wasn't yet sure. But would Theo threaten a child?

My child?

I had to believe he wouldn't. He was off, but not *that* off.

Still, why the hell had he used *my* name to visit Wendy? There had to be a reason. Theo never did anything without a reason.

Unless it hadn't been Theo.

Tom was in Boulder with Evie and the new baby.

Larry... Where the hell was Larry?

He hadn't been home when I went to his place earlier.

Didn't matter. Theo was the only one who could be

mistaken for me. We were roughly the same size, had the same coloring.

Damn, again!

I squealed into the driveway to the ranch house, slammed the door of my truck, and raced inside.

Two officers sat in the living room with my mother and mother-in-law.

"Where's Daphne?" I demanded.

"She's in your bedroom. Jonah just went to sleep in his cradle."

I didn't stop to talk. I ran to the master suite, through the sitting area, and into the bedroom. Daphne lay in bed, one hand on Jonah's cradle, rocking it gently.

"Thank God." I rushed toward Daphne, sat on the bed, and pulled her into my arms.

I'd promised Daphne and her father that I'd protect her and the baby.

I hadn't done a very good job.

Daphne sniffled against my shoulder.

"Don't cry, baby. I'm here now."

"I'm not crying. Not really. Why is this happening? Why? Who would threaten an innocent baby?"

"I don't know, Daphne, but I'm going to find out, and I'm going to take care of it. I promise you that."

She sniffled again. "I can't lose him. He's everything to me. Everything I never imagined. I can't lose our baby."

"Our baby will be fine. Trust me. I promise."

If it killed me, I'd keep that promise. I'd protect Daphne and our child, no matter what I had to do.

Even if I had to become my father. I winced at the thought, but it was no less true. I'd do whatever was necessary.

I held her for a few more minutes, soaking in her love and warmth. Then I sighed and pulled back. "I have to go talk to the officers, baby."

She sniffled once more and nodded.

"You okay here?"

"Now that you're home I am."

"I'm here, and I'm not going anywhere. I'll come to bed when I can." I stood and left the room.

Mom had made the officers a pot of coffee. "I sent Belinda home," she told me. "She'd stayed past her normal hours to talk to the police, and she wanted to stay longer because she felt so bad about not remembering much about the kid who brought the note."

"She's better off at home," I said. "Though does it strike you as odd that she couldn't remember any characteristics of the kid?"

"Not really. Do you remember everyone who comes to the door with a package?"

"I suppose not."

I had no reason to suspect Belinda had anything to do with this. She'd been in my family's employ for over ten years.

The events beginning with Murph's death had me on edge. I looked at everyone with skepticism and doubt.

In my head, everyone was a suspect.

I'd quickly learned to trust no one.

I poured myself a cup of Mom's coffee and walked to the living room.

"Mr. Steel." One of the officers stood and held out his hand. "I'm Officer Will Grant. We spoke on the phone."

I nodded.

The other officer stood. "And I'm Fred Ericson."

I shook both of their hands.

"How is your wife?" Ericson asked.

"She's doing as well as can be expected. Please, sit back down. We have a lot to talk about." I turned to my mother-in-law. "If you don't mind, Lucy, I need to speak to the policemen alone."

She stood, looking visibly relieved. "I think I'll go to bed. This has all been a bit . . . much."

"I want some privacy," I said to the officers. "Please follow me."

I led them to my father's office. No, *my* office. For the last month, it had been *my* office. I was the Steel in charge now.

I knew it. I just didn't always *feel* it.

I took a seat behind my father's desk and directed the officers to sit down across from me.

"I have a lot to tell you," I said. "So let's start at the beginning."

CHAPTER FORTY-TWO

Daphne

"Daphne"—Mazie peeked into the bedroom—"phone call. It's Patty. She wants to make sure you're okay."

I nodded. "I'll take it in here."

I hadn't heard the phone ring. I'd turned off the ringer once Joe drifted off to sleep. Now, I rolled over to Brad's side of the bed, where the phone was, and picked up the receiver.

"Hi, Pat."

"Daph, Ennis and I have been so worried."

"Brad came home."

"Thank God! What does he think?"

"I don't know. He's talking to the police now."

"Keep us posted, okay?"

"I will."

"And if you want to cancel the dinner tomorrow night, we understand. You have a lot going on."

"Are you kidding? Having dinner with my only two friends in the world is the one normal thing in my life. Don't you dare not come."

"All right. We won't miss it. Love you."

"Love you too. Bye."

I hung up the phone and leaned back over to check on the baby. He was so beautiful. He didn't have that wrinkled newborn look. No. My little dove was perfection personified.

"I'll protect you," I said out loud as I lightly laid my hand on his sleeping body. The movement of his little chest as he breathed comforted me. "I'll always pro—"

Crash!

A scream lodged in my throat. Something had come through the window, and shattered glass lay everywhere. I scanned the room wildly. A rock lay on the floor.

A piece of glass nearly the size of my hand had landed on Jonah's back.

So close to his little neck.

My heart raced wildly, and my skin prickled with fear.

This time I screamed.

The crash hadn't woken the baby, but my scream did.

I froze. I had to hold my baby. But glass. Glass everywhere. Shards. Big shards and tiny shards.

"Daphne!" Mazie came running in. "What was that?"

I opened my mouth to respond, but nothing came out. Nothing except another blood-curdling scream.

Mazie snatched Jonah out of his cradle, the large piece of glass falling onto his small mattress.

"What in the world? Brad! Brad! Come quick!"

"Where is he?" I finally squeaked out.

"In the office with the door shut." She handed Jonah to me. "I'll go get him."

"A rock." I pointed. "Someone threw a rock through the window." I gulped. "It could have … It could have landed on the baby. The piece of glass. It almost … My baby. My baby." I cuddled little Joe to my breast as he continued to wail. "Please don't hurt my baby."

"Honey, he's okay. We'll find out who did this. The police

are still here. I'll get them."

"My baby, my baby..." I repeated the words again and again.

"Brad!" Mazie shrieked. Then she ran out of the room.

Time passed in a haze. I held my baby and tried to calm him to no avail. Finally, I unbuttoned my shirt and tried to nurse him.

He resisted at first but finally latched on and calmed down.

My baby. Had to protect my baby.

Brad stormed in then. "Daphne! Are you okay?"

Two officers followed him. My breast was exposed, but I didn't much care at the moment.

"Mrs. Steel, what happened?" Officer Grant asked.

Again, I opened my mouth, but nothing came out. The words were in my head, but I couldn't seem to get them out of my throat.

"Daphne, please," Brad said. "Tell us."

"A rock. A rock came through the window. A piece of glass hit... the baby. Brad, our baby!"

"God! Is he all right?"

"I got him calmed down. It landed on his back." I gasped. "It didn't cut him."

"Thank God. You and little Joe get out of here."

Officer Grant picked up the rock. "How long ago?"

"I don't know." I gulped. "Not long."

"Get in the squad car," he said to Ericson. "See if you can find whoever did this. I'll stay here and take the statement."

"Got it." Ericson left quickly.

"Did you hear anything before it happened?" Grant asked me.

I shook my head. "I'd been talking to Patty on the phone."

"Patty...?"

"Patty Watson. My friend. She and her boyfriend were here earlier when the note came."

"This is bullshit," Brad said. "You need to find out who did this. What if that rock had hit Daphne or the baby?"

"These things are usually meant as a scare tactic," the officer said.

"I don't give a rat's ass. A shard of glass landed on my five-day-old child."

"I understand, Mr. Steel. We'll do everything we can." He turned to me again. "Can you tell us anything else that might help? Did you see a shadow? Did you happen to look out the window? Anything, Mrs. Steel?"

"I want my baby."

"He's right here, Daphne," Brad said.

I looked down. Joe was still nursing. Right. "I mean, I want him safe. I ... I need to leave this house."

"This is your home," Brad said. "Damn it! I won't be chased out of my own home!"

"I'd advise getting a security system installed right away," Officer Grant said.

"Out here in the middle of rural Colorado? My father never believed in anything like that."

"We live in a different time now, Mr. Steel. You've had two threats to your child tonight."

"I want to leave," I said again.

Brad nodded. "First thing in the morning. I'll have something top of the line installed."

"Good. That will help. Mrs. Steel, is there anything else you can tell me that might help us?"

I shook my head.

"All right. If you think of anything, call me right away. I left several of my cards on the table in the kitchen. We'll be on this."

"Th-Thank you," I stammered.

My baby. My precious baby.

I'll protect you. I'll die protecting you.

CHAPTER FORTY-THREE

Brad

Fear sliced through me like a butcher's knife through a tender cut of beef.

But the rage outshone the fear.

I was angry.

Really angry.

Angrier than I had been when someone killed Murph at my wedding, and I was raging about that.

Whoever the fuck was messing with my wife and child had incurred more than my wrath.

They'd incurred my unadulterated hatred.

This was beyond even Wendy's capabilities. She was a mess, but she wouldn't threaten a baby.

Who would?

Who hated me *that* much?

I had no idea.

But someone was fucking with me.

Once more, I missed my old man. Not because he and I were ever close, but because he'd know how to handle this. George Steel knew how to get his hands dirty and then clean them to sparkling before anyone was the wiser.

I needed to be George Steel.

I'd vowed to protect Daphne. I'd promised Jonathan.

I could take care of her, take care of Jonah. I had the money to give them whatever their hearts desired.

But could I truly protect them from some outside force that seemed determined to haunt us?

I hadn't been able to protect Murphy, and he'd paid with his life.

I walked around the bedroom. Shards of glass lay over the carpet. Grant had taken the rock with him as evidence.

But he'd find nothing. Already I knew this in my gut. Whoever was behind this had covered their tracks.

Which made my job all the more difficult.

"Baby," I said to Daphne, "you and little Joe need to sleep somewhere else tonight."

"I'm not sleeping anywhere but next to you."

"Of course. I'll sleep with you. I need to move his cradle. Okay? Until we get this glass fixed, we can't sleep in here."

Where I slept tonight mattered little, because I wouldn't be sleeping anyway. I'd lie awake all night and watch over my wife and child.

They would never be harmed on my watch.

★ ★ ★

By noon the next day, I'd contracted someone to install bulletproof glass in all the windows in the main ranch house and the guesthouse, I'd ordered a state-of-the-art security system to be installed as soon as possible, and I'd hired a bodyguard for my wife and son. Cliff would arrive soon. He'd stay in one of our guest rooms and would be part of the household. He'd also be Daphne's driver.

She'd balk at the intrusion, but their safety was paramount.

Until I neutralized whoever or whatever was threatening them, they'd be watched and protected at all times.

Now, I perused the files in my father's cabinet. He'd whispered the combination to his personal safe to me before he died. In the safe, I found the key to his always-locked file cabinet.

Since his death and little Joe's birth and everything else that had occurred in the last month, I hadn't had the time to look through the files. Now? I had to find any secrets my father might be hiding. The Future Lawmakers were not behind this attack on my child. I didn't believe it for a minute. They were young and greedy, but they weren't killers. They no longer needed my money, and none of them would hurt a baby. Not even Wendy.

I'd given it a lot of thought. They were businessmen, first and foremost, and hurting an innocent child would not result in any profit.

But someone had made the threats.

I'd always known the Steels had a few skeletons in their closet. Now it was time to unearth them.

These were my father's personal files.

All the ranch files were in three other cabinets, none of them ever kept locked.

This cabinet had always been hands-off to everyone except George Steel.

What are you hiding, Dad?

I opened the top drawer. It was stuffed with hanging file folders housing thick manila files. This cabinet had four drawers. Did my father truly have this many personal files?

Apprehension gripped me as I let my hand hover over the sea of manila. Which one should I grab first? And would it lead me down a dark path from which I could never escape?

Didn't matter.

My wife and son were depending on me to keep them safe, and if knowing what hid in these files could help accomplish that, I had to look at them.

I had no choice.

I'd turn twenty-three in a month. Not even a quarter of a century old. But I felt like I'd already lived a lifetime of threats and fears.

I had to suppress the fear.

My old man hadn't been afraid of anything—especially not losing someone close to him.

Why? Because he'd never gotten close to anyone.

He loved my mother once, and in his own way, he loved me. He would have loved Jonah, too.

But not the way I loved Daphne and my child.

George Steel hadn't been capable of that kind of love. I'd learned that kind of devotion from my mother.

Take a file, Brad. You're procrastinating.

I sucked in a breath and grabbed a file folder.

None of the folders were marked, so I had to look inside to see what the file contained.

I opened the folder . . . and nearly lost my footing.

This file was all about *me*.

CHAPTER FORTY-FOUR

Daphne

Little Joe had gone to sleep after his noon feeding, and I sat in the family room watching game shows. I didn't want to think about anything serious, so Bob Barker and *The Price Is Right* were a nice distraction.

My mom had gone to the greenhouse with Mazie. Mom had really taken to the greenhouse. I wished she had one at home. I enjoyed the greenhouse as well, but I hadn't gotten out there since Joe had arrived.

Belinda puttered in the kitchen.

I jerked when the doorbell rang.

"I'll get it, Miss Daphne," Belinda called.

I wasn't expecting anyone, but I shivered anyway. I hadn't been expecting anyone last night either, when that message had arrived.

I peeked into Joe's bassinet. He was sleeping soundly. Then I walked upstairs to see who was at the door.

A large man—a *very* large man—stood in the entryway with Belinda. I froze in my tracks.

"This is Clifford Danes," Belinda said. "He's here to see Mr. Brad."

Clifford Danes nodded at me. "Are you Mrs. Steel?"

I swallowed. "I am."

"Nice to meet you. Seems I'm your new bodyguard."

I lifted my eyebrows. "My . . . what?"

"Your husband hired me."

"He did?"

"I'll get Mr. Brad," Belinda said. "Have a seat, Mr. Danes." She motioned to the formal living room.

I stood in the foyer for a few minutes. Was I supposed to talk to him? This bodyguard? A bodyguard I didn't want?

Or did I? I'd do anything to protect my child.

So instead of sitting down in the living room, I walked back through the hallway to the family room where Joe slept in his bassinet. That was where I belonged—watching over my baby.

I sat down and glued my eyes back to *The Price Is Right*.

I'd let Brad handle this bodyguard business.

I hadn't slept well last night after all the commotion. Whenever I nodded off, Joe woke up. I closed my eyes.

★ ★ ★

"Baby?"

I jerked my eyes open. Brad stood over me, nudging me.

"I'm sorry to wake you, but there's someone you need to meet."

Right. My bodyguard. I peeked into the bassinet. Joe still slept soundly. "I can't leave the baby."

"Okay. I'll bring him down here."

A minute later, Clifford Danes stood over me. He was a few inches taller than Brad and even more muscular. The man was a mountain.

"We met," I said.

"Cliff is armed with two weapons at all times," Brad said. "He's also a third-degree black belt in karate and a champion kickboxer. He'll be living in the guest room across from my office."

"Not right next to our room?" I said incredulously . . . and a little sarcastically.

"I thought you might want more privacy than that."

"Thanks." I resisted an eye roll.

Really, this was sweet of Brad to get protection for me and the baby.

"He'll be your driver, as well," Brad continued. "You and the baby aren't to go anywhere without Cliff."

I was too tired to argue. I simply nodded.

"Good. I'm glad you agree. Cliff, I'll show you your room, and you can get settled in."

I checked on Jonah. He was making those baby oinking sounds that were so cute. I laughed out loud. I'd have to tell Patty. She'd know if it really sounded like oinking. That meant he was waking up, and he'd probably be hungry. I pulled him out of the bassinet and kissed the top of his head. Then I inhaled.

Had anything ever smelled as sweet as baby Joe's head?

Never.

Even the most fragrant flower in Mazie's greenhouse couldn't compare.

I unbuttoned my shirt and settled him in for his feeding.

The phone rang again.

"Miss Daphne, it's for you," Belinda called. "It's Ennis Ainsley."

"Okay, tell him to hold on a minute." I situated Joe so he could still nurse and then got up to grab the extension in the family room. "Hi, Ennis."

"Hey, love. Patty's not back from shopping yet, so we may be late for dinner."

"Wow. Is it dinnertime already?" I looked at my watch.

"We're due at your place in a half hour, which means we need to leave now. She took off after lunch to shop."

"Snow Creek isn't that big."

"You know Patty. She's got the shopping bug. I expected her back at the hotel by now."

"I'll tell Belinda you might be a little late," I said. "Let me know when you're on your way."

"Will do. Thanks for understanding."

"Patty dragged me out shopping a couple days after I first met her. She's a born shopper. See you soon."

I hung up and sat back down, settling Jonah in for more of his feeding. "Belinda!" I called.

"Yes, miss?" She stood at the top of the small staircase.

"Ennis says he and Patty are going to be late for dinner. She hasn't returned from shopping yet."

"Okay. Not a problem. Keep me posted."

"I will. Where's Brad?"

"He's in his office with the new bodyguard. They've been in there awhile."

"Okay."

Jonah had nodded off to sleep. I set him in his bassinet and buttoned up my shirt. Then I walked to the office to let Brad know about Ennis and Patty. I knocked.

"Come in." Brad's voice.

I opened the door. The bodyguard stood next to Brad, perusing papers on his desk.

"Hey, baby," Brad said.

"Ennis and Patty are going to be late for dinner."

"Oh? I forgot they were coming."

"I guess you've been preoccupied," I said.

"Just bringing Cliff here up to speed. He comes highly recommended."

"I'm sure he does."

"You and your baby will be safe on my watch, Mrs. Steel."

"Please, call me Daphne."

"Whatever you prefer," he said. "I'll try not to intrude on your day-to-day activities any more than I have to."

"I understand."

"Thank you for being so understanding about this, Daphne," Brad said. "I just want you and little Joe safe."

"I understand," I echoed myself. "Will you be staying for dinner, Mr...?"

"Danes. Call me Cliff, Mrs. Steel. Er... Daphne."

I nodded.

"Cliff will eat in the kitchen with Belinda," Brad said.

I nodded again numbly.

I hated feeling numb. Numbness made me feel colorless, like those pale-green blooms in Mazie's greenhouse. One day I'd have to remember to ask her why they were her favorite.

"I'll let you know when Patty and Ennis get here." I left the office, closing the door behind me.

I returned to the family room to check on Joe. He was sleeping soundly. Mom and Mazie came bustling in from their trip to the greenhouse.

"Hey, honey." Mom kissed my cheek. "I'm going to take a quick shower before dinner. Mazie and I did some transplanting, and I'm filthy."

"Take your time," I said. "Ennis and Patty are going to be late."

Mazie was in the kitchen chatting with Belinda. Now, while I had it on my mind, I'd ask her about the pale-green tulips.

"Hi there, Daphne," Mazie said. "How's the baby?"

"He's good. He's sleeping."

"Good. I'll go take a look at him."

I smiled. Or tried to, anyway. Smiling was difficult after last night's events. "I want to ask you something first."

"Sure. What is it?"

"Why are those pale-green tulips your favorite?"

She lifted her brow. "That's an interesting question."

"Brad told me, and I just wondered, because to me they seem so . . . sad."

"I suppose they do seem a little sad next to the brighter colors. Brad told me the yellow are your favorites."

"Yeah. They remind me of the sun."

"So they do."

"The pale-green ones remind me of the moon, which reminds me of . . . " I stopped. I'd been about to say darkness. Did Mazie even know about my junior year?

"They're called green spirit. Maybe it's the name I like." She smiled wistfully. "But I like the color as well. I don't see sadness when I look at them. I see something that reminds me that the darkness has its own beauty."

I dropped my mouth into an O. Her words spoke to me, offered me something about the flower—and myself—that I'd never considered before.

"When you embrace darkness," she continued, "and learn not to fear it, you can begin to see it in a different way. After all, only the most beautiful stars shine in the dark." She laughed. "Am I making any sense at all?"

"Actually, yes," I said. "I never thought of it that way."

"Most people don't. Most people fear the darkness. But the darkness has a lot to teach us. I should know."

Was that an invitation to ask what she meant? Belinda stood at the counter, ripping lettuce for our salad.

"Don't fear it, Daphne," Mazie said. "It's part of you. It's part of everyone. Now, I need to clean up before your friends arrive." She left the kitchen.

Part of me.

My junior year was part of me, part of my history. Had Brad told Mazie about it?

I'd never forget what Mazie had said. I vowed then to learn from everything in my life, find the stars among the darkness, the roses among the thorns.

But I still liked the yellow tulips best.

CHAPTER FORTY-FIVE

Brad

After Cliff got settled in his room, I returned to my office.

I hadn't had a chance to look through my father's file about me.

On top was my birth certificate. Of course I'd seen it before, and of course my father would have a copy of my birth certificate. Not a huge deal. So why was this file so fat?

I pushed the birth certificate aside. Copies of my report cards from grade school through college, except for the last semester that I'd just completed. Dad had died before then.

After those, my medical records. I was healthy as a horse and up-to-date on all my vaccinations. Okay. What was the purpose of this file?

I moved the medical records out of the way and—

The Future Lawmakers Club.

One page. A simple list of all the members and the names of their parents. That was it.

Okay. Strange.

Next page: *See separate files for more information.*

My heart sped up a little...but only a little. I wasn't overly surprised that my father had kept files on the Future Lawmakers.

The rest of the file on me consisted of invoices and ledgers.

The fucker had kept a file on how much I'd cost him over the years. Seriously.

Had he really been upset that he couldn't have more children? Seemed the one he had was nothing but an expense to him.

I perused the ledgers. Man, every diaper was accounted for. Even my part in the food bill over the years.

Then—

"Oh my God," I said out loud.

My father had an account of every payment I'd made to the Future Lawmakers. Out of my own accounts. His name hadn't been on them since I turned eighteen. How would he have—

This was George Steel.

He didn't follow the rules.

He got what he wanted no matter what, and apparently what he wanted was to keep very close tabs on how his only son spent his money. Not just my investments in the club, but every other payment I'd made over the years since I turned eighteen.

Every fucking payment.

The dinner I'd shared with Daphne at Tante Louise in Denver? There it was.

Every time I'd picked up the tab for Murph or anyone else? There it was.

Something as mundane as a monthly insurance payment? All there in black and white.

What the hell else had my father kept tabs on?

I pushed my file aside and grabbed another one out of the drawer. If only he'd marked them, but no, I had to pull them out and open them to see what they were.

Dr. Devin Pelletier.

Oddly, the file wasn't thick. Dr. Pelletier was well-educated and considered a pioneer in psychiatry. He'd authored several textbooks and even a bestseller. He'd given therapy to a handful of celebrities at his former office in Aspen. No wonder my father had chosen him. According to this file, his integrity was unquestioned.

Except when you show him the green, apparently. Or when you point a gun at him.

I closed the file and grabbed another.

Harrison Faulkner? No idea who that was, but all of these merited a look.

Frederick Jolley? Never heard of him.

Gloria Mathias. That was Theo's mother. Why would my father have a file on her?

Jonathan Wade… Shit. Daphne's father. Also Larry's father. What did *he* have to hide?

Lucy Wade. Lisa Wade.

Daphne Wade.

He had a dossier on Daphne.

All of this, and I hadn't even found the individual Future Lawmakers yet.

This was going to be a long night. I spread the files out on my desk and—

A knock on the door.

"Yeah, come in."

Daphne opened the door and entered.

"Hey, baby."

"Ennis just called again. Patty's still not home. He's getting worried."

I looked at my watch. An hour had passed since we were supposed to have dinner. I hadn't noticed because I'd been involved with my father's files.

"Where did she go?"

"She was just shopping in town. He's going to go look for her."

"She probably found a shoe sale at Mariah's or something," I said.

"Brad... I'm worried too. I know Patty's a shopper, but she's not rude on purpose. This isn't like her."

"I'm sure she'll turn up."

"Brad..."

I looked up. Daphne's eyes were glazed over. She truly was concerned.

"After everything that's gone on since yesterday, I'm really worried. We already lost Sean."

My heart thudded. Murphy. Daphne actually thought...?

Reality slammed into me like a freight train. "I'll call the police."

I made the call quickly.

Then, to Daphne, "Call Ennis. Tell him to stay at the hotel. Not to go out looking for Patty."

"I can't."

"Fine. I'll do it."

"No, Brad. That's not what I mean. Ennis already left."

"Shit. All right." I stood. "I'm going into town."

"Brad, no. Please."

"Something stinks about this, Daphne. You stay here. Cliff will keep you and the baby safe."

She stumbled a little but caught herself by grabbing the edge of my desk. I raced to her, taking her into my arms.

"Come on," I said. "Be strong for me."

"You don't really think..."

"I don't know, baby. But like you said, this isn't like Patty."

She nuzzled into my shoulder. "Why? Why is this happening?"

"I don't know," I said again, "but I promise you I'll find out what's going on, and I will stop it. Trust me."

She nodded against me. "I trust you."

I kissed the top of her head. "Tell Belinda to go ahead and serve dinner for you, Mom, and Lucy. Don't wait up for me."

She nodded again.

I pulled away slightly and met her gaze. "Daphne, trust me."

She didn't smile. Simply said, "I trust you, Brad."

★ ★ ★

I found Ennis wandering around Snow Creek.

"I've checked everywhere," he said. "It's like she disappeared into thin air."

"Have you called her parents? Maybe she . . . "

"Took off?" He shook his head. "I already thought of that. But after the morning we had, I doubt it."

"Good sex?"

"Better than good. And we said I love you for the first time."

"You think she got cold feet?"

"No. Plus, Patty isn't one to mince words. If she wanted to leave me, she would have told me."

I nodded. I didn't know Patty well, but Ennis's impression sounded on the mark to me. "I don't like this."

"Neither do I, mate. I'm worried. Really worried."

"The cops are on it. I called them. Have you seen them wandering around?"

"Honestly, I haven't noticed. I've only been looking for red hair."

"I get it. They're going to want to talk to you."

"Hey, wait." He lowered his eyelids. "You don't think . . . "

"I don't know. But like you say, Patty wouldn't just leave."

"Steel, I'm beginning to regret the day I ever laid eyes on you."

A spark of anger lit inside me, but I tamped it down. What could I say? He'd watched a man—one of my most treasured friends—die at my wedding. He also knew about both of the threats against my newborn son. To him, if Brad Steel cared about you, you were toast.

I said nothing.

"Look," Ennis began. "I didn't mean—"

"Yeah. You did."

"Okay, I did. What the hell is going on?"

"I'd tell you if I knew."

"You've got to know someone who has it out for you."

I knew one, but she was a nonissue. And even Wendy had her limits. She loved me. She wouldn't intentionally cause me grief.

Would she?

Again, a nonissue. She was locked up and medicated.

Tom was in Boulder with his wife and newborn. He now knew what fatherhood felt like, which meant he wouldn't be threatening someone else's child.

Larry was Daphne's brother. Plus, he was the most innocuous of the three. This wasn't him.

And Theo? Yeah, Theo was always the wild card, but he also wasn't stupid. He knew I had the resources to protect those I loved.

"I'm working on it," I finally said.

"Steel, you've got to do better than that. The woman I love is—"

"I know. I'll do what I can." I shook my head. "This will kill Daphne."

"Not as much as it will kill me. We were talking about going to London to meet my folks. Then touring the continent."

"I know, man. I'm sorry. You're right. It will affect you worse. I'm walking over to the police station to file the report. You want to come along? They'll need to talk to you anyway."

He didn't respond, simply nodded.

We walked in silence the few blocks to the station.

CHAPTER FORTY-SIX

Daphne

Brad returned before midnight with Ennis in tow.

I was awake, as Joe had just woken up for a feeding.

"Ennis is staying with us now," Brad said.

"Patty?" I asked, wide-eyed.

"She's missing," Ennis said.

My heart dropped to my stomach. "No . . . "

"Not officially until twenty-four hours have passed," Brad said.

"Not officially?" I asked. "You think that makes a difference?"

"No, baby, I don't. Ennis and I have been talking to the cops for the last couple of hours. They've checked every shop in Snow Creek and even went around the residences in town and knocked on doors. Patty's gone."

"And no one saw her?"

"Not that we've found yet. I'm so sorry, baby."

"No, just no." I laid Joe in his bassinet, my heart pounding. "This can't be happening."

Ennis's eyes glazed over. "It is, love. I wish it weren't, but it is."

"But how . . . ?"

"We'll find her," Brad said. "I asked you to trust me."

"I do trust you, but so did Patty." I swallowed. "So did Sean."

Brad's facial muscles went rigid. Maybe I shouldn't have brought up Sean, but I couldn't help it. Brad hadn't protected him.

"You should get to bed," Brad said to Ennis.

"Why? I won't be able to sleep. Besides . . . I'm going to have to call her parents."

"That can wait until morning," Brad said.

"If your child were missing, would you want to wait until morning to find out?" Ennis turned to leave the room.

"Wait!" My eyebrows shot up. "Maybe they know where she is. Maybe she went home."

"She's not," Brad said. "I already called them earlier this evening and posed as a friend from school. They haven't heard from her. If she'd flown home, she'd have called them with the information."

No. I wouldn't give up hope. "Maybe not. Maybe she wanted to surprise them."

"There's one way to find out," Ennis said. "I'm calling them now."

"Use my office," Brad said. "You want me to come along?"

"No, I'll do it alone. I just wish I knew what the hell to say."

"Wait, Ennis," I said. "Don't call them."

"I have to, Daphne."

"But she's . . . She's not . . ."

"She's missing, love. They're her parents. They have a right to know."

"No, Brad. Please."

"He's right, baby. He has to make this phone call."

"No. No. No." My voice sounded oddly robotic, as if it

were coming from somewhere other than my body.

"I'm sorry." Brad's voice.

At least I thought it was Brad's voice.

Then I didn't think at all.

★ ★ ★

"Daphne! Daphne!"

Voices buzzed around me, but I could only make out one word.

Daphne.

Daphne.

Daphne.

My world became a bubble. Something needed me. Something was forcing me back to this life that was too difficult to bear.

White walls. Always white, because color might prove too distracting to some.

The deli owner's daughter. She was lucid but quiet. Everyone thought she was completely bonkers, but she wasn't. She was actually really logical, always keeping order. She'd talked to me once. She'd said, "You're really pretty. I'd like us to be friends." But I'd waved her away. I didn't want to be the girl who befriended the crazy person.

The crazy person.

Weren't we all crazy?

After all, we were all here.

The candy striper. She followed the orderlies around, insisting she was helping them. She painted stripes on her gray sweats during art class once. She'd been banned from art class after that.

The scary guy. He was only sixteen—we were all minors at this facility—but his arms were covered in tattoos. He looked dangerous, and I stayed far away from him. He stared at me constantly, though, his stark blue eyes seeming to melt the clothes off my back. But he never spoke to me.

The paperboy. Had he been a paperboy on the outside? No one knew, but he spent all his time folding newspapers and then delivering them to each door. The orderlies collected them at the end of the day and gave them back to him the next day, when he began again.

Who were these people?

How had I forgotten them?

I'd spent a year of my life with them, and somehow, they'd all vanished from my mind.

Now they seemed so real. I could see them like a motion picture playing inside my head. They were more real than the buzzing and squeaking around me.

I hated being here.

Hated being around these people.

Though I didn't hate them.

I just hated being colorless.

That was how we all were here. Colorless. All the same. Treated the same by the orderlies and nurses. Even by the doctors.

Same. All the same.

Black and white.

No color.

I didn't know their names. They were the paperboy, the deli owner's daughter, the rebel. No names, only labels.

How did they label me?

I never knew.

So clearly they appeared inside my head. So much clearer than the blurred images rushing around me.

It was easier to stay here.

These people were colorless. Not distracting.

They didn't bother me, and I didn't bother them.

Daphne.

Daphne.

Daphne.

The sound seemed to come from the TV. That big color TV in the rec room where we had social time. Except none of us talked to each other. Only the TV, and occasionally the candy striper asking someone if they needed a bedpan or the deli owner's daughter saying, "What else can I get for you today?"

Daphne.

Daphne.

Daphne.

"Leave me alone!" I yelled at the candy striper.

Daphne.

Daphne.

Daphne.

Then a cry.

A baby's cry.

Who would bring a baby here?

But it wasn't any baby.

The images came into focus.

"Daphne, baby. Please."

The voice. I knew the voice.

"Jonah needs you."

I snapped into reality.

My baby. He was crying. Jonah was hungry.

I grabbed him out of Brad's arms and snuggled him. Within a few minutes, without me opening my blouse, he settled back down to sleep.

Because of me.

I was my child's comfort.

Me.

Daphne.

I held my precious child, kissed his tiny forehead.

And I remembered.

I remembered the deli owner's daughter.

I remembered the candy striper.

I remembered the scary guy.

I remembered the paperboy.

I *remembered*.

They hadn't been my friends, but I'd spent a year of my life with them. Why was I remembering now, when an *actual* friend was missing?

Dr. Payne said that memories could resurface, and if they did, there'd be a reason.

Why now?

I kissed Joe's head once more and then inhaled his sweet baby scent.

It was time.

Time to face my past.

If I truly wanted to never be a colorless flower, I had to face it *all*.

CHAPTER FORTY-SEVEN

Brad

"I'm fine. I just freaked out over Patty for a bit." Daphne cuddled baby Joe in her arms.

I wasn't convinced, but at least she was back.

"Go ahead," I said to Ennis. "Use my office, like I said. I'll stay with Daphne."

He nodded and left the room.

"Baby," I said. "I'm so sorry about Patty."

"We'll find her."

"I truly hope so, but you need to face the possibility that we won't."

"I can't lose another friend, Brad. I already lost one. My best friend in high school moved away and I never saw her again."

"I know," I said. "You've told me."

Her eyebrows shot up then. "Brad!"

"What, baby?"

"You can find Sage for me!"

My mouth dropped open.

Sage. Daphne didn't know the truth.

And I couldn't tell her.

All I could say was, "I'll try, baby. I'll try."

She smiled. God, she was radiant. And her eyes—that look

in her eyes that said, *Thank you, Brad. I believe in you. I know you'll find her.*

I felt like a piece of shit.

"Thank you, Brad. You'll find Patty, and you'll find Sage. I know you wouldn't let anything happen to my friends."

"I'll do my best."

The lie lodged in my throat.

I couldn't find Sage.

But I'd do my damnedest to find Patty.

I just hoped she was alive when I found her.

★ ★ ★

Once Daphne and baby Joe had fallen asleep, I returned to my study. The files were still splayed out on my desk. Ennis had come in here to call Patty's parents. Had he looked at any of these documents? If he had, he didn't say anything to me.

He'd probably been too focused on telling his girlfriend's parents that she was missing.

He'd gone straight to his room after that.

I doubted he was sleeping. I considered knocking and asking him if he wanted a drink but then decided against it.

He needed to be alone with his worry.

As did I.

I was worried not simply about Patty but also about Daphne. Could I lie to her? Tell her I'd exhausted every resource at my disposal and still hadn't found Sage?

Would she believe it?

She didn't know the kind of power my money wielded. Indeed, I hadn't known myself until I saw my father in action with Dr. Pelletier. A normal person who pulled a gun would be arrested.

George Steel hadn't been a normal person. His money had protected him.

His money—which was now *my* money.

I could tell Daphne, after a few months, that Sage had disappeared. After all, eight months had passed since Murphy's death, and I was no closer to an explanation.

I eyed the open files on the desk. Was the answer in here somewhere?

And if so . . . where? Where to begin?

I sighed. The answer to Murph's death wasn't in these files. My father had only been gone a month. If the answer lay here, he'd have uncovered it.

Unless . . .

Unless he hadn't *wanted* to uncover it. Unless my father had known all along . . .

No.

He was an asshole, but he was loyal to me. He wouldn't have had a friend of mine killed, and he certainly wouldn't have helped someone else do it.

Would he?

This was a man who'd pounded on his wife because she couldn't give him more children.

This was a man who'd forced his young son to watch a beloved calf be slaughtered.

This was a man who'd held a psychiatrist at gunpoint.

This was a man who'd probably committed myriad more unspeakable acts that I couldn't even begin to fathom.

Acts I could probably find in these files.

Fear gripped the back of my neck.

These files held secrets. My father's secrets.

These files could help me . . .

They could also hinder me. The fear gripping me wasn't of what my father had done, but what the knowledge of what he'd done would ultimately do to me.

Power.

My father had power—power that was now mine to wield.

Power could do a lot of good in the world, if a person handled it well.

Most people didn't. Power often led to corruption.

Had that happened to my father?

Temptation hung over me—temptation to take all my father's private files out back and burn them in a huge bonfire. Hell, I could roast marshmallows over it and make s'mores. I'd never had a s'more before. My father never took me camping. No one had.

The thought was comforting, but that was all it was—a thought.

I couldn't do it. I needed this information. I needed to know what I was dealing with.

With no more hesitation, I chose a file at random.

Jonathan Wade.

Daphne's father.

What did George Steel have on him?

I opened the manila folder. First was his birth certificate. Then his marriage certificates to both Lisa, Larry's mother, and Lucy. His employment records. One arrest record—a DUI when Daphne was a toddler. He'd lost his driver's license for six months. Funny, he still drank. Though he did seem to hold his liquor well. Hell, after what his daughter and now his wife had been through, he probably didn't drink nearly enough.

Then his financial records... Basic stuff. Checking account, savings account, money market account. All totaled about thirty-five thousand dollars. Not a lot, but more than many people had. Daphne had gotten a scholarship to Stilton. Good thing, as her parents couldn't have afforded it.

Jonathan's health insurance had covered most of Daphne's hospitalization during her junior year of high school. Still, Jonathan and Lucy had paid twenty percent of the bill, which amounted to about a hundred thousand dollars. Where had they gotten that kind of money? The billing records for the hospital were all marked paid. Lucy had quit working that year as well.

Yeah, that was a big question mark.

Of course, did it have anything to do with Murphy's death? Patty's disappearance? Definitely not. Still...my curiosity won out, and I decided to investigate Jonathan further. After all, I was married to his daughter.

My father was nothing if not thorough. Underneath what I'd found were Jonathan's bank records for the last twenty years. Good. Easy enough to see where an extra hundred grand had come from.

But...nothing.

Just his paychecks and Lucy's, until she stopped working, were accounted for. Next I checked his credit card accounts. No charges at all to the facility. How had that hundred grand gotten paid?

Either Jonathan had paid cash, or someone else had paid the bill.

I ruled out cash. Why would he pay cash when he could so easily write a check? More likely, he would have made smaller payments over time. But he didn't do any of that.

Deduction—someone else had paid the bill.

But who?

A relative, perhaps? Did he or Lucy have any relatives with that kind of money?

My mouth dropped open.

He did.

His son. Larry Wade.

Larry was a millionaire due to his investments with the Future Lawmakers. Tom, Theo, and Wendy hadn't told anyone, including their parents, about the fruits of their labor. But Larry? He and I had never been close, and we didn't talk a lot.

Could Larry have paid for Daphne's treatment? If so, I owed him one.

Mental Note: Get in touch with Larry.

Of course, the last time I'd tried that, I'd run into Theo at Larry's place.

I'd gotten off track quickly. My goal was to figure out who had threatened my son. He was protected for now, housebound with the best security available. After that, my goal was finding who had killed Murphy and who had taken Patty. The latter was far more important—Murph was already dead, so I couldn't save him. I hoped I could figure everything out in time to save Patty, but I had the sinking feeling all the events were related.

Someone was fucking with me—fucking with me through those I loved—and I wouldn't stop until I found out who and put a bullet between his brows.

CHAPTER FORTY-EIGHT

Daphne

After breakfast, once baby Joe had a full belly, I left him in the care of Mazie and my mother and walked to the greenhouse.

I did my best thinking among the plants, and right now, I needed to think. Why had those "friends" from the hospital come back to me? I had no idea, but I wanted to know why. Did they have something to tell me? To teach me? Or was I chasing unicorns?

Mazie's tulips were always in bloom—both inside and outside, now that spring was here. For some reason, I preferred to enjoy them here, inside the greenhouse. I shook my head. That didn't make a lot of sense. Flowers were meant to be outside, swaying under the sun and absorbing its rays.

So why did I enjoy them more in this enclosed space than I did outside in Mazie's beautiful garden?

And that was when it hit me—why I'd remembered those patients at the hospital. We were like the flowers in the greenhouse—enclosed, not in the perfect place, but still existing. We were still people.

I'd never bothered to learn their names.

In fact, I hadn't even remembered their existence until now.

They were telling me something, though, I was sure. What

were they telling me about Patty? Maybe even about Sage? Had I been a good friend? Maybe I didn't try hard enough to keep in touch with Sage after she moved.

No. Not true. I'd written five times, and she never replied once.

As for Patty... well, I'd been enamored with Brad since the first night of school. Then, a month later, I was pregnant. Weeks after that, I was married and had left school. But I'd been a good friend to her those couple of months. Hadn't I?

Maybe I hadn't.

Maybe I'd been too consumed with myself and my own problems.

Maybe that had been my problem at the hospital too.

Patty hadn't been found. Brad had been up all night in his office, going over his father's files. Why he thought that might help Patty, I had no idea, but I didn't ask questions. I wanted my friend back.

And deep inside me—that place I never allowed myself to go—I was frightened. Frightened that something terrible had happened to her, just as it had to Sean.

Just as it had to... *me.*

Anxiety and depression. Those were the two reasons I'd ended up in the hospital for so long. Bullies had beaten me, sent me spiraling downward. Then Sage moved away.

Funny I didn't remember the bullies, but there was so much else I didn't remember, so I didn't think much about any of it.

Until now.

I remembered those people at the hospital.

Something horrible had sent them there. Perhaps anxiety and depression, yes, but something had caused the anxiety and depression.

Just like something had caused it for me.

The bullies.

The bullies I didn't remember.

Could a person spiral down into severe anxiety and depression just by being bullied once? For years at a time, sure, but *once*?

I had no memory loss before junior year. I'd been picked on a few times, just like any other kid, and I hadn't become anxious or depressed.

What had truly happened? If only I could remember . . .

My brows shot up. I didn't have to remember, because someone else did, and she was here on this ranch.

My mother.

I left the greenhouse.

Mom and I were going to talk.

★ ★ ★

I fed the baby and spent some time with him after lunch, and then I cornered my mother. I'd tread softly. She'd just been through a rough ordeal herself recently, and I didn't want to make anything worse.

But I had to know for sure what had sent me into such horrid anxiety and depression that I'd ended up hospitalized for most of my junior year.

Brad was still busy in his office. I didn't want Mazie to interrupt us, so I took Mom into the master suite I shared with Brad. I laid Jonah in his cradle and then turned to her.

"Mom, I need to talk to you."

"What about, honey?"

"First, how are you? I mean, how *are* you?"

"I'm fine."

"No more suicidal thoughts?"

"No, sweetie. I'm good now. I'm so sorry I put you and your father through that."

"Was it because of me?" I winced. I wasn't sure I wanted the answer, but I had to know.

"No. Of course not."

"Mom..."

She sighed. "I always wondered what I'd say if either you or your father asked me that straight out."

"The truth, Mom."

She sighed again. "No. My answer stands. It wasn't because of you. Rather, not *solely* because of you."

I swallowed, feeling icy. "What does that mean, exactly?"

"I've talked at length with my therapist, and we feel I was trying so hard to be strong for you, and once I found out you had Brad and you were going to build a life, it was like a load had been lifted from my shoulders."

"But why would that make you—"

She gestured me to stop. "It sounds senseless, I know. But I'd held back on letting the depression take me because of you, and once you were no longer my responsibility..." She shook her head. "Even now, the words sound ridiculous, but if you were in my head, you'd understand."

"I want to understand, Mom, and I think I can. I've been through the same thing."

"I know, honey."

"I'm starting to remember some things."

She went rigid and her cheeks lost their color.

"Mom?"

She didn't respond.

"Mom? What's wrong?"

She closed her eyes, seeming to brace herself. Then she opened her eyes and met my gaze. "What are you remembering, Daphne?"

"Some of the people from the hospital."

Her shoulders relaxed. "Oh. Good. Thank God."

I wrinkled my forehead. "Thank God?"

"Just . . . thank God you're finally starting to remember, is all. It must be a load off your mind."

"Not really. I have a lot more questions, actually."

She cleared her throat. "Oh?"

"Yeah. Dr. Payne told me memories would come when I was ready to face them or when I needed them. Why would I be remembering the other patients now?"

She cleared her throat again. "That's probably a question for Dr. Payne."

"He's not here."

"Are you seeing a therapist in Snow Creek?"

"No. There's been too much else going on with the marriage and pregnancy and then George's death. I haven't had time to think about therapy. And now, with Joe so little . . . He needs me."

"I'm here. I can watch Joe for you while you go into town to see a therapist."

"You won't be here forever, Mom. Dad needs you back home."

"When I leave, Mazie will be here. She loves that baby as much as I do."

"True. Is there even a therapist in Snow Creek?"

"One way to find out." She picked up the phone book that sat next to the phone on the end table in the family room.

She leafed through it. "Here we go. Maryann Masters, family therapist."

"I don't need a family therapist. I need a psychologist."

"Okay. Here's one. Devin Pelletier. He sees patients at Maryann Masters's office once a week in Snow Creek. Looks like he's based in Grand Junction, though he has an office in Denver too."

"Devin Pelletier? What are his qualifications?"

"He's a psychiatrist, which means he has an MD. Also he's licensed as a clinical psychologist."

"That sounds a lot like Dr. Payne."

"He's in tomorrow. Should we call and make you an appointment?"

"What will he charge me?"

"I have no idea. Probably a hundred bucks an hour. But Daphne, money is not a concern for you anymore."

Oh, yeah. I forgot that a lot of the time, which didn't make sense, since I lived in this mansion.

"I'll call his office." My mother began dialing the phone.

"Mom . . . wait."

She looked up. "What?"

"I need to talk to you first."

She replaced the receiver. "What about?"

"The . . . bullies. The bullies who sent me into such horrible depression that I had to be hospitalized for a year, Mom. The bullies who happened to have all moved away by the time I went back to school. None of it makes sense, and I don't remember any of it."

"I know that, honey. It's normal. You had a concussion, and you lost your memory of that time. We've explained all this to you a hundred times."

"There's something else," I said.

Mom whitened again and swallowed audibly. "There's nothing else, Daphne."

I sighed. "Fine. I'll need to call Dr. Payne and get my records transferred. I want this new doctor to have all my relevant information so he can best help me."

CHAPTER FORTY-NINE

Brad

I'd called Larry every hour since I'd reviewed Jonathan's file. He wasn't answering. Why didn't he have one of those newfangled answering machines? All I needed to know was whether he'd funded his half sister's psychiatric treatment.

Because if he hadn't, Jonathan had gotten the money somewhere.

I'd read through Daphne's file. All her medical records were there, including the account of what had happened to her that horrible night. I'd retched while reading it but had managed not to puke all over my desk. Dry heaves only, thank God. Her friend Sage's records were in Daphne's file as well. I found myself thanking the universe that Daphne hadn't been harmed as badly.

Still, Daphne had been harmed.

Violated by three different men. She had been beaten so badly that the eyelid on her right eye had puffed up and turned inside out.

And yes, there were photos.

Of *all* of it.

Thank God for her concussion.

The rest of the file was thick—records from her year-long hospitalization, no doubt. I couldn't look anymore. I just couldn't. She didn't remember any of it anyway. I didn't want those memories plaguing me any more than they already were.

I gathered all the medical records, including Sage's, tucked them into my briefcase, and left my office.

Daphne and her mother were in the family room, talking.

"Hey, baby," I said from the top of the small staircase. "I'm going out for a while."

"Okay. Where?"

"The north quadrant."

"Dressed like that?"

I looked down at my suit and tie. "Uh...yeah. Meeting with one of the veterinarians. He's looking at some stock."

"You should change into jeans and your boots," Daphne said.

"No time," I said. "I'll be back soon."

I left the house and got into my truck. My father's trusty lighter rested in my pocket. I turned the key in the ignition and drove for a few miles until I found a desolate spot on the property.

I got out, taking the file, and gathered some dead brush. I built a small fire, and then, one by one, I tossed in Daphne's and Sage's medical records.

The horrors of that night went up in smoke.

It was the only way I could protect the woman I loved.

★ ★ ★

Back in my office, my father's personal line—now my personal line—rang.

"Hello, this is Brad Steel," I said into the phone.

A throat cleared. "Mr. Steel, this is Dr. Devin Pelletier."

Dr. Pelletier. I'd read his file, but I'd only met him once . . . when my father pulled a gun on him.

"Dr. Pelletier," I said, "what can I do for you?"

Silence.

"Doctor, I'd like to thank you for helping my father and me deal with the . . . uh . . . Wendy Madigan situation . . . and also, I want to apolo—"

Another throat clear. "Mr. Steel, that's not why I'm calling."

"Oh . . . then what?"

"My secretary scheduled an appointment for me at my Snow Creek office tomorrow. For your wife."

My jaw dropped. "Daphne?"

"Yes. Daphne Steel. She'd like to start therapy with me. I felt I should let you know."

This time I was silent.

"I won't be keeping the appointment, of course. I'll call her and cancel."

"And tell her what?"

"That I'm not accepting new patients at this time. My secretary made a mistake."

My heart pounded. I'd just destroyed her medical files, but I didn't have the only copy. Her therapist back in Denver had them, as well as the hospital where she'd spent her junior year of high school.

I had to destroy them all.

"Doctor," I said, "I don't want you to cancel."

"I'm afraid I must. Given my . . . er . . . relationship with your late father, I don't feel I'm the best professional to treat your wife."

"Trust me," I said. "You are."

"I'm afraid I can't—"

"I'll make it worth your while," I said.

"Mr. Steel—"

"I know your reputation, Doctor. My father has a file on you. You're the best, which is why he worked with you in the first place. Granted, your integrity leaves a little to be desired, but believe me when I tell you that you did the right thing helping to get Wendy Madigan put away."

"I'm afraid—"

"Please, let me finish. My wife and child are my whole world. I'll do anything for them, and I've got my hands full at the moment with ... other issues. Daphne needs help—help I can't give her. You're good, and you're here. She won't have to be away from the baby more than an hour or so at a time if she goes to therapy here in Snow Creek. You're the best choice."

"I can't—"

"Please, Doctor. You'll never be threatened again. My father is dead."

"I'm not the best choice, Mr. Steel."

"You are."

"I have a history with your family."

"Can you recommend someone else, then? Someone who can come to Snow Creek and treat my wife? He or she will be handsomely compensated."

"I cannot. Not in good conscience."

Life sometimes threw you curve balls. This was one of those times. I was the head of the Steel family now, and the job of protecting my family was mine.

My family included my wife—my wife, whose medical records I'd read, nearly making myself ill, and subsequently burned to keep them from her forever.

This was the legacy left to me by George Steel—the man who sired me.

The man who created the Steel empire.

Now it was up to me to make it bigger. Grander.

And to protect those who were mine.

"I understand your issues with my father, Doctor," I said calmly and devoid of emotion. "Believe me, I had my own issues with him. But this concerns my wife, and I'll do everything I can to see she gets the best treatment available. So it may interest you to know that my father left everything to me. All of his money . . . and all of his guns."

CHAPTER FIFTY

Daphne

"You can get my records from Dr. Mitch Payne," I said to Dr. Pelletier after he'd closed his office door, giving us privacy for our first session. "He's in Westminster."

"I'll do that," he said, "first thing tomorrow morning. You'll have to sign a release on the way out. For now, what can I help you with, Mrs. Steel?"

"This is difficult for me, Doctor," I said. "It took me a while to get comfortable with Dr. Payne, and now I need to begin again."

"If you feel you should be seeing Dr. Payne, I certainly don't want to interfere."

"No. I want to see someone here in town. Dr. Payne is in Denver."

"I'm sure your husband could arrange for him to have an office here in Snow Creek," Dr. Pelletier said.

A touch of snideness laced his voice. Or was I imagining it?

I cleared my throat. "No, I'm sure you're very competent, Doctor. I'd like to talk, if I may."

"Of course. That's what I'm here for. Please, proceed."

"I have a history of anxiety and depression. I was... hospitalized most of my junior year in high school. Apparently

I was bullied by a couple of girls at school, and they beat on me a little, but not enough to do any significant damage."

"I see."

"The problem is that I don't remember any of this. Apparently I got a concussion and lost the memory of the incident plus a couple days before."

"Retrograde amnesia," he said. "Not uncommon from a concussion, especially if the patient loses consciousness."

"I probably did, though I don't know for sure."

"Of course. Because you don't remember."

"Well, I wouldn't remember anyway if I lost consciousness."

He smiled. "True. So what brings you in here today? Are you having trouble dealing with your prior hospitalization?"

"No. I mean, sort of. I don't remember most of that year, and I always thought it was because of the medication I was on."

"What medication was that?"

"I don't know, honestly. I was a minor at the time. I pretty much did what I was told. You can get those records from Dr. Payne."

"Yes, of course."

"Anyway, just the other day I remembered something. Or I should say, someone. Or . . . more than one."

"What did you remember?"

"The patients who were at the hospital with me. Only I didn't remember their names. I don't think I ever knew their names, or I never bothered to learn them." I quickly relayed the information I'd remembered about each person.

"So you knew them only as these nicknames you made up."

"Yes. Correct."

"And you have no doubt that this is a real memory?"

I widened my eyes. "You mean there's such a thing as a fake memory?"

"The human mind is a delicate thing," Dr. Pelletier said. "It's hardly infallible. Sometimes we make up scenarios to fill in what we don't recall. It's a defense mechanism and is well documented. You can actually be certain that something is true, when in fact, it didn't happen at all."

"You mean because I have a history of mental illness."

"Not at all, Mrs. Steel. This is common in people who don't suffer from mental illness. Most everyone does it to some degree."

I sat, my jaw dropping. Truly? Could I have made up those patients at the hospital?

I shook my head. "These people were real. I'm sure of it. Once I remembered them, I remembered everything about them. Except, of course, their names, but I don't think I ever knew them."

"Surely the doctors and nurses at the hospital called them by name."

"I don't know. I don't recall."

"Mrs. Steel, trust me. The doctors and nurses called these patients by name. They did not call them paperboy and deli owner's daughter. How do you know this girl's father owned a deli, anyway?"

"I'm not sure."

"There must be some reason you remember her as being associated with a deli."

"Honestly, I don't know."

"Did you ever go to a deli?"

"Yeah, when I lived at home with my parents. There was this great New York–style deli a few miles from our house. We went there a lot for lunch on weekends. I used to love to watch the workers slice the meats to put on sandwiches."

Dr. Pelletier nodded and made some notes.

"How can I prove to you that this memory is real?" I asked.

"Nothing can be proven without factual corroboration." He continued writing.

"Then let's get the factual corroboration."

"That's impossible."

"Why?"

"Because records of other patients are strictly confidential. I can't access them unless I'm a treating physician on the case. This is especially true where minors are involved."

"Oh." I bit my lip.

"But let's go on the assumption that these memories are real," he said. "Why do you think you're remembering them now?"

"That's kind of why I'm here," I said. "Dr. Payne told me my memories might come back, and when they did, there would probably be a reason."

"There can be," he said. "What's been going on in your life lately?"

I sighed. There was no easy answer to that question. What *hadn't* been going on?

"I have a week-old baby whose life has been threatened twice. A good friend of mine is missing. Another friend died at my wedding eight months ago, and we don't know why or who was behind it. My husband is always working. Oh . . . my mother attempted suicide after I told her I was pregnant and getting married."

Dr. Pelletier stopped writing and met my gaze. "I see we have a lot to talk about, Mrs. Steel."

CHAPTER FIFTY-ONE

B r a d

My flight to Arizona was uneventful. My PI had located Larry and his girlfriend, Greta, in a bed-and-breakfast in Sedona. And yeah, I walked in on them while they were doing it.

Not a sight I ever wanted to see again.

"Steel! What the fuck?" Larry rolled off Greta and wrapped a sheet around himself, leaving her totally exposed. What a gentleman.

I averted my eyes. "Get dressed, both of you. I need to talk to Larry alone."

"We're kind of in the middle of something here," Larry said.

"Believe me, I can't unsee that. This is important. You have two minutes."

"Now listen here—"

"Larry, *you* listen here. I'm not just a friend anymore. I'm your brother-in-law, and I need your help. I'll make it worth your while."

That got him. I could almost see the dollar signs in his eyeballs.

"All right. I'll be with you in a minute."

I closed the door and waited in the hallway.

True to his word, Larry came out dressed in jeans and a

Queen T-shirt, his feet bare.

"Get some shoes on," I said.

"What for?"

"We're going for a walk."

Larry rolled his eyes but went back in the room, returning a few seconds later wearing Chuck Taylors. "Let's go, then."

Sedona was a beautiful city with its perfect red rock formations. I wanted to bring Daphne and little Joe here. They were both so beautiful. They belonged in a place like this.

"Can we stop for a bite?" Larry asked. "I need to carbo-load."

"Too much information, man," I said. "But sure."

We found a small sandwich shop, ordered, and got a table.

"What the hell was so important that you needed to interrupt me fucking my fiancée?"

I widened my eyes. "Fiancée?"

"Yeah. I proposed last night. Greta accepted."

"Congratulations, man."

"Thanks. She's coming to Phoenix with me when I start law school in the fall."

"Cool. So you'll be a kept man like Simpson?"

"Nah. I'm not going to make Greta work when I've got seven figures in the bank."

"You're a better man than he is, then."

"Yeah, you don't have to go too far for that." Larry sipped his Coke.

I lifted one eyebrow. "Oh? What makes you say that?"

"Come on, Steel," Larry said. "You're not blind."

No, I wasn't. Perhaps I hadn't given Larry enough credit. I'd always considered him the least intelligent of our little group. Of course least intelligent among the Future Lawmakers was still damned smart. He'd gotten into law school.

"Anything you want to tell me, Lar?" I asked.

"Nothing you don't already know."

I nodded. "We'll get to that. For now, I have a simple question for you."

"Shoot."

"Did you pay for Daphne's hospitalization?"

His brows nearly flew off his forehead. "What?"

"You heard me."

"Hell, no. My dad has insurance."

"His insurance is pure indemnity, not one of those newfangled HMOs. It only paid eighty percent, and his share amounted to over a hundred grand."

"Where did he get that kind of money?"

"That's what I'm trying to figure out. My first thought was you."

"Nope. He never asked."

"Of course," I said more to myself than to Larry, "because he doesn't know you have money."

"Right."

"Okay, then. Who does your father know who could have given him that kind of money?"

"How do you know he didn't just pay it himself? Over time?"

"I have his financial records."

Larry opened his mouth, but I gestured him to be quiet.

"Before you freak out, I found them in my old man's files. I didn't get them myself."

"Why the hell would your father—"

"I have no idea. I can only guess that he had Jonathan investigated after Daphne and I told him she was pregnant. He kept files on everyone, from what I can see."

"On your friends too?" Larry wrinkled his forehead.

"Oh, yeah. There's one on everyone in the club. I haven't looked through them yet. I'm more concerned with Daphne at the moment, and also finding Patty and figuring out who's responsible for Murphy's death."

"Whoa, whoa, whoa. Hold up. What's up with Patty?"

"She's missing. For two days now. She went shopping in Snow Creek and never returned."

"Snow Creek? Someone invaded that little town? Hardly a hub for criminal behavior."

"Apparently it is now."

"And still no information on what happened to Sean?"

"No, and I've had the best investigators on it. My father hired them after the wedding. But I need to get back to why I'm here. Who does your dad know who could have paid for Daphne's medical bills?"

"I have no idea, man. We weren't exactly close. I didn't see my dad a lot, and I hardly ever saw Daphne. I never really knew why she ended up hospitalized for so long that year."

"You don't know what happened to her?"

"Only a little. The story I heard was that she was bullied by a couple of girls."

He didn't know. Unless he was lying.

But maybe he wasn't.

Maybe, to keep the truth from Daphne, Jonathan and Lucy kept it from everyone else as well.

Except... *Wendy* knew.

A conversation from months ago speared into my head.

"You and I, Brad. We're connected. We'll always be connected. Someday, we'll have that baby that was stolen from us in high school."

"No, we won't."

Her miscarriage had been tragic, but it had also been a blessing in disguise. I didn't want to be bound to Wendy through a child. If I could excise her from my life with a sharp scalpel, I would, and I'd live with the scar, no matter how deep.

And it would be deep.

"Oh, we will. You can't avoid destiny, Brad."

"My destiny lies with someone else."

"Daphne?" She shook her head. "There's so much you don't know."

"I know everything."

"About her year in London?"

I didn't want to discuss Daphne with Wendy, but I couldn't resist shoving it in her face. "She told me all about it."

"Then you know she wasn't actually in London."

"As I said, she told me all about it."

"That's sweet. Really. But there's no way she told you all about it. There are things even she doesn't recall."

"What the hell are you talking about? If you know something, you better fucking tell me."

"Sorry, you set the rules, so you get to live by them. You said no more deals. You want to know the truth about your sweet little slut? You won't get it out of me. Besides, it's not my story to tell." She turned and flounced toward the doorway.

"You're telling me," I said to Larry, "that you don't know what happened to your sister?"

"Sure I do. The bullies. But that's it. Dad didn't tell me much else. I was already in college, and he was dealing with Daphne in the hospital. We didn't talk about it."

"Would it surprise you to know that Daphne doesn't remember what happened to her?"

"No. Dad told me about the concussion."

"Would it surprise you to know that the problem was way more than a couple of bullies?"

His eyes widened slightly.

"And would it surprise you to know that Wendy seems to know what happened?"

He let out a guffaw at that one. A true guffaw. "Steel, nothing that Wendy knows or does *ever* surprises me. It sure as *hell* shouldn't surprise you."

"You really don't know what happened to Daphne?"

"Only what my dad told me. Are you saying that's not what happened?"

"Not at all. I'm just wondering where your father got that kind of money to pay his share of Daphne's medical bills."

"He didn't get it from me."

"Would you have paid it if he'd asked?"

"That's a moot point, Steel. He didn't ask. He doesn't know I have money."

"I got my answer."

Larry was right. It was a moot point. Why did it matter that Larry wouldn't have paid for his half sister's medical bills? Who really cared, in the long run? I already knew that Larry, Tom, and Theo were all profit-driven.

I didn't understand it, and I probably never would. Money had never been an issue for me. I had it in abundance.

I cleared my throat. "I found Theo at your place in the city a few days ago."

Larry lifted his brow.

"He said he was looking for you. Does he have a key to your place?"

"Yeah. We all have keys to each other's places, you know,

if we need to crash."

I nodded. "Did you know he visits Wendy at Piney Oaks?"

"Yeah."

"And that he's using my name?"

"Why would he do that?"

"I have no idea. I thought *you* might."

"Dude, I'm clueless."

Yeah, he was. In more ways than one.

"Have you been to see Wendy?"

Larry shook his head. "We were never that close. She's more in tune with Theo and Tom. And, of course, you."

"She and I were over a long time ago."

"I get it, man. I do. I'm just not sure she does."

"True enough."

"You two sure were hot and heavy back in high school, though. Or have you forgotten about how you were joined at the hip and made out during passing period every damned day? Like you couldn't wait until school was over."

"We were kids."

"It wasn't that long ago, man."

"Larry, trust me. It was a lifetime ago."

He didn't have any more information for me. I'd found out what I'd come for. He hadn't paid for Daphne's hospitalization, and he didn't know who had.

None of this had anything to do with finding Patty or solving Murph's case.

I'd come down here because of my own curiosity about Daphne's father. Did it really matter who had paid for Daphne's treatment? What mattered was that she'd gotten the treatment.

I was going home, where I'd solve the mystery of Murph and Patty for good.

CHAPTER FIFTY-TWO

Daphne

"I love Patty," I said, "but I feel like I should be feeling worse than I do."

"How so?" Dr. Pelletier asked.

"I have so much else going on. I have a baby who needs me, whose life has been threatened, and my husband is always working. When I'm not taking care of baby Joe, I'm napping. I had a really tough pregnancy."

"Are you and Patty close?"

"As close as we could be, I guess, after really only knowing each other for a couple of months before I left school to get married."

"Tell me, Mrs. Steel, have you ever had a close friendship other than with Patty?"

"There's Patty's boyfriend, Ennis, but I only knew him for the same time I knew Patty."

"Anyone else?"

"Only once. Her name was Sage. She moved away during the summer between our sophomore and junior years of high school."

"The summer before you were hospitalized."

"Yeah."

"Did losing her have anything to do with your depression?"

"I don't know. I'm sure it didn't help. I wrote to her. Five letters, and she didn't answer any of them."

"She was young."

"So was I. We were the same age. If I could write, why couldn't she?"

"I can't answer that, Mrs. Steel."

"Could you call me Daphne, please? I'm nineteen. I don't feel old enough to be Mrs. Steel."

"But you *are* Mrs. Steel. I find it best to keep a professional distance with my patients."

"Okay." I twisted my lips. "Maybe I never got over losing Sage, but that's not enough to send someone into a tailspin."

"Maybe it was, combined with the bullying."

"But I don't even remember the bullying. How can something I don't remember send me reeling?"

"I've said it before. The human mind is a delicate thing. It may not recall actual events, but somewhere, deep in its recesses, it recalls the feelings."

I lifted my eyebrows. "I don't understand."

"No one truly understands the human mind, Mrs. Steel. Not even professionals like me. Especially professionals, to be honest. We study and study and study, read theory after theory, only to be more confused. I can tell you this, though, with regard to your friend Patty. You feel like you should be feeling worse than you are. I think your mind may have trained you not to get too close to a friend again because of the heartbreak you felt when Sage didn't write you back."

I lifted my eyebrows again. "Hmm."

"You were hospitalized for most of your junior year. What happened your senior year?"

"I went back to my high school."

"And...?"

"I didn't have any friends. People seemed afraid to approach me, and I heard a lot of whispering."

"Did they know you'd been hospitalized?"

"No. The story was that I'd been in London studying abroad with a relative."

"Do you think you imagined the whispering?"

I shook my head. "Absolutely not. I heard more than once that I was a 'little off.'"

"I see. How did you handle all of that?"

"I threw myself into my studies. I'd always been an excellent student, and this time I truly worked hard. I studied for my college prep tests too, and I became a national merit scholar. I got a full ride to a very competitive college."

"Then that's all good."

"Yes. It seemed so. Except I left college after two months because of my pregnancy."

"You can return to school."

"Not to Stilton, where my scholarship is. It's in Denver, and I live here now."

"You can go anywhere. Money is hardly an issue for you."

I shook my head. "College isn't in the cards for me. I'm a mother first. My baby needs me."

"You can be a mother and a college student, Daphne."

"You called me Daphne."

"I did. I'm sorry."

"Please, I prefer it. I know I'm young. I hardly seem like a missus."

He smiled. "Okay. If it means that much to you, Daphne. You worked very hard for your scholarship. Are you sure you're ready to give up college?"

"My baby is the most important thing in my life. I never knew true love until I had him."

"Are you saying you're not in love with your husband?"

"Oh, no. Of course I am. But my feelings for my child are even more intense in a totally different way. There's nothing I wouldn't do for him."

"Would you say your child is more important to you than your husband?"

Would I? "I'm not sure. You really can't compare the two. They're like apples and oranges."

"If you had to choose," Dr. Pelletier said, "which one would you choose?"

"Between my husband and my baby?" I rounded my eyes. "You can't be asking me that."

"I *am* asking you that."

"I can't imagine my life without Brad."

"So you choose Brad?"

"No." I shook my head vehemently. "I'd choose . . . I can't believe I'm saying this. I'd choose my child. I'd choose Jonah."

He smiled. "Most mothers would make that choice if they had to."

"Oh!" I heaved a relieved sigh. "You scared me for a minute there."

"It doesn't mean you love your husband any less. It just means you're a normal mother who will do anything to protect her child."

I nodded. "What does this have to do with Patty? And Sage?"

"You've been through a lot in your short life, Daphne. As a psychiatric professional, I need to make sure you're fit to raise a child."

"What? That's not why I'm here."

"Doesn't matter. I'm still bound by my ethics to do the right thing. You're young, but you'll be a good mother. Your baby is very lucky, and he should always be your first priority."

"He is. That's why I need to figure the rest of this stuff out. So I can be my best for him."

"Which is why you're here, of course. Now... when did you write Sage those letters?"

"I wrote them"—my mind raced—"while I was in the hospital."

"All five of them?"

"Yeah."

"How is it that you remember writing five letters, but you don't remember so much else about your stay?"

"I... I don't know, Doctor."

"When was the last time you thought about those letters to Sage?"

"Before now? I'm not sure."

"But they came to your mind when you remembered the other patients?"

"Yeah. They did."

"I think this is probably all related to your friend who's currently missing. I'm sorry that a friend had to disappear for your memory to kick in."

"Yeah. Me too."

"Our time is up for today, Daphne, but I assure you that we *will* get to the bottom of this."

"Thank you, Doctor. My husband is trying his hardest to find Patty. I wish I could help him, but I think the best thing I can do for my baby and myself is to work through my own issues."

"You're on your way," he said, smiling. "Your child is lucky to have you."

"I'm the lucky one." No truer words. "I'll do anything for my little dove. *Anything.*"

CHAPTER FIFTY-THREE

Brad

Theodore Mathias

I stared at the name on the file I'd just opened. It was twice as thick as the files on the other Future Lawmakers, which made me pause. He was a year older than I was, and his birth certificate indicated his parents' names were Niko and Gloria Mathias. He had one sister, Erica, who was engaged to Rodney Cates. I flashed back to when I'd first found all the files. My father kept a file on Theo's mother. *Mental note: Check that out.*

Medical history was unremarkable, and his school records were of course commendable. He didn't attend college, which was odd for someone of his intellect. But why should he? He was making scads of cash with his Future Lawmakers investments.

Would they continue to make that kind of cash now that I'd divested?

I sighed. Not my problem. I'd only looked at the first three pages of what appeared to be at least a hundred, when my phone rang.

"Brad Steel," I said into the receiver.

"Mr. Steel, it's Jason Morey."

Good. One of my PIs. "Yeah? What do you have for me?"

"Not good news, I'm afraid."

My stomach dropped. "Out with it, then."

"We found Patty Watson."

I consciously regulated my breathing. "And . . . ?"

"I'm sorry. She's gone."

Fuck. My heart nearly stopped. What was I supposed to tell Daphne? And Ennis?

"Under what circumstances?"

"The usual. Beaten. Raped. Then bludgeoned in the head. It's not pretty."

"Damn." I shook my head. "Have you called the cops?"

"Not yet. We're waiting for your go-ahead. We found her body wrapped in a tarp in an old barn about two hours south of Snow Creek. It was just luck that we stopped to look. We pretty much thought it would be a dead end."

"Who owns the property?"

"That's the funny part, Mr. Steel."

"Uh . . . nothing about this is funny at all from where I'm standing."

"Sorry. Bad use of the word *funny*. When you've seen as much crap as I have on this job, you get a little numb to it."

"Just spit it out."

"The unusual part is that the owner of the property is . . . *you*."

The receiver slipped from my grip and thudded on top of Theo's file. I hastily retrieved it.

"Say what?"

"It's part of the Steel property. Just not part of the actual ranch."

"Fuck. Seriously?"

"Seriously. I checked ownership of the legal description myself."

"Listen," I said, "do *not* call the police. You got me?"

"Mr. Steel, I have to—"

"How does a hundred grand sound to you?"

"Is this a bribe?"

"I really don't like the word *bribe*, Mr. Morey," I said. "Think of it more as payment for a service."

"For me keeping my mouth shut. I see. And just what am I supposed to do with the body?"

"Leave it where it is. I'll take care of it."

"You've got to be kidding me."

"Do I sound like I'm kidding? Give me all relevant information now, over the phone. Do not write anything down. You got it? I'll have the money wired to you after this phone call."

"I'm going to hell, aren't I?" he said.

"For taking money you can use for your family and the greater good? I doubt it." I quickly jotted down where to find Patty's body. "This conversation never took place," I said to Morey.

"Got it."

I ended the call and arranged for the wire transfer. Now . . . how to clean up this mess?

George Steel would know. I'd bet my fortune he'd cleaned up messes far worse than this one. I'd create a story, bring in Patty's parents—after paying them off, of course—and convince both Ennis and Daphne that Patty had joined the Peace Corps and gone off to Africa, met someone, and never looked back.

Daphne was fragile. Murph's death had nearly broken her, and they weren't even close. Patty? I'd have to pull a

Jonathan—keep Patty's death from her like he'd kept Sage's.

This would be my legacy—part of it, at least.

To protect those I loved from the evils in this world.

Daphne was too perfect for these evils, and I had the ability to protect her. My need to protect her was greater than anything I knew, and I'd felt it the first time I'd laid eyes on her.

I jerked out of my chair when someone knocked on the door. "Yeah?"

The knob turned. Daphne stood in the doorway. "Hi. I'm back."

"Back?"

"From therapy?"

Right. Her appointment with Pelletier. I'd get the scoop from him. He was being well paid to help my wife . . . and to keep me informed. "How did it go?"

"I'm not sure. But I'd like to keep going."

"Of course. How's the baby?"

"He's good. I'm going to feed him now. I just wanted to let you know I was back."

"Okay, baby. I'm glad it went okay."

She nodded and closed the door.

I drew in a deep breath.

Man, marriage was complicated.

Life was complicated.

At least it was when you were George Steel's surviving heir. He'd left a fucking mess for me.

I had to step up my game. Patty was gone, and I had no idea who'd killed her or why. Same as I had no idea who'd killed Murphy or why.

PIs could find the bodies—and in Murph's case, the body was already around—but not figure out who or why.

Which meant only one thing. Whoever was behind these deaths covered their tracks very well. Well enough that even George Steel couldn't uncover them. He'd been on Murph's death since it happened, and . . . nothing.

I had to become *better* than George Steel.

I had to create a legacy that could never be toppled and that was capable of anything.

Quickly I'd learned that type of legacy couldn't be created doing things the legal or even the ethical way.

So I made a choice then and there.

A choice that I'd protect those I loved no matter what the cost.

Yes, I'd made that proclamation before, but this time I vowed to stop at nothing.

No matter the cost.

And it would be costly, but if I proceeded intelligently, my child wouldn't pay the price for my sins.

★ ★ ★

Did you ever see a dead body?

I asked the question silently to my dead father as I slowly approached the lump covered in a blue plastic tarp.

Darkness had fallen, and the ray from my flashlight shone against the blue of the tarp.

I had to look. Had to make sure this was truly Patty Watson.

Nausea clawed up my throat like lava from an acidic volcano. I inhaled through my mouth, holding my nose. This was an old barn and wouldn't smell good anyway.

Plus, I'd never smelled a dead body before. I didn't want to start now.

I won't get sick. I won't get sick. I won't get sick.

Too late.

I dropped to my knees and retched. When my throat stopped spasming, I inhaled involuntarily through both my mouth and nose.

The stench.

Old barn. Feces. Rot.

I retched again.

I was still ten feet away from the tarp-covered body.

"Did you ever have to do this?" I said aloud to my father in his grave. "Help me. For God's sake, help me."

No help came, of course. I didn't believe in ghosts.

"I'm here."

I jerked.

The voice was crackly, but familiar.

"What the fu—"

Someone grabbed me from behind and slipped a hand over my mouth. I jerked wildly. I could take most men, but my attacker had the element of surprise on his side.

"Quiet," he roared. "I'm not here to hurt you. I'm here to help."

"Who the fuck *are* you?" I demanded. Of course the words came out as nothing, since his hand was still clamped over my mouth.

"I'm going to let you go now. *Do not yell.*"

My gun was strapped to my ankle. As soon as the attacker loosened his hold, I bent down and grabbed it, turned, and held it on him.

The assailant was masked. "You don't want to do that," he said.

"I assure you that I do."

"No, you don't." He removed the black ski mask.

I'd dropped my flashlight when he first grabbed me, but now I knew why the voice was raspy but familiar.

George Steel stood in front of me.

My jaw dropped.

"It's me, son."

"You're . . . dead." Except the words didn't come out. They floated around in my head, repeating themselves again and again.

"It's me. I'm not dead."

"But how . . . "

"It was time for me to step down, let you and your children run the Steel family. Besides . . . I can accomplish a lot more dead than alive."

"You're crazy," I said, shaking my head. "A complete loon."

He guffawed. "I've been called a lot worse."

"But I have . . . I have all your money. Your assets."

"You have all the Steel assets, son. Do you really think I didn't hide a thing or two away over the years?"

"Enough to fake your death, apparently."

"Your mother is better off without me. We both know that."

"You didn't have to be such a tyrant."

"You're right. I made a lot of mistakes, but I built Steel Acres legitimately, and I've left it in a good place. You have the chance to make it huge."

"I plan to. I've already got major investments in place. I'm going to take it into nine figures. Maybe ten."

"You can do it."

"Why didn't *you* do it?"

"I wasn't the man for the job. You are."

I shook my head. "This is nuts. Why would you pretend to die? The heart attack?"

"Son, money can buy just about anything."

"You bought your own *death*?"

"In a manner of speaking. I'll be of much more use this way. My legacy is in good hands with you."

"I'm twenty-three."

"You're more of a man at twenty-three than most are at three times your age. You have a wife and a child. Something to live for."

"You had that too."

"I did. And I stayed around until I was sure you could handle everything."

"Why not just walk away, then? Why orchestrate your own death? Or fake death? Or whatever the fuck it is you did?"

"Because, Brad, something's going on. I haven't been able to put my finger on it quite yet, but I know I'll be better able to figure it out without anyone watching me."

I gestured to the tarp-covered body in the corner. "Please tell me you had nothing to do with this."

"I did not, of course. I'm not a killer, and even if I were, I certainly wouldn't harm anyone who's important to you or your wife."

"So it *is* Patty, then."

"It is. I'm sorry, son."

"Damn. Why is she here? On our property?"

"My people recovered the body and brought her here at my instruction."

"Wait ... Your people?"

"A select few who are in on my little secret."

"Who did this? Who's behind this?"

"I don't know yet."

"Is it related to Murphy's murder?"

"I believe so."

"Why? Why would anyone want to hurt two innocent people?"

"Because they're important to you, Brad."

"Me? Who— Oh, fuck."

"I can't be sure it's her. She's under constant supervision, and she's heavily medicated."

"Who else, then?"

"That's what I'm trying to figure out. Whoever it is moves like a panther. Untraceable. Which is why I'm better off flying under the radar. I'm able to do that if everyone thinks I'm dead."

"You really think I can keep this from Mom?"

"I'd think you'd be happy to."

I sighed. He was right. My mother was happy now. She had a grandson to dote on, a new daughter-in-law, and her tyrant of a husband was finally gone.

"How do I get in touch with you?"

"You don't. I'll find you when I need to."

"And … now?"

"It was time for you to know. Go home. Tend to your wife and son. Take care of your mother. Leave this to me."

It was tempting. Really tempting. But—

"No way. I'm all-in now. Murph and Patty were my friends. I've already decided … "

"Decided what?"

"I can't tell Daphne about this. I'm going to figure out a way to make it look like Patty left the country."

"You think you can pull that off?"

"Didn't you say it yourself? Money can buy just about anything?"

"I want better for you," he said.

"Right. If you wanted better for me, you wouldn't have pointed a gun at Dr. Pelletier's head while I was standing right there."

"I was making a point."

"Yeah. The point that money can buy anything."

"You missed that point, son. Money can buy just *about* anything. When money can't get you what you want, a threat against someone's life can. Life trumps money any day. It took me a while to learn that lesson."

"You say you wanted better for me. I call bullshit."

"I did, Brad. I wanted a lot better for you. Unfortunately, I may not get my wish."

"I want better for *my* son."

"I know you do. I hope you get it."

"I will. I fucking will. But for him to thrive, he needs his mother whole. This will destroy her."

"She's stronger than you think."

"She spent a year at a mental hospital, Dad."

"I know that. Doesn't mean she's weak."

"Her father thinks she is."

"Does her father know her better than you do?"

"Hell, yeah, he does. She and I haven't even known each other for a year. It's insane!"

"Jonathan Wade isn't who you think he is, son. Be careful."

"Jonathan Wade loves his wife and his dau— Wait. What are you saying? Who paid for Daphne's treatment? Do you know?"

"I don't. But I'm trying to find out."

CHAPTER FIFTY-FOUR

Daphne

Two months later ...

Ennis had gone back to London after Patty left him, and so far, Brad hadn't been able to locate Sage for me.

I was alone.

Alone with no friends.

But I did have my adorable baby. Jonah was nearly three months old now, and he was a beautiful chubby little boy. Mazie had shown me some photos of Brad as a baby, and Joe was a dead ringer for his dad. His smiles warmed my heart. I was still nursing him, and soon I'd add some solid food to his diet. No more threats had been made against him, and although Cliff still hovered over us, I was beginning to feel normal again. Well, sort of. Dr. Pelletier and I were still working together. It was a slow process, but I felt better.

My mother was back in Denver with my dad, so Mazie was my sole help with the baby, while Belinda took care of the household.

Then there was Brad ...

He was gone most of the time.

But tonight he was coming home from a three-week business trip, and I had plans.

My doctor had given me the green light to resume sexual relations.

It had been so long. Because my pregnancy had been problematic, we hadn't made love at all during the last trimester.

Five months since I'd been intimate with my husband.

I'd lost all my pregnancy pounds—thank you, nursing—and I was ready for an evening of passion.

Joe was in Mazie's care for the evening. I sat in the bedroom clad in a lacy pink negligee, waiting for my handsome husband.

I closed my eyes, slipping into dreamland.

★ ★ ★

"Baby."

I jerked awake.

Brad hovered over me, his jaw unshaven, his eyes tired and sunken.

"I'm home, baby."

I cupped his cheek, letting his stubble scratch my fingertips. "Welcome, home."

He pressed his lips to mine. "I've missed you so much. You look beautiful."

"I . . . fell asleep."

"I know. The plane was late. I'm sorry, baby. I'm beat."

"But—"

"In the morning. I promise."

I sighed and sat up. "I'll go check on the baby. He's spending the night in the nursery with Cliff."

"You had this all planned," he said. A statement.

"I did. It's okay."

But it wasn't okay.

It wasn't okay at all.

★ ★ ★

Five a.m. came quickly. Joe was on a strict schedule. He slept through the night now, if you called eleven to five sleeping through the night.

I sat with him in the rocker in the nursery, feeding him. He was so big now, so different from that little bundle I nursed those first few days.

He was beautiful. I dreamed of having more babies just like him once he was older. Of course, to have babies, my husband had to actually be around to make love to me.

Last night still disappointed me. Brad couldn't help it if his plane was delayed, but I was upset anyway.

I jolted slightly when the door to the nursery opened and a sliver of light came in.

"Hey," Brad said.

"Morning."

"How's he doing?"

"He's great. Hungry."

Baby Joe tugged on my nipple urgently.

"I'm a little jealous," he said.

"Don't be."

"I'm sorry about last night, Daphne."

"Don't be," I echoed.

"I was beat. I'm still beat, but it's five. Rise and shine and all that."

I nodded.

"How long until he's done?"

"Until he falls asleep." I looked down. Joe's eyes were closed. "Sometimes I just sit in here after he falls asleep, holding him close like this. It's calming. Settling."

Brad sighed. "I haven't given you much calming lately."

"No."

Did he expect me to deny it?

"I love you, baby."

"I love you too."

"Come to bed with me."

"The baby..."

He lifted a sleeping Joe from my arms and planted him in his crib. Then he took my hand and helped me out of the rocker. "Come on. Please."

I followed, smiling.

I'd do anything for my husband, forgive him anything.

Anything.

★ ★ ★

"We're going to make up for lost time," Brad said as he laid me gently on our bed. "I'm going to touch, kiss, and lick every inch of your beautiful body, wife."

My breasts tingled and my nipples hardened. All over, my skin erupted in icy prickles as warmth coursed between my legs.

Only months had passed, but I felt like a virgin yearning for the first touch from the man I adored.

"God, please," I whispered.

"Anything you want, baby. Whatever you want. I want what you want."

"Just kiss me."

His lips came down on mine.

I opened for him, letting the velvet of his tongue twirl against my own. It started as a gentle kiss, an exploring kiss, but soon it was a mass of lips, teeth, and gums.

It was a ferocious kiss, a kiss too long denied.

I poured all my love for Brad into that kiss, all my longing, all my desire.

All my complete devotion to him and our family.

He trailed his hand under my lacy nightie, grabbing one breast. It tingled as a drop of milk leaked out.

Wait.

I squirmed.

This was wrong.

Those breasts weren't Brad's anymore. They were—

He pinched a nipple, and I bucked beneath him.

Still his.

They had a dual purpose now.

He broke the kiss and trailed his lips over my jawline and neck. "So beautiful," he groaned. "I've missed you so much."

"I've missed you too," I whispered.

"I want to make this good for you," he said, "but I can't wait, baby. I just can't."

He turned over quickly, releasing me, and disrobed in what seemed like two seconds.

Then he was inside me, thrusting, thrusting, thrusting...

The completeness, the utter wonder.

I'd nearly forgotten.

Then—

"God!" He plunged in deeply, releasing.

And it was over.

What I'd anticipated for so long was simply over.

Turned out I didn't have to worry about whether my breasts belonged to Brad or the baby. After a single grope, he'd gotten on with his fucking.

For that was what it had been.

A fucking.

This hadn't been lovemaking.

It had been a fuck, pure and simple.

"Brad..."

"Hmm?" He rolled off me and covered his eyes with his arm.

I need more. The words hovered on the tip of my tongue.

I've missed you. I've missed us.

Finally, I spoke.

"Nothing."

CHAPTER FIFTY-FIVE

Brad

My beautiful wife deserved better than a *wham, bam, thank you, ma'am*.

Once I began, though, I couldn't stop myself. A pure physical reaction had taken over when my mind had raced toward the information I'd uncovered during my last trip.

Anything to chase away the thoughts. I'd had to get inside her, fuck her. Use her.

I wasn't proud of myself at the moment. Indeed, I hadn't been proud of myself since I'd found out my father was alive over two months ago and had been keeping his secret.

I had no choice, though.

For Daphne. For my child. For my mother.

Everything I did was for them.

The bed rustled as Daphne got up. "I'm going to shower. Then see to the baby."

Daphne in the shower, her lush body wet as trickles of water dribbled over her.

The sight in my mind's eye made my cock twitch again. I could go with her, fuck her again against the shower wall while the warmth of the pelting water rained down on us. She would let me.

No.

She deserved better. I'd let her shower in peace, and tonight, I'd arrange for us to have a romantic dinner alone. We'd go out. Or I could send my mother out. Either way, I'd make it happen.

I rose and dressed quickly. Time to get to the office.

★ ★ ★

"What did you find out?" I said into the phone.

"Did you do what I asked?" my father said. "Make sure there's no bug on your office line?"

"I did."

"Good work." He cleared his throat. "She's getting out."

"Fuck."

"They can't keep her there any longer. She's been a model patient."

"She's conning them."

"Maybe so."

"What about Pelletier?"

"That's part of the issue. He thinks I'm dead, so he feels the threat is gone."

Apparently he hadn't taken my guns comment seriously. Who could blame him? I wasn't George Steel, and I'd told him his life wouldn't be in danger. Besides, Dr. Pelletier was doing wonders for Daphne. I needed him.

I'd known this day would come. I'd been hoping Wendy might do something horrible to prolong her commitment, but I hadn't held my breath. She was too smart for that.

"I can't threaten Pelletier," I said.

"Why not?"

"Because he's treating Daphne. She needs him, and I need her whole."

"You have to let her be, son," he said. "You can't hide everything from her. If you never give her a chance to be strong, she won't be."

"Daphne's *my* responsibility. I'll handle her situation the way I see fit. My child needs his mother."

"Your child needs a mother who has a grip on reality. How can she have a grip on reality if you're constantly hiding it from her?"

"Enough!" I slammed my fist on my desk. "I made a vow to protect my wife, and I will do it. I know her better than you or anyone else does."

"Fine. I'll let it drop. There are more important matters. At least there haven't been any more threats against your son."

I breathed a sigh of relief. "I know. Thank God. I'm still not convinced Wendy hasn't been a part of this the whole time."

"I'm not convinced either," he said, "though I can't find any evidence that she has."

"If anyone can cover her tracks, it's Wendy Madigan."

"She's been locked up, son."

"I know. And now she's getting out. Which means things will get worse."

"Maybe not. Maybe she actually healed at the hospital."

"Please." I scoffed.

"Then find another doctor to replace Pelletier," he said. "Make him an offer he can't refuse so he'll keep Wendy hospitalized."

"Dad, does it have to be like this?"

"You have another choice."

"What's that?"

"Let Wendy be released. See what she does. Maybe she'll finish school. Get a job. Maybe she'll leave you behind."

"If she's not behind all this shit—and I still think she's got her hands dirty—then who is?"

"I've been working on that. She may well be involved. I just don't know yet."

"You've been working on it for a year. If we haven't figured it out by now, how will we ever?"

"We will. I'll leave no stone unturned. How are things with the ranch?"

"Profits are great. My new financial guy has us invested in some ground-floor deals. We're going to make a killing."

"I knew you'd be the one to take this business to the next level."

"Yeah, we'll be richer than God." I rolled my eyes. "I'd trade it all for the safety of my wife and child."

"Then you know what you have to do."

I exhaled slowly. "Yes. I know."

"I'm sorry, son."

"I'm sorry too. This is all on me. Me and those damned Future Lawmakers. Fuck. Why didn't you stop me?"

"Because a man has to learn from his own mistakes."

"I was a kid."

"You were eighteen by the time you began giving them money, Brad. That's a man."

"In my defense, I got paid back ten times over."

"You did, and I'm glad you got out when you did."

"I had to. They were getting into drugs."

"They were. They *are*."

"Tom and Larry are both going to be lawyers. I don't get it."

He laughed. "Lawyers are notoriously unscrupulous."

"Not all of them."

"I suppose you can find a couple good apples in the bushel. I tried."

"Really? You tried?"

He laughed again. "Not really. I needed attorneys who were willing to leave their scruples on the doorstep."

I nodded, knowing he couldn't see me. I had nothing else to say.

Except for one thing.

"Thank you, Dad."

"For what?"

"For working so hard all those years. And for doing what you're doing now, trying to find out who's behind all of this horror."

"You don't need to thank me."

Again, I said nothing.

"I've got to go, son. I'll talk to you next week. Same time. Be sure to pick up."

"Can't you give me any way to contact you?"

"We've been through this. I have to keep moving. I'll call you."

"Fine." I hung up the phone a little more harshly than I meant to.

CHAPTER FIFTY-SIX

Daphne

He was gone again.

Only out on the ranch, this time, checking on things. He was the owner, after all. He'd be back for our romantic dinner.

He'd promised.

I had no reason to believe he would renege.

I was making my way to the nursery to check on Joe when the doorbell rang. Mazie was in the greenhouse.

"I'll get it, Belinda," I called and walked to the door.

A young man stood on the porch.

"May I help you?" I asked.

"I have a delivery for Bradford Steel."

"I'm his wife. I can take it."

"Okay." He handed me the white envelope.

I closed the door and fingered the smooth paper.

Take it to his office.

Just take it to his office.

I walked through the foyer and down the hallway leading to Brad's study. I opened the door and was about to lay the envelope on his desk, when—

Hmm. The seal had been broken and was only glued at the tip of the triangle. Without thinking, I ran my finger under the seal and broke it without tearing the paper.

Nicely done.

Don't, Daphne. Don't.

But as soon as I noticed the broken seal, I knew I was going to look inside.

I pulled out the single sheet of paper.

My heart was beating like a racehorse inside my chest. My ears thrummed with the beat, as if someone were pounding on a bass drum inside me.

I unfolded the paper.

"Miss Daphne?"

Belinda. I scrunched the paper up and hid it inside my fist. "Yes?"

"Who was at the door?"

"No one. I mean"—I held up the envelope—"a message for Brad. I'm taking it to the office."

"Okay." She smiled and went about her business.

I ran into the library and uncrumpled the wad of paper in my hand.

Dear Brad Steel,

How important is it to you that your wife never finds out what happened to her? How much are you willing to pay?

I'll wait for your call.

A friend

I gulped.

His wife? I was Brad's wife. Something had happened to me? Something I didn't know about?

My heart dropped into my stomach.

My hands shook as I attempted to smooth out the

crumpled paper. I couldn't put it back in the envelope now. Why had I even looked?

What could I do?

Nothing had happened to me. Except . . . there was still a lot I didn't remember. A phone number was written on the bottom of the paper.

There was one way to find out what this was about.

I'd call the number.

"Hello?"

"This is Daphne Steel. Brad Steel's wife."

A throat cleared. "Mrs. Steel. What can I do for you?"

"You can tell me where the hell you get off trying to extort money from my husband."

The words left my throat before I could think about them. I wasn't going to allow this to happen to my husband, to our family.

I became a lioness, fierce and protective.

I was no longer timid Daphne Wade, a colorless flower.

I was Daphne Steel, a full yellow bloom.

And I was angry.

Passionately angry.

"I beg your pardon?"

"I got your message. Let's come to terms *now.*"

CHAPTER FIFTY-SEVEN

Brad

I picked up the phone in my truck when it rang. I didn't give this number out to just anyone, so I knew the call would be important.

"Steel," I said.

"Mr. Steel, it's Dr. Pelletier."

"What's the word, Doc?"

"Given your father has held me at gunpoint, I don't think you should be calling me by a nickname."

"I'm paying you a shit ton of money, so I'll call you what I want. I hope you have good news for me. How much longer will Wendy be committed?"

"She won't be. That hasn't changed. She's been a model patient, and she's getting out sometime next month."

Fuck. I'd tried everything, and no dice. "What do you want, then?"

"I want to talk to you about your wife."

My heart softened. Daphne. "I'm sorry. Is she all right?"

"I told you after our first session that she had remembered some of the patients who were with her when she was hospitalized."

"Yeah."

"The facility finally got her old records to me. Apparently

there was some turnover in the records department that caused the delay."

Damn. I'd paid that department a lot to get those records unsealed and to Dr. Pelletier. Delay my ass. Good thing I hadn't gone with my first instinct months ago and had them all destroyed.

"Some heads are going to roll. But at least you have them now. You can review them and help her even more."

"I *have* reviewed them, Mr. Steel. That's the issue."

"Okay..." My stomach churned. "I assume there's something in there I should know."

"There's a lot in there you should know," he said, "but the most alarming is that your wife was heavily medicated."

"I assumed so. That explains why she has such significant memory loss from that time."

He cleared his throat. "That could be a partial explanation, yes."

"What other explanation could there be?"

"Her diagnosis."

"I know what her diagnosis was. Anxiety and depression."

"Anxiety and depression were some of her symptoms, but her actual diagnosis was dissociative identity disorder."

"Dissocia— What?"

"It's also known as multiple personality disorder."

"What the hell is that?"

"Did you read the book *Sybil*? It came out a few years ago."

"I was in college for the last several years. I didn't have time to read for pleasure, and I doubt I'd read some girlie book. What the hell are you talking about?"

"Dissociative identity disorder is the new name for split personality."

"I'm still not following."

"Your wife was kept heavily medicated," he said. "And even when she wasn't medicated, she had limited interaction with other patients. I always thought it odd that she remembered the patients but not their actual names. Now I have an explanation."

My heart dropped into my stomach. "What's the explanation, then?"

"The patients are all *her*. Aspects of her. Different personalities."

The receiver dropped out of my hand and thudded onto my lap. I quickly picked it up and put it back to my ear.

"Mr. Steel? Are you there?"

"Yeah, yeah. I'm here."

"It's a classic case. She has memories of these so-called separate people. The memories are becoming more vivid."

Multiple personalities. My Daphne. My Daphne whose own personality was the sweetest in the world. Why hadn't Jonathan told me?

Jonathan Wade isn't who you think he is, son. Be careful.

I swallowed. "What does this all mean?"

"It means"—he cleared his throat—"she's likely to dissociate again."

EPILOGUE

B r a d

Present day . . .

The guard clanked his key against my cell. "You have a visitor, Steel."

"It's not visiting day."

"What can I say? He made it clear he had to see you." The guard pointed to his pocket.

Of course. Money talked. How well my father had taught me that lesson.

It had to be Talon. He was the only person who ever visited me, and I hadn't seen him in over a month.

I held out my hands to be cuffed—one of the prices I'd paid so those who'd helped me over the years could go free. No minimum security for Brad Steel. I was treated like a serial killer, except I didn't have to wear a Hannibal Lecter mask and be rolled around on a dolly.

The guard led me to the visitor area and cuffed my left hand to the bar so my right was free to use the phone.

I picked up the receiver. "Talon," I said.

I jolted when the voice on the other end spoke back.

"It's not Talon."

Only then did I focus my gaze on the person on the other side of the glass.

Jonah.

My firstborn.

Like looking in a mirror twenty-something years ago.

The son for whom I'd created my legacy—my legacy that had turned to nothing more than smoldering ash.

Oh, the money was still there. My family was set for many lifetimes.

But at what cost?

"Joe," I said simply.

"I'm here for only one reason," he said, "and it's not to make peace."

I cleared my throat. His attitude didn't surprise me, and I'd given up hope long ago that my firstborn would ever forgive my indiscretions. Not even a glimmer of hope remained.

"Understood."

This time he cleared his throat. "I just had an interesting conversation with my mother."

I lifted my eyebrows at his use of the word *interesting*. I'd taken care of Daphne since her complete break with reality over twenty years ago. Conversations with her were always the same, centered on her two sons away at camp—even though we'd never sent our children to camp—and her baby, Angela, which was Marjorie's original given name until we changed it after she defied all odds and lived—not becoming an angel—despite being born prematurely.

I said simply, "Interesting?"

"Yes. Very interesting."

"I assume you didn't come here only to tell me it was interesting."

He paused a moment. Then, "I debated coming at all. I almost didn't."

Did he expect me to commend him? Tell him I was glad he'd come? I was, but what was he truly after?

"Just say what you came to say, son."

He winced when I said "son."

Too bad. He was still my son, and I was still his father. That would never change, nor did I want it to.

"Sometimes Mom seems to come back to reality," he said.

"She has a minute of lucidity every once in a while," I said. "Unfortunately, they never last long."

"Marj and Talon have seen them a few times. I've only witnessed one, and it happened today."

I nodded. "And you've come to tell me about it."

"Yes. It was . . . troubling."

"I'm sorry to hear that."

He cleared his throat once more. "She said she'd been keeping a secret. A big secret. One that was destroying her."

I widened my eyes. Daphne had never said anything to me about a secret before. "Did she say what it was?"

"No. She faded out into her own little world before I could get any more information."

"I see."

"You say she's had moments of lucidity in the past."

"Yes."

"Has she mentioned a secret?"

"No, she hasn't."

"What kind of things has she said?"

"Usually she recognized me and got angry for things I'd done in the past."

He rolled his eyes. "There was certainly no shortage of those."

I couldn't fault him for his not-so-subtle dig. He was right.

"Through everything, I always loved her," I said. "I still love her."

"You had a strange way of showing it."

"Everything I did was for—"

"Her protection. I know. I've heard it all before. I didn't come here to rehash old news. I came here to find out what you're still hiding."

"I'm not hiding anything," I said.

"Bullshit."

"All I have is my word."

"Your word sucks."

"I've lied in the past. I'm not lying now."

"That's what a liar would say."

"For Christ's sake, Jonah, do you really think I'd be here, rotting in prison for the rest of my life, if I still had any lies left in me? I'm paying the price for my sins, and it's no less than I deserve. But I did it all—"

"For us. Spare me."

"Think what you want. I have no control over you. I haven't since that bastard Tom Simpson first taught you how to handle a gun."

"I'm no fan of Tom Simpson. He was a psycho degenerate, but at least he taught me. It's been a useful skill over the years. For the life of me, I never understood why you wouldn't."

"I had my reasons."

"Reasons that are no longer relevant. Come clean, why don't you?"

I sighed. "I once taught someone, and it was the worst thing I ever did."

"Worst thing? To teach someone how to shoot? That was worse than faking your own death not once but *twice*?"

"It was one of the first dominoes to fall. Teaching her had disastrous consequences."

"Her? Fuck. You're talking about Wendy Madigan."

"If I hadn't taught her how to handle a gun, she wouldn't have—"

"Save it, Dad. Wendy Madigan was a psychopath. She would have still been a psychopath if you hadn't taught her to shoot a gun."

"Everything she did can be traced back to me teaching her."

He shook his head. "I can't believe I'm about to say this, but give yourself a break. You didn't turn her psycho."

Maybe I hadn't, but I'd had more than a hand in it. Jonah didn't know all that had transpired between Wendy and me, and now was not the time to get into it. I'd lied when I told him and his siblings about Wendy moving away after sophomore year.

I hadn't been able to bear telling them I'd stayed with her during high school, that I'd been at her side when she'd miscarried. Instead, I'd fabricated a story about her almost dying from a ruptured fallopian tube due to an ectopic pregnancy. Had I been trying to gain sympathy?

No one was more unworthy of sympathy than I was, yet I couldn't resist trying to get a little from my children.

I'd admitted to them that I'd sold my soul, but I hadn't been able to admit that I'd stayed willingly and returned to her again and again. That hadn't changed until I'd met Daphne.

When had lying become so easy?

Many, many years ago.

I said nothing for another minute, and then, "How's my grandson?"

"He's good."

"And Melanie?"

"She's good as well."

"Your brothers and sister? Spouses and kids?"

"We're all fine, Dad. We're dealing with everything." He shook his head. "This was a waste of time."

Again I said nothing. It hadn't been a waste of *my* time. I'd seen my firstborn—the child for whom I'd begun creating my legacy—and I was thankful. I gazed at his handsome face now beginning to show some signs of age. Gray at his temples, crow's feet in the outer corners of his dark eyes. Silver lacing his stubble.

I memorized every inch.

For I knew, deep in my soul, that this was the last time I'd ever gaze upon it.

CONTINUE THE STEEL BROTHERS SAGA
WITH BOOK FIFTEEN

#1 *NEW YORK TIMES* BESTSELLING AUTHOR

HELEN
HARDT

A STEEL BROTHERS NOVEL

DESCENT

MESSAGE FROM HELEN HARDT

Dear Reader,

Thank you for reading *Legacy*. If you want to find out about my current backlist and future releases, please like my Facebook page and join my mailing list. I often do giveaways. If you're a fan and would like to join my street team to help spread the word about my books, please see the web addresses below. I regularly do awesome giveaways for my street team members.

If you enjoyed the story, please take the time to leave a review on a site like Amazon or Goodreads. I welcome all feedback. I wish you all the best!

Helen

Facebook
Facebook.com/HelenHardt

Newsletter
HelenHardt.com/SignUp

Street Team
Facebook.com/Groups/HardtAndSoul

ALSO BY HELEN HARDT

The Steel Brothers Saga:
Craving
Obsession
Possession
Melt
Burn
Surrender
Shattered
Twisted
Unraveled
Breathless
Ravenous
Insatiable
Fate
Legacy
Descent

Blood Bond Saga:
Unchained
Unhinged
Undaunted
Unmasked
Undefeated

Misadventures Series:
Misadventures with a Rock Star
Misadventures of a Good Wife (with Meredith Wild)

The Temptation Saga:
Tempting Dusty
Teasing Annie
Taking Catie
Taming Angelina
Treasuring Amber
Trusting Sydney
Tantalizing Maria

The Sex and the Season Series:
Lily and the Duke
Rose in Bloom
Lady Alexandra's Lover
Sophie's Voice

Daughters of the Prairie:
The Outlaw's Angel
Lessons of the Heart
Song of the Raven

Cougar Chronicles:
The Cowboy and the Cougar
Calendar Boy

ACKNOWLEDGMENTS

I did something in *Legacy* that I've never done before as a writer.

I began the descent of Brad Steel from hero to anti-hero. It was a challenge, and I thought a lot about other famous anti-heroes as I wrote—Walter White, Jaime Lannister, even Scarlett O'Hara. Brad's true *Descent* will happen in the next book, of course, but I've sowed the seeds in *Legacy*. Like Walter, Jaime, and Scarlett, Brad will do anything to protect those he loves—and that protection sometimes comes at a tragic cost.

Huge thanks to the following individuals whose effort and belief made this book shine: Jennifer Becker, Audrey Bobak, Haley Boudreaux, Keli Jo Chen, Yvonne Ellis, Jesse Kench, Robyn Lee, Jon Mac, Amber Maxwell, Dave McInerney, Michele Hamner Moore, Chrissie Saunders, Scott Saunders, Celina Summers, Kurt Vachon, and Meredith Wild.

Thanks also to the women and men of Hardt and Soul. Your endless and unwavering support keeps me going.

To my family and friends, thank you for your encouragement.

Thank you most of all to my readers. Without you, none of this would be possible.

Descent will be here soon!

ABOUT THE AUTHOR

#1 *New York Times*, #1 *USA Today*, and #1 *Wall Street Journal* bestselling author Helen Hardt's passion for the written word began with the books her mother read to her at bedtime. She wrote her first story at age six and hasn't stopped since. In addition to being an award-winning author of romantic fiction, she's a mother, an attorney, a black belt in Taekwondo, a grammar geek, an appreciator of fine red wine, and a lover of Ben and Jerry's ice cream. She writes from her home in Colorado, where she lives with her family. Helen loves to hear from readers.

Visit her at HelenHardt.com

ALSO AVAILABLE FROM

HELEN HARDT

THE BLOOD BOND SAGA

ALSO AVAILABLE FROM

HELEN HARDT

SEX AND THE SEASON SERIES

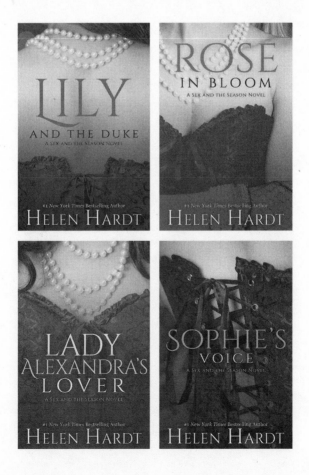